W9-BYR-404

VICTORIA FORESTER

The BoY WHO KNEW EVERYTHING

FEIWEL AND FRIENDS
NEW YORK

A FEIWEL AND FRIENDS BOOK
An Imprint of Macmillan

Feiwel and Friends books may be purchased for business or promotional use.
For information on bulk purchases, please contact the Macmillan Corporate and
Premium Sales Department at (800) 221-7945 x5442
or by e-mail at specialmarkets@macmillan.com.

Library of Congress Cataloging-in-Publication Data Available

ISBN: 978-0-312-62600-6 (hardcover) / 978-1-250-08021-9 (ebook)
978-1-250-08930-4 (international edition)

Book design by Anna Booth

Feiwel and Friends logo designed by Filomena Tuosto

First Edition: 2015

10 9 8 7 6 5 4 3 2 1

macteenbooks.com

PROLOGUE

*T*HEY FLED FASTER THAN THEIR HEARTS could beat. His mother led him to the cave at the top of the mountain, where they huddled panting in the dark and listening for His inevitable footfalls.

"What will He do to me?" The boy's teeth chattered.

"Shhhhh," she assured him. She was all he had and he was all she had. They had only been given eleven short years together—not nearly enough.

"Where is Father going to take me?"

"I don't know. Somewhere that I can't find you. But He will erase your memory and you won't remember me or your home. It won't hurt."

"It hurts now," he said. The silence prickled his skin and he itched at it but then fell still again, listening. "But why is He doing this?"

"Your father has lost Himself . . . He is the Dark One."

Then they heard His footfalls on the mountain

outside the cave. The boy clung to his mother with his life.

She knew these were their last moments together and she wanted to give him something: she chose hope.

"Listen closely and mark my words," she whispered. "There is a prophecy. It speaks of a girl who can fly and a boy who knows everything. The prophecy says that they have the power to bring about great change. The day will come when they will stop your father and we can be together again."

"But when will that be?"

"Soon. I hope. Very soon."

The boy thought about this girl who could fly and this boy who knew everything and he promised to hold them in his heart where He could not make him forget.

"Please," he prayed. "Please let them come very, very soon."

Part I

ONE PROBLEM WITH BEING A GENIUS— and there are many problems—is that there is an overwhelming need on the part of adults to "assess" you, which is just a tricky way of saying they want to figure out exactly how smart you are and why you are smart and where your smarts come from. (And silently ponder the unspoken question that doesn't appear on any test but hangs heavy in the air—"For heaven's sake, why can't I be as smart as you?")

Conrad Harrington III was in the middle of his third assessment of that day by yet another ninny, who called herself an expert, and even though he was only seven years old he still had better things to do than answer her silly questions, which not only were boring but took up a lot of his valuable time.

"In a candy store there are two times as many jelly

beans as there are gummy bears and four times as many licorice whips as there are jelly beans," said the ninny. "If there are a hundred and thirty-six lollipops and there is the same number of lollipops as there is licorice, how many jelly beans are there?"

"Thirty-four."

"You build a house with four square walls each with only southern exposure. A bear shows up. What color is the bear?"

"White."

"How many of each animal did Abraham take on the ark?"

"None, Noah built the ark."

"In this number sequence—"

"I don't know."

"I haven't finished the question."

"I still don't know." Conrad slumped back in his chair and glared.

"Complete this number sequence: one, eight, twenty-seven, forty-eight," the ninny persisted. She introduced herself as Dr. Hilda Hamish and she was short and puckered. At some point in her life, probably when she was five, her face pulled itself into a concerned question mark and it had never managed to free itself in all the time that followed.

"I don't know," Conrad repeated, and looked out the window.

The ninny pursed her lips anxiously; she had promised to complete her assessment that evening, but if she couldn't get the boy to cooperate she would be stuck. He was a scrawny seven-year-old with a head that was too large for his body, serious eyes, and a sad mouth. At that moment he had his arms crossed over his chest and a stormy look on his brow. She considered how to proceed and decided on a different tack.

"Your father told me that you like numbers."

Conrad turned on the poor woman. "And did you believe my father?"

The ninny was taken aback, but instead of dismissing the question out of hand she actually thought about it. "Your father is a very smart man."

"No, my father is an important senator and he is powerful in Washington, but that doesn't make him smart; there is a difference."

"Oh," she said nervously, and looked down at her assessment test, trying to figure out which question to ask next and how to get this process back on track.

"Do you know why you are here?" Conrad pressed— he would be the one asking the questions now.

"Of course," she sputtered. "Your father wants to know how he can better help you grow and learn."

"Wrong again." Conrad rolled his eyes at her obtuseness. "Today is my seventh birthday, but my father canceled my party because he's angry with me."

She looked at him questioningly and he admitted, "I hacked the Defense Department mainframe and reprogrammed an orbiting satellite. The president found out, and now my father sees me as a threat to his political career." Conrad leaned forward in his chair and bore down on the flustered woman. "He is using you to help control me."

The ninny's face flushed bright red and her mouth puckered into four different questions before giving up completely and turning her eyes back to her forms.

"Perhaps we'd better go back to language comprehension." She quickly flipped her pages about.

"There is something you should know about my father," Conrad whispered.

The ninny shifted uncomfortably, her face almost cracking in half as it endeavored to fully transform into the question mark it longed to be. "What is that?" she asked.

"My father has a terrible secret."

"A secret?" she whispered.

"Yes. He tries to hide it, but I'm going to find out what it is."

A forest fire of goose bumps exploded up her neck. "What sort of secret?"

Conrad held her gaze. "He's—"

Suddenly the door to the room flung open, causing Dr. Hamish to jump out of her skin. Standing in the doorway was Senator Harrington. He was a man who'd been packaged to perfection—tall, blond, athletic, and topped with a walloping serving of charm and charisma. He was John F. Kennedy crossed with Brad Pitt, and when he smiled, he dazzled.

"Thank you, Dr. Hamish, that will be all for today," said the senator, smiling.

"Oh, Senator Harrington?" The ninny scrambled to her feet, even more flustered than before. "You surprised me."

"He was listening the whole time," said Conrad. "He does that."

"Oh," she said. "Oh."

"It's been a long day." Senator Harrington took Dr. Hamish's hand and guided her toward the door. "My assistant will show you the way out."

"But the assessment . . . ?"

Before Dr. Hamish knew what was happening she was escorted out of the mansion and deposited, with all conceivable politeness and charm, of course, onto the sidewalk of their Washington, D.C., brownstone. From his playroom window Conrad could see her still shuffling her papers on the street and suddenly found himself feeling sorry that she was gone and sad that he would never see her again: there was an honesty about Dr. Hilda Hamish that he was thirsty for. With his father looming over him he had little time to consider this, though.

Folding his arms across his chest, Senator Harrington leveled Conrad with a hard stare. "There is a woman downstairs. Her name's Dr. Letitia Hellion and she wants to take you away to her school. She says that she can help you—make you better."

"Mother won't let you send me away."

"Because you're my son, I'm going to give you a choice," the senator continued. "You can go with this Dr. Hellion right now, or you can come with me and I'll take you to the president. You will tell the president that you didn't reprogram that satellite and that it's all been a big mistake."

"But Father, that satellite was falling out of its orbit," Conrad explained for what he knew was the third time. "If I hadn't reprogrammed it, it would have crashed over Seattle."

"I will provide the president with credible evidence that someone else was responsible and that they used you as a patsy. You'll act like a normal seven-year-old boy and make him believe it."

"You mean act stupid."

Once again Senator Harrington completely ignored Conrad's remark and pressed his own agenda. "From now on you will do as I say, when I say, and stop this." He pointed to his head.

"Just stop?" Conrad repeated, thinking about how he would stop thinking.

To Conrad's surprise Senator Harrington suddenly softened, reaching forward and taking his young son's hand. "Connie," he said gently, and smiled encouragingly, and his smile dazzled: it said "you're my guy" and "come be on my team" and "you and I share a special secret" and also a little bit of "agree with me and everything will be okay."

"I can help you. But you have to work with me, not against me. I forbid you from ever interfering like that again. You have to understand: bad things happen and no one wants your help. Who cares if the satellite crashed? They're called accidents for a reason. Why make it into a problem?"

Conrad sat back in his chair and looked at his father with amazement. "But if people get hurt doesn't that make it wrong?"

"Why don't you let me decide what's wrong?" The senator's smile now coaxed. "Don't you want to have your birthday party?"

Conrad looked at his father and for one glorious moment thought that he would let him decide, would stand at his side and be his best buddy and grow in the warmth of his companionship and approval. He would go to the president, and while his father lied about what happened to the satellite he would play with a small truck, making loud engine noises; he would look the other way and act as his father told him to. He would get his big birthday party.

The moment passed.

"I guess I'm too old for birthday parties now," Conrad said finally.

Senator Harrington's smile melted into a hard line and he got to his feet. A pain began bubbling in the back of his head and he pushed it with the fingers on his right hand. "There's a reason these things happen, reasons you don't understand," he barked with a strange, angry voice. "No one wants you to get involved."

"You mean someone wanted that satellite to crash?"

"No! No." The senator's composure was slipping and with effort he took himself in hand by straightening his tie and brushing the creases from his pants.

"You leave me no choice, Conrad." Senator Harrington turned away. "I'm sending Dr. Hellion up now."

"But Father . . ."

Senator Harrington walked out of the room and out of Conrad's life without missing a beat. As Conrad stood alone and helpless, despite the vast resources his genius provided him, he wondered what he was going to do without a father to father him.

*C*ONRAD HAD FOUR LONG, AGONIZING years to consider and reconsider his conversation with his father while he suffered under the control of Dr. Letitia Hellion. Dr. Hellion had taken it upon herself to collect all things exceptional and under the guise of "helping" was systematically eradicating the world of anything that she deemed to be abnormal. In her opinion, Conrad's extreme intelligence was definitely abnormal and thus a threat to society as a whole and to Conrad as an individual. Day in and day out, year after year, Dr. Hellion used every means at her disposal (and her arsenal was indomitable) to force Conrad to relinquish his intelligence and embrace normalcy.

There was no doubt in Conrad's mind that his father would have left him at the mercy of Dr. Hellion indefinitely had Piper McCloud not arrived. Like Conrad, Piper was exceptional: she had the ability to fly. With her long brown hair and sky-blue eyes Piper was like a well-meaning tornado stuffed into a china teacup. Thanks to Piper and her flying, Conrad was able to finally plan an escape that not only set the two of them free, but all the other kids under Dr. Hellion's control too.

But of course the price of his freedom was the reminder that he had no home to return to: his father wouldn't take him back. Once again Piper stepped in and saved the day by offering up her home and family. Betty and Joe McCloud lived on a humble farm in remote Lowland County and, like Piper, they were honest and good-hearted country folk. They soon came to love Conrad like their own son and Conrad adjusted to the pace of life on the farm and began to flourish. He built a laboratory in the old barn and got to work on his pet "time travel" project; he helped Joe with the farm work and ate up every last bite of Betty's amazing country cooking. All of a sudden Conrad was smack dab in the middle of a real family; he had loving adults looking out for him and over him, and he had the company of his good friend Piper, who could always be counted on to come up with some crazy scheme.

For instance, that very day Piper had happened to uncover a fabulous secret that Conrad was trying to keep from everyone: it was his twelfth birthday. Not only had Piper discovered this, but she had planned a surprise birthday party for him. With the greatest care she had secretly invited all of their friends and had planned everything so that at just the right moment they would leap out on her unsuspecting friend and yell—

"SURPRISE!" Piper mouthed the words, not allowing sound to escape.

Before the sun had touched the clouds that morning, Piper had slipped from her bed, tingling with excitement. Conrad had the little bedroom next to hers, and she was careful to be very quiet when she opened her bedroom window. As soon as her feet lifted off the ground, the thrill of taking to the morning sky made her soar.

It was the beginning of November and the air was crisp and she flew fast and far over the forest. They had enjoyed an Indian summer that kept the leaves on the trees late that year, and the foliage burned red, yellow, brown, and orange in hues so bright and vivid it took Piper's breath away. The wind picked at the leaves and tossed them about in passionate tangos. Piper swooped down over the trees and went low, as low as she dared, and dodged this way and that through the festival of color.

Piper allowed the twists and turns of Clothespin Creek to lead her back to home and family. It contented Piper to fly over the simple farms of her neighbors, where she could see the sheep and cattle grazing and hear the roosters crowing.

When Piper reached her farm she circled above it. It still amazed her to see all that had changed on the farm. When Conrad had first arrived at the McClouds' they had twenty rocky acres of farmland and not much else. No sooner had Conrad moved in than he began urging Piper's father to adopt revolutionary farming techniques, which had lifted his crop yield from poor to overabundant. As the money came in, Conrad advised Joe McCloud to buy the hundred acres of swampland that bordered their south field. It was with amazement that Millie Mae Miller, the town gossip, reported to her sewing circle that somehow Joe had devised a way to irrigate the swamp, drain the water into a reservoir, and then plant crop after bountiful crop. In no time flat the McClouds had gone from subsistence rock farmers to the most prosperous landowners in the county. Joe now had a shed stocked full of the most up-to-date farming equipment of every description, the herd of cattle had tripled in number, and the sheep were bursting from the fields.

The simple clapboard farmhouse had undergone its own Cinderella-like transformation. The peeling, eroding structure had been revived with a splashy coat of bright blue paint. White shutters and flower boxes had been added around the windows and a flowering vine danced up through lattice.

Circling one last time, Piper quickly dove down and

landed on the roof of the old barn. Wiggling through a hole in the cupola, she arrived in the hayloft to find Myrtle waiting for her.

After Piper and Conrad had escaped from Dr. Hellion's evil institute, all of their exceptional friends had gone their separate ways. It was quite a task getting the word out quietly about Conrad's surprise party that morning.

Myrtle, a painfully shy beanpole of a girl, was the first to arrive. Of course, Myrtle would be first since she could run faster than the speed of light. She was sitting on top of a large rafter, her feet dangling impatiently.

"Myrtle! You're a sight for sore eyes!" Piper swooped down and settled next to her. "I can't wait to see the look on Conrad's face when he sees you all here."

"You sure he doesn't know?" Myrtle was very shy and she spoke softly and tilted her head downward in an effort to hide beneath her thick brown hair.

"Nope." Piper shook her head with certainty as she crossed her heart with solemnity. "My lips are sealed."

Piper showed Myrtle where she had stowed boxes of decorations and the girls began to decorate the hayloft with streamers, bright signs, and balloons. No sooner had they begun than Nalen and Ahmed Mustafa, mischievous identical twins and weather changers, arrived, followed soon after by Daisy and Jasper. Piper was particularly happy to see her good friend Violet, who could shrink to the size of a teacup. Violet, with flashing brown eyes and a dark complexion, was soft-spoken but fiercely loyal and surprisingly courageous.

With her super strength, Daisy set to effortlessly tossing the hay bales around, arranging them to Piper's specifications while Ahmed and Nalen hung the streamers from the rafters and Jasper and Violet blew up balloons until their heads felt dizzy.

And some things never changed—Kimber and Smitty showed up bickering. They bickered just as much as they ever did when Piper first met them at Dr. Hellion's school. Smitty had just had a growth spurt and his mother had slapped a pair of braces on his teeth, but his X-ray vision was as sharp as ever. Sharp enough to sneak peeks at Kimber's underwear, despite the electricity that Kimber wielded in her fingertips. Over the course of the last year Kimber's wild red hair had mellowed into a rich auburn color and her freckles had faded to reveal milky-white skin that hinted at the striking young woman she would one day become. Which did not mean for a second that her wicked temper had in any way mellowed; indeed, she was just as hotheaded as she'd ever been.

Piper hugged them both gleefully. "Conrad didn't see you come, did he?"

"No way. No one saw us," Kimber reported confidently.

"The cows saw us," Smitty corrected.

"Fine." Kimber sighed irritably. "No one saw us who can talk. Jeez, do we have to fight about everything?"

The last and final member of their group to arrive was Lily Yakimoto, and she would have been there sooner but she had to fix her hair—twice. Lily was nine years old and prided herself on her spotless appearance. Her hair hung in ringlets, her shoes gleamed, and she allowed only the finest silk dresses to grace her delicate form. She often used her keen telekinetic powers to arrange the ribbons in her hair or to retie the hard-to-reach bow on her dress.

"Five minutes," Piper warned in a loud whisper. "Conrad always comes in here before breakfast to check on his experiments." She nodded to the center of the loft where Conrad had set up a makeshift science lab. Despite the fact that he'd cobbled together odds and ends of computers and other random high-tech equipment, which regularly had stray bits of hay raining down on them, the effect of the entire arrangement was strangely awe-inspiring—in a mad-scientist sort of way.

The finishing touches were completed with the balloons dangling from the walls and the streamers pinned on the hay and the rafters. Violet handed out party hats and blowers and then Piper ordered them into hiding places. As she crouched down in the hay, Piper held herself gleefully. Every pair of eyes rested on the barn door as they silently waited, ready to jump out.

"ACHOO!" A loud sneeze blasted through the barn. Jumping up, Piper looked about. "Shhhhh!"

"ACHOO!"

Piper spotted Lily holding her two hands over her face and bending over. "ACHOO!"

"Lily, you have to be quiet!" Piper whispered frantically.

"I can't—ACHOO—help it!" she whined. "This hay is—ACHOO—making me sneeze. ACHOO."

"Maybe she's a-allergic," Myrtle whispered.

Piper had never considered this. "Are you allergic to hay?"

"ACHOO!" Lily's eyes were running by this point and her face was getting red and puffy. She nodded her head miserably.

"Here." Piper tossed Lily her sweater. "Sneeze as quietly as you can into this."

"Someone's coming," Smitty warned, using his X-ray vision.

"Places, everyone," Piper whispered.

Once again everyone crouched down and listened

to the approaching footsteps. A moment later the barn door swung open.

"SURPRISE!" Piper shouted, jumping out and throwing brightly colored confetti. All around her the other children did likewise while Kimber used the electricity in her fingertips to create a sparkler effect.

"SURPRISE! SURPRISE!"

"Happy birthday!"

Standing before them, with the life near scared out of him, was none other than Piper's father, Joe McCloud.

Now it was Piper's turn to be surprised. "Pa? What are you doing here?"

Joe clutched his chest and took several steps back, using the wall for support. When he could gather himself he pointed to the bags of chicken feed stacked against the wall.

Piper's shoulders fell. "Oh no, it's Tuesday. Feed day." Piper suddenly remembered that on Tuesdays Joe always collected the chicken feed he needed for the week.

"But where's Conrad?" Kimber wanted to know.

"I'm right behind you," Conrad said clearly.

At the sound of his voice all the children swiveled around to discover Conrad languidly leaning against the back wall with an amused smirk on his face. His blond hair was tousled and in need of a haircut, but the erect way he held himself and the precision with which he dressed belied his keen attention to detail. He was, without a doubt, the only person in the entire barn at that moment who wasn't surprised. Poor Joe felt as though his life had just flashed before his eyes.

"Surprise," Conrad said evenly.

Piper's face sank. "You knew! How'd you know?"

"Simple," Conrad said. "You didn't eat your piece of apple pie last night."

"You knew I was throwing a surprise birthday party because I didn't eat my apple pie?"

"Of course. You didn't eat because you were excited. I knew you were excited because of the way you wiggled your baby finger." He demonstrated with his own baby finger. "And then there was the purple marker on your hands. Obviously you'd been making something— but you don't usually do crafts. Which meant there was a special reason that you were doing them, and the only thing special that was going on was my birthday. It was pretty obvious."

Piper shook her head and sat down hard on a hay bale. "You're impossible."

"Sorry." He nodded to Lily and tossed her a box of allergy medicine. "Take two of them now and then two in another four hours."

"You knew Lily was allergic to hay too?" Piper was not only disappointed now but also exasperated.

"Of course. Didn't you?" Conrad paused. "But the one thing I couldn't figure out was how you knew it was my birthday. I never told any of you, nor do you have access to any information that would tell you. So how'd you find out?"

Piper smiled, triumphant.

"Well?" Conrad waited on her answer.

Suddenly a lone voice started singing "Happy Birthday." Conrad looked about, surprised. A cake with twelve candles brightly burning on top appeared from around the corner of a stack of hay. It floated through the air, heading straight for Conrad.

Jumping to her feet, Piper clapped and sang. The other kids joined in.

"Happy birthday to you!"

As the cake approached, a man began to materialize so that all could see that the cake was not floating but was being held in his hands. He was not a young man but somewhere in his middle years. Now that he was visible it was possible to see that he was wearing fatigue pants and a black T-shirt. He had the intense look of a harried soldier but for the moment a smile was on his lips.

"J.," said Conrad, recognizing him; he was surprised but not happy. "I should have known."

"MY MOON AND STARS, WHAT'S GOING on here?" gasped Betty McCloud. She'd been feeding the chickens when she heard the commotion and arrived at the barn just as Conrad was blowing out the candles. Her startled eyes couldn't make sense of the gathered kids, a strange man holding a cake, and Joe with his face as white as a sheet.

"It's Conrad's birthday, Ma," Piper chirped excitedly. "We're surprising him and I didn't want to tell you in case he found out."

Birthdays were serious business for Betty. "Lands' sakes, child, your birthday? Why didn't you tell us?" She bustled about, giving kids hugs and reaching for Conrad. "I'd best get a birthday breakfast on for you youngens and we'll need ice cream to go with this cake." She took the cake out of J.'s hands and headed for the house, gathering up the kids like a clucking mother hen corralling her unruly and overexcited chicks. Piper was in the middle of the clutch when she noticed that Conrad and J. were off by themselves talking quietly. The hard lines brewing around Conrad's mouth told Piper that they were not enjoying a joyous reunion.

"Who asked you to butt in?" Piper heard Conrad say in a low voice.

"I'm not butting in," J. said defensively. "I'm just looking out for you and Piper. I check in from time to time to make sure that you're doing all right. That's it."

Conrad turned to Piper, who was now nervously standing between them as though she was anticipating the need to break up a fight. "J.'s been visiting you? And you didn't tell me?"

Piper's cheeks flamed red. "J. came a few times. Maybe three or four," she stammered.

J. had the ability to make himself invisible and was always off on some crusade or another. He had tried to rescue Piper when Letitia Hellion had first come to take her away and then again from the school. But despite his extraordinary ability, J. was no match for Dr. Hellion. Piper had a soft spot for J.'s frantic, intense ways and his clandestine comings and goings. Conrad, on the other hand, had no such soft feelings and regarded J. and his lone-wolf ways with suspicion at best and outright hostility at worst, which was why it wasn't exactly a priority for Piper to "mention" J.'s unexpected visits.

"I didn't think you'd be interested," Piper said.

Conrad snorted at her lame excuse and turned back to J. "How did you know it was my birthday?"

J. threw his hands up. "It's not exactly top secret information."

"And it's not exactly common knowledge, either. Are you spying on me?"

"I wouldn't say that." J. chose his words carefully and spoke them slowly.

"Then what *would* you say?"

J. considered what to tell Conrad. J.'s life was about things that were hidden, and he traded on who knew what and when. He had been a small boy when he learned that he could make himself invisible, and on that first day of wondrous invisibility he had sat in the kitchen quietly watching his mother do the dishes. She was unaware that he was close by, and he marveled at the simple act of observing her unseen. All of a sudden for no reason that he could see she stopped doing the dishes and started to cry. It was a gut-wrenching cry that she managed to achieve without making any sound whatsoever, as though it was something she had long practiced. J. was shocked that his mother had such a deep sadness inside of her and had never guessed she was hiding it from him and the rest of his family. Less than a minute later his father and sister had returned home and his mother resumed washing the dishes as though nothing at all was the matter. J.'s mother was a revelation to him. She was keeping secrets from those she loved most, and it soon became clear to J. that everyone was keeping secrets. Most of the secrets were small, inconsequential things, but some of the secrets were big and important.

From that day forward J. watched from the shadows, collecting information and looking for hidden truths. The older he got, the more he watched and the deeper the truths he followed. Just recently he had realized that Piper and Conrad were connected in some way to a mystery, and he made it his mission to find out how and why.

With a deep sigh, J. decided to tell Conrad none of this and answered his angry question with a shrug.

"Spying is a strong word," J. said.

"That's not an answer!" Conrad pressed.

"It was me," Piper confessed quickly before things escalated further. "I was worried about you because of the election. All you do is work in your lab and listen to the election coverage, and I asked J. if he knew anything about it."

"You?" Conrad was dismayed. "The election?"

A new president was about to be elected, and for the

last year Senator Harrington had been mounting an impressive presidential bid. The closer the election came the more Conrad had watched and listened to the things his father did and said. Seeing the way Conrad watched his father had made Piper worried for some reason she couldn't exactly pinpoint.

"I saw the way you were looking at your father on the television and so I asked J. to find out about him." Piper swallowed hard. "And I guess I thought that if he became president you'd want to go home, and I didn't want you to go."

"You make no sense, Piper. This is my home now."

"Really? You mean it?"

"Really. Unless, of course, you drive me crazy, which at this moment presents itself as a distinct possibility."

Piper's relief turned into a smile and she slugged Conrad's shoulder good-naturedly. "C'mon, who doesn't like a birthday party? It's fun!"

"If you say so." Conrad allowed himself a half-smile.

As the tension dispersed J. pulled a file from his backpack. "This is for you." He offered Conrad the file.

Conrad made no move to take it. "What is it?"

"Consider it a birthday gift. It's the information Piper asked me to get on your father. You need to read it." J. stood with the file outstretched.

"No, thanks."

"Your father is not who he says he is," J. said quietly, as though he might be overheard.

"My father's secrets don't concern me anymore."

"If you say so." J.'s tone plainly communicated the opposite message.

"But Conrad," Piper pleaded, taking the file out of J.'s hand and offering it to him, "take it. It might be important."

"Do you even know his name?" Conrad pointed at J.

Piper shrugged. "His name is J."

"J. is not a name; 'J' is a *letter*." Conrad spoke to Piper but glared at J. "And we know nothing about him or where he's from or what he does or knows. Because he won't tell us. How do we know he's not hiding something from us?"

"Because . . . because," Piper stuttered, "because he's J."

"That's not good enough for me," Conrad snapped. "And this is my birthday party and I'm supposed to be eating cake and acting happy. So if you'll excuse me—" Conrad turned on his heel and marched out of the barn, leaving J. and Piper in the wake of the awkwardness of the exchange.

"I guess he doesn't like surprises," Piper offered, her cheeks pink. "I'll give this to him later." She tucked the file beneath her arm. "I know he'll appreciate it when he's not so . . . well, so Conrad."

J. sighed and gathered his things, hoisting his backpack over his shoulders. "You can lead a horse to water—"

"—but you can't make it drink," Piper finished.

J. headed for the door, Piper hot on his heels.

"You're leaving? Already? Can't you stay longer?" Piper pressed him. "Don't you want cake?"

"There are urgent matters." J. strode purposefully into the farmyard. "I have a source and this time I think I'm getting close."

"You mean to finding out about that secret place where everyone is like us?" Piper asked excitedly and perhaps too loudly.

"Shhhhh."

"Sorry." J. had been telling her for months that he was hot on the trail of information that was leading him to a hidden community of people who were all exceptional. It was thrilling to think about.

"Will you tell me when you know?" Piper whispered.

J. was already turning himself invisible, but Piper was able to see him tip his head. "You'll be hearing from me soon."

CONRAD'S BIRTHDAY BREAKFAST WAS A higgledy-piggledy affair. With eleven youngens packed around the McClouds' breakfast table telling jokes and jostling elbows for greater room while reaching over one another to get at the hot blueberry muffins, crisp bacon, cheesy omelets, hotcakes, and waffles it was a mercy no one was maimed, or worse. At one point little Jasper, who normally didn't make a peep, laughed so hard at a joke of Smitty's ("What's the last thing that goes through a bug's mind when he hits a windshield? His butt!") that he went red in the face, brayed like a donkey, and snorted egg out of his nose. This, in turn, caused such hilarity that Kimber gave herself a jolt of electricity and Daisy accidentally broke her chair into bits when she burped unexpectedly—and in an alarmingly smelly way. When everyone had finally calmed down and eaten more than they could possibly hold,

Betty served cake and ice cream and shooed them away and told them to play outside, and for heaven's sake not to cause any more mischief.

Next, Piper gathered everyone around Conrad on the porch for presents. Conrad proceeded to shake each of the strangely shaped objects and pointedly guess, in a hopeful way, that they might contain weapons-grade plutonium for his time machine. To which everyone rolled their eyes and assured him that no one was going to give him plutonium for his birthday. Conrad pretended to be disappointed but dug into his gifts with good humor.

Lily gave Conrad a silk tie, which was met with groans that she stubbornly ignored as she loudly explained how it was the very latest fashion from Paris. Ahmed and Nalen whipped up a small windstorm that tidily snatched the tie away in the hopes of putting an end to Lily's fashion lesson. Undaunted, Lily telekinetically retrieved the precious tie while at the same time "accidentally" tipping the Mustafa brothers' drinks into their laps (which was Lily's way of politely reminding them not to mess with her or, and perhaps more important, a fashionable silk tie).

Violet gave Conrad an extremely rare coin that she had dug up in her latest archaeological adventure. But it was Myrtle's present that caused an uproar. On one of her recent jaunts across the globe Myrtle had stumbled

across a pygmy rhinoceros. He was a box-shaped creature no larger than a football, and Myrtle had clumsily
wrapped him in a package so that when Conrad opened
it, startling him out of his nap, he immediately chomped
down on Conrad's fingers.

"Owww!" Conrad jerked his hand away but the tiny
rhinoceros refused to release his fingers. Fortunately Daisy
was able to gently pry its jaws open and Jasper quickly
healed Conrad's bleeding appendages, at which point
they were all finally able to get a good look at the pug-
nacious little fellow. He was a muddy gray color and his
skin was all wrinkled up and leathery. He made a snuffling sound when he breathed and he was stamping about
clumsily knocking his horn into things.

"I named him Fido," Myrtle offered tentatively, trying to gauge Conrad's reaction. "But you can call him
anything you want."

Conrad grew very silent and looked at Fido, who
was at that moment biting the bottom of his jeans and
growling playfully. Conrad was by no means under any
illusion; Fido was snappish, dangerous, and unquestion-
ably one of the ugliest creatures he had ever seen, yet
still he was struck dumb by the presence of him.

As Conrad's silence stretched into an uncomfortable
length Myrtle shifted nervously and looked to Daisy for

help. Daisy didn't know what to say and so she nudged Jasper.

"D-d-don't you like him?" Jasper asked meekly.

Conrad looked up at his friends with a suspicious shine in his eyes. "I've never had a pet before," he said. "My father wouldn't allow it." Conrad swallowed hard. "I think this is the best birthday I have ever had."

"Yippee!" Conrad's friends cheered with excitement and relief, and of the entire group Piper made the most noise.

Fido was once again startled by the unexpected clatter and suddenly a pair of wings snapped out from beneath the folds of skin on his back. He bolted into the air, flapping about in erratic patterns. This development was such a startling revelation it struck many of the kids dumb.

"I forgot to mention"—Myrtle shrugged—"Fido can fly. I think he's part bat."

Conrad grinned, watching the crazy creature bumping into trees and bumbling through the air.

"He's fast!" Piper was delighted and immediately took to the air after him.

The rest of the day was taken up with games and Conrad getting to know his first pet so that by the time the sun set everyone was tuckered and laughed out. When the kids had all gone home Piper found Conrad hunched over his workbench diligently tinkering with a white oval device the size of an ostrich egg, which he called TiTI (short for Time Infinity Travel Instigator). Fido snored loudly at his feet, twitching at odd moments.

"Whatcha doing?" Piper asked, perching next to Conrad.

"Just putting on the finishing touches." Conrad didn't take his eyes from TiTI, turning it over and using a very small laser to cut precise incisions on the mechanism within.

"Are you really going to be able to travel through time with that thing?" Piper's nose wrinkled up.

"No, it's not possible to travel through time." Conrad had explained this to Piper a thousand times already. "I'm bending time. TiTI distorts time and allows the person holding it to move to different places on the space-time continuum."

"Uh, okay."

Conrad could see that he would have to explain it again at some point in the not-so-distant future because Piper was too busy placing a brightly wrapped package on his worktable and nudging it toward him.

"You forgot to open my present," she said.

Conrad shook his head. "Piper, you didn't have to—"

"I know I didn't have to. I wanted to, you genius-dummy. So, open it already."

Conrad sighed and tugged the paper away. Inside was a glass canister and inside that canister were several complicated mechanisms surrounding a small vial of silver liquid.

"You didn't!" Conrad gasped. *"Plutonium?"*

"I'm your best friend." Piper grinned and clapped her hands excitedly. "Just 'cause I can't understand half of the crazy things you're talking about, it doesn't mean I'm not listening."

"But . . . how did *you* get weapons-grade plutonium?"

Piper shrugged. "J. has a few contacts . . ."

"J.!" Conrad snorted, anger flaring hotly in his cheeks. "I should have known."

"But now you can try out TiTI just like you wanted," Piper said quickly. "Where it came from doesn't matter. Don't spoil the present. It's the thought that counts."

A crooked smile played with Conrad's lips and he swallowed his anger. "Thank you. It's just what I wanted."

"See?" Piper said smugly. "Surprise birthday parties are pretty fun. I guess that means I do have good ideas."

"You're something else, Piper McCloud. I'll give you that."

Conrad gently placed the canister on a shelf and

returned to his work while Piper gauged her words and waited for just the right moment.

"You know, Conrad," she said with forced nonchalance, "I was talking with some of the others, and they're having a hard time out there." Piper nodded to the outside world. Ever since the kids had escaped from the school they'd scattered to the winds in pursuit of their dream jobs. Unfortunately they didn't get to see one another that much anymore and most of the kids were running into problems, particularly as they had to carefully keep their special abilities secret.

"Last week Violet got stuck inside an Egyptian sarcophagus on an archaeological dig. Now, if Smitty had been there and used his X-ray vision she would have known that was going to happen before going in. And then last month when there was that freak flooding in Colorado, Jasper and Myrtle were trying to save a herd of deer and Ahmed and Nalen didn't know they were there and started a windstorm to dry things out but blew the deer away and Jasper hurt his hands. Then there was the time—"

"I get it. I get it," Conrad cut her short. "There have been mistakes."

"Those wouldn't have happened if you'd been in charge. Now, I'm not the only one who is thinking this," Piper continued carefully, "but it just might make more sense if we all worked together. You know, as a team." She waited on Conrad's reaction.

"Sure, if you want to." Conrad kept the majority of his attention on TiTI. "Go ahead."

"No, I mean all of us." Piper pointed at herself and then Conrad meaningfully.

"You mean me?" Now he gave Piper his full attention.

"Of course. Why not you?"

"Because I don't want to." Conrad put his equipment down and walked away. Piper followed him.

"But you have so many great plans and you always figure things out and we'd get so much more done. Together we could make a big difference."

"A big difference to whom? Or what?"

"Everyone. Anyone. Think of it!" Piper's face was animated with the possibilities. "We've been blessed with these abilities and we've gotta use 'em as a blessing."

"Thanks but no thanks."

"But why not?"

"Because my work is here." Conrad pointed to TiTI.

Piper looked around the dusty old barn. "So you plan to just hide out here for the rest of your life working on this . . . stuff."

"It's not 'stuff.' And yes. Why not?"

"Because we need a leader, Conrad, and that leader is you," Piper admitted. "We can't do it without you."

"Sorry." Conrad returned to his table, placing his back to Piper. "You'll have to find someone else."

"There aren't exactly a lot of super geniuses just hanging around the corner store."

"Things happen for a reason," Conrad said quietly. "No one wants us to get involved."

Piper wanted to argue her point more when the dinner bell rang loudly.

"Supper's up!" Betty called. "Come and git it!"

AREA 63 IS A HIGH-SECURITY PSYCHI-atric hospital that houses criminally insane patients who pose a threat to national security. They are considered by the United States government to be the most dangerous people in the world.

It is located just outside a sleepy Massachusetts town in the center of two hundred acres of heavily guarded woods. Most, if not all, of the residents of the town have no inkling of its very presence, which is not strange since it cannot be found on any map, no one in the govern-ment will acknowledge its existence let alone its loca-tion, and no prisoner has ever escaped, been released, or gone missing.

If J. was a moth then Area 63 was his flame.

Patient X, his target, was at the center of Area 63, and to get to her J. was going to have to pass through no less than seven security checkpoints. Being invisible didn't automatically open doors for you. Indeed, invisibility only got you so far in this world, as J. discovered early in the game. You needed other skills like cunning and stealth and intuition and practical skills too. After all, those locks weren't going to pick themselves, and a bloodhound could catch an invisible person almost as easily as a visible one. It had taken a lifetime of hard work for J. to develop the skills that would allow him to tackle a security behemoth like Area 63.

Sweat was pouring down his face and he grunted softly as he pulled himself through a ventilation shaft in the heart of the beast. J. silently opened a hatch and dropped down to the floor. The instant he closed the hatch a security sensor was activated and an alarm sounded. J. positioned himself and waited patiently. Exactly four seconds later a door opened, just as J. knew it would, and he released the rat that he'd stashed in his backpack. The overexcited bloodhound went howling after the rat and J. invisibly slid through the open door, right past the guards. Security checkpoint number three was now behind him.

J. didn't celebrate, didn't pause; his thoughts remained only on Patient X. He must get to Patient X.

Six months earlier J. had heard about Patient X for the first time. It was a night like any other for J.; he was on the move as usual and had a long train ride to Boston. It was late, and with a first-class compartment at his disposal he'd made himself comfortable. No sooner had he stretched out and turned invisible than a middle-aged man bumbled into his compartment and locked the door, unwittingly trapping J. in the corner.

Confident of his aloneness, the man had immediately opened his briefcase, dug through his files, and begun dictating voice memos into his smartphone.

"Patient Jones is experiencing tics and sleeplessness. Decrease haloperidol to three milligrams two times daily, add plasmapheresis as needed."

J. glanced at the man's briefcase, catching sight of the tag on it—DR. HARRISON ANTHROPE. J. sighed to himself. *So much for getting some sleep.*

For the next twenty minutes J. did his best to block out the monotone drone of Dr. Anthrope, but the man had a voice so irritating that it came as no surprise to J. that his patients all seemed to be heavily medicated. At that moment J. would have taken whatever medication Dr. Anthrope offered if only he would stop talking.

"Now on to Patient X," Dr. Anthrope continued, pulling a thick red file from the bottom of his case. "Patient X persists in her delusions. She has elaborate and detailed fantasies of a hidden utopia where everyone has superhuman abilities."

J. sat up in his seat, lightning coursing through his veins.

"Patient X is unable to explain where the imaginary people get their abilities, but claims to have one herself," Dr. Anthrope continued. "She refuses to demonstrate this ability. She is strangely persuasive and influences those around her in disturbing ways. She continues to be a danger to the staff and herself. I recommend no further treatment, no medication, and complete isolation."

J. noticed that Dr. Anthrope's hand was shaking, as though the mere thought of Patient X was causing him trepidation.

"Patient X must have the highest security. Under no circumstances can she be allowed to have contact with any other patients. Only those staff with a level four TS SCI security clearance may address her directly."

Dr. Anthrope abruptly turned his smartphone off, wiped the sweat from his brow, and leaned back in his seat as though spent. He stared out the window into the darkness for long moments.

J. wished he could crawl inside the man's head and know all that was there to be known. Needless to say, when Dr. Anthrope departed the train in Boston the red file of Patient X was mysteriously absent from his briefcase.

It had taken months for J. to plan his route through Area 63, accounting for all eventualities and timing it down to the last second. Standing at the threshold of

Patient X's door, J. tingled to be so close to what he hoped was his holy grail.

Gently cracking open the door six precise inches, J. slid inside the room of Patient X. She was sitting on the floor, her back to him. As she rocked back and forth her forehead made a soft thudding noise against the padded walls. Everything was white: the single mattress that rested on the floor, the linens, her pillows, and her gown. In sharp contrast her hair was raven black, tangled and matted about her shoulders. He watched her closely, considering his options.

"I can hear you breathing," she said. Her voice was low and musical.

J. was disappointed; he had wanted to observe her for a while before making himself known. She continued to rock, the thud of her head against the wall a metronome of sadness marking time infinite.

J. turned visible and placed his backpack upon the ground. He didn't want to scare her so he stayed put. "What is your name?" he asked kindly.

"My name doesn't matter, Jeston. That is not what you came here for."

J.'s breath caught, jagged and hard like a knife against the back of his throat. "What did you call me?"

She rocked and rocked. "Jeston, Jeston, Jeston."

The sound of his name spoken aloud ignited a fury

inside J. He felt exposed and was barely able to contain the urge to rush forward and beat this strange creature into silence.

"Shhhh," he said, and his voice was no longer soft.

"Jeston, Jeston, Jeston."

Would she never stop saying it? "How do you know my name?"

"How do you not know mine? Jeston. Jeston. Jeston."

J. bolted across the room, jerking the woman around and grabbing her by the shoulders. "*Stop* saying my name!" he growled.

"Jeston," she whispered one last time.

J. saw her face then—her sharp green eyes, pale skin, and thin lips. The lips were the only thing that looked different, and only because she wasn't wearing lipstick. The sight of her made him feel like his eyes had been harpooned.

"Letitia?" He released his hold on her, his hands on fire. "Letitia Hellion."

She neither confirmed nor denied it but sat passively, making no movement.

"But you died. You're dead. You fell . . ."

"I wanted to die. I prayed for death, but he wouldn't let me."

"Who wouldn't let you?"

"Him." She wanted to say his name but it wouldn't

come into her head. This frustrated her and she started to rock back and forth again. "Him, him, him."

"Who is *him*?"

"The one who made me into a monster. He made me live and remember everything. He likes the fact that I suffer. If I didn't know and remember I wouldn't suffer as I am. He is . . . a shadow."

J. was too shocked to organize his thoughts, too confused to think about the fact that his time was running out and he must hurry.

"A man who is a shadow?"

She rocked faster. "I want to go home. He won't let me go home."

"I could take you home."

She grabbed at him like a drowning swimmer. "You can take me? Yes. Yes. But . . . do you know where it is?"

The confusion J. felt was apparent on all his features. "If you tell me . . ."

She immediately released him and turned away. "Fool. Stupid. Do you think I'd be here if I could remember that?" She rocked again, holding her head.

Without warning, a powerful emotion washed over J., filling him with an expansive happiness and relief. It was so strong he felt weak. He had never allowed himself to acknowledge what Letitia's loss had meant to him. They had had their differences but family was family.

"I missed you, sister," J. said. She didn't respond and so he sat next to her. "Why didn't you tell me that you could fly? When did you first find out?"

It took several moments for his words to penetrate into her head and for her to find a response. "It started when I was seven. I hated it. I didn't want to be like you. I wanted to hide it."

He nodded; hiding it and pretending it didn't exist would have been much easier. He understood all about that.

"And then there was Sarah . . ." Letitia murmured, unable to finish her thought. Of course with J. she didn't need to explain more. J. knew all about the day that Letitia had flown with their younger sister, Sarah, and there had been a terrible accident when they got caught in a rainstorm. Sarah had slipped out of Letitia's hands and fallen to her death, and Letitia had never forgiven herself or flown again.

"Mom and Dad will be glad to know where you are," J. said, changing the subject.

"They aren't our real parents," Letitia said matter-of-factly and without missing a beat. "They adopted us. They were the ones who called you Johnny, but that wasn't your real name, not the one you were born with."

"*What?* What did you say?"

Letitia was suddenly sharply lucid. "Don't you

remember anything? Nothing?" She watched him closely and saw that he didn't, and then sighed. "Which is worse? Knowing and not being able to have it, or not knowing and never understanding what could be?"

Her rocking returned and she slipped away again.

An alarm sounded and J. remembered that his time had been limited, only now he didn't care. Like his sister's, his time had become infinite. He gathered his things and turned invisible, staying close beside her.

"I want to know what you know," he told her.

"Jeston. Jeston. Jeston," she said.

J. liked the way his name sounded on her lips.

6

*C*ONRAD'S FATHER ANNOUNCED HIS DEATH on national television. Everyone was watching. Especially Conrad. It is a very peculiar feeling to have your parent declare your death when you happen to know that you are still very much alive.

It was a day like any other on the McCloud farm. Before the sun rose Piper had taken Fido out to stretch his wings. As soon as they had returned to the farm Fido immediately went to Conrad, who was in his lab working on TiTI. Conrad had grown used to the snuffling and bumbling of his new pet and even let him sleep at the foot of his bed. For his own part, Fido didn't like to let Conrad out of his sight and had calmed down considerably as he grew accustomed to the routine of farm life.

After lunch, Conrad, with Fido at his heels, helped Joe with a fence that needed fixing in the back field. By the time that was done and the animals fed for the night, Betty was ringing the dinner bell.

"Piper, I expect you to eat more than that," Betty fussed, filling Piper's plate with another helping of fried chicken. "Conrad, there's a fresh pair of socks on your bed. You've been growing again; I swear your feet is a whole size bigger than last week, so I figured you needed more."

"Thank you, Mrs. McCloud."

Betty was always doing small special things for Conrad. Ever since he'd come to live with them something had told her that the boy needed a little extra mothering. For all of Conrad's smarts, he seemed a little lost to Betty, and she took it upon herself to make him feel cared for, even if it was just making sure he had warm socks and a clean shirt to wear.

"And no feeding that—" Betty searched for just the right word to describe Fido, who sat begging at Conrad's feet. "That—pet or whatever it is at this here table."

"Yes, Mrs. McCloud."

Unseen by Betty, Piper slid a small piece of driftwood about the size of a banana in front of her father. "Saw that when I was out flying," Piper said quietly. "Knew right away that it was made just for you, and I picked it up."

Joe McCloud was as quiet as his wife was chatty.

A small sigh, a nod of his head, or shrug of his shoulder was all it took to get Joe's point across. He was the favorite person to go to when someone needed to talk things out. As Joe fixed a fence or ploughed a field or mended a feed trough it was a common sight to see him trailed by one kid or another talking a mile a minute about something that was on their mind. It was a rare day when they walked away from Joe not feeling one hundred percent better, too.

His gentle hands, weathered by the sun of the summer and the snows of the winter, turned over the piece of wood and nodded. If he wasn't a farmer and he didn't call his whittling a hobby, some fancy city person might actually say that Joe's wood carvings were art.

Joe tucked the piece of wood appreciatively into his pocket and Piper touched his hand with her small pale one.

After two slices of Betty's fresh apple pie, the McCloud clan, both by birth and adoption, gathered around their newly acquired television. It was the night of the national election and Betty was eager to learn the results. As usual, she was as chatty as she was round and had opinions about all the candidates and wasn't afraid to share them.

"Now, that there Senator Harrington would make a fine president. That's who got my vote." Betty nodded approvingly as Senator Harrington's face flashed across the television screen. "He talks nothing but the truth, and I like that. Folks have gotta be able to trust their president, and I say Senator Harrington is as honest as the day is long."

As much as she hated to admit it, even Piper could see why her mother felt kindly toward Harrington. There was something about the way Harrington talked that made you want to listen to him—and believe in him. He was almost hypnotic.

Suddenly Betty squinted and leaned forward to study the screen with a renewed intensity. "I declare, I din't notice this 'fore but this brand-new TV is so sharp it makes me see that Senator Harrington looks a heap like our Conrad. Don't he, Mr. McCloud?"

Joe McCloud nodded quietly, looking between the television and Conrad.

Piper squirmed uncomfortably. What would her parents think if they knew that Conrad really was the son of Senator Harrington? Betty and Joe had never asked where Conrad came from. To them he was simply a youngen who needed a place to stay and a family to keep him safe, both of which they were glad to provide.

"Senator Harrington's a big phony," Piper said quickly and with passion. "Sure, he's got blond hair like Conrad, but lots of folks do. And I wouldn't trust him farther than I could throw him." Piper spoke more harshly than she meant to and she cast her eyes in Conrad's direction to see his reaction. Conrad was sitting with Fido on his lap, petting him absently; his eyes fixed on the television screen, his face intense and unguarded, as though he had forgotten that anyone was around. Piper could see naked longing in his expression, as if he was drinking in every image of his father and was thirsty for more; as if he wanted to climb through the television and stand next to him.

Piper could imagine but never know what it must feel like to have your father heartlessly abandon you and never want to see you again. As much as Conrad acted nonchalant, something like that had to hurt.

For the better part of an hour the family watched the results come in and the analyses accumulate until finally they braced for the big announcement.

"And winning the election by a landslide," the reporter on the television told them excitedly, "is Senator Harrington. I repeat, Senator Harrington is officially the president elect of the United States of America."

Betty clapped excitedly. A flush spread across Conrad's face and it seemed to Piper that he was looking at his father with pride.

When President Elect Harrington came forward with his wife, he also introduced his four-year-old daughter,

Althea. Piper knew that it was the first time Conrad was catching a glimpse of his baby sister, who was born after Dr. Hellion had taken him away. She stood very still, holding her mother's hand as the cheering died down and Harrington launched into his victory speech.

"I believe in action and results. I am a can-do man and this is a can-do nation." President Harrington was tall with square shoulders and a handsome face. No question, Conrad was his spitting image.

"The recent death of my son was a hard test for my wife and me to overcome," he continued. "But—like this great nation—we found a deeper strength inside of us. We found strength in our pain and used it to move us forward to reach for something better."

Piper was aghast. "Did he just say his son *died*?"

Conrad's face drained of all color.

It was one thing to reject your son; it was another thing to declare him dead in front of the entire world.

Conrad was not stupid: he knew that he wasn't dead. He rationally and factually knew that he was very, very much alive. Which made it all the more strange that he suddenly felt the life seep out of him.

7

BY SPRING CONRAD HAD A LINGERING cough that wracked his thin shoulders and caused his entire body to bend. Dark circles lined his eyes and he had somehow managed to lose even more weight so that his clothes hung like a defeated flag about his body. To Piper he looked like he was being habitually starved and whipped, neither of which was true.

Conrad walked slowly and kept his eyes down as they left the Lowland County Schoolhouse. He bent forward to counterbalance the weight of his book bag against his bony back.

"What you got in that bag?" Piper chirped, bobbing next to Conrad, as though her sheer enthusiasm might rescue his low spirits. "A small planet?"

"Math homework." Conrad switched the lump of a bag to his other shoulder.

"*You* have homework?" Piper rolled her eyes. "Conrad, that's plain crazy."

"Actually," he explained, "there's nothing crazy about it. Most kids find math very challenging."

"Most kids haven't hacked into the United States Defense Department mainframe and reprogrammed an orbiting satellite. And most kids haven't figured out a way to bend the space-time continuum so—"

"Most kids at twelve years old—"

"You're *not* most kids." Piper stopped suddenly and blocked Conrad's path. "You're not even some kids. You're in a group of one—you're a super genius."

"Not anymore." Conrad stepped around Piper and continued down the path.

Piper sighed deeply: *That again.*

Ever since that darned election Conrad had become a different person. The very next morning Conrad couldn't even get out of bed and didn't go to his workshop in the barn. Long days passed where Conrad just sat in his room, staring out the window with Fido curled at his side.

Of course, when you have a brain that is soaring like a jet sitting on top of your shoulders and it suddenly grinds to a halt, there are consequences. Conrad developed blinding headaches; his head hurt so much that he couldn't eat or get out of bed. His room had to be absolutely dark and he would lie perfectly still until the throbbing had eased enough for him to sit upright. Gradually he became accustomed to the pain and convinced Betty and Joe to let him go to the local country school. It was a basic place, but Conrad thought it might be good for him to attempt simple tasks like the other farm children of Lowland County to clear the fog that had settled over his brain.

He worked very, very hard at the Lowland County School, but as far as Piper could tell, the closer Conrad came to normal the sicker he got. When Piper had first met Conrad he was puffed up with anger and devious plans. His blond hair caught the light and framed his handsome face while his body, like his mind, was always in motion toward some greater purpose. That Conrad was a distant dream, and the person who walked next to her as they left the schoolhouse was shrunken and dull, like central casting had sent a bad stand-in for the real thing.

As another coughing fit wracked Conrad he dropped his book bag and held onto a tree trunk for support. He had already entered the wood that bordered the playground, and Piper leaned over, concerned.

"Maybe you should go see Doc Bell again. You've had that cough for months now."

"I'm okay."

"You look like something the cat dragged in."

"I left my throat drops in my desk," Conrad said through a cough.

"I'll get 'em," Piper offered quickly.

"No, I should—"

Piper turned on her heels and was gone before he could argue. When the coughing fit subsided Conrad slowly straightened up and once again began walking into the wood.

Just as the path rounded a bend and he was out of view of the schoolyard a branch snapped loudly. It was immediately followed by sharply rustling leaves. Moments later Rory Ray Miller emerged from the bushes, flanked by his four brothers.

Rory Ray was seventeen and bulky from hard work in the fields. His callused hands toyed with a tree branch, pleased with its weight and heft. It annoyed Rory Ray, more than he was already annoyed, that Conrad didn't look scared and wasn't trying to run away. It was only further confirmation of what Rory Ray felt about Conrad, which was that there was something wrong with him. He knew Conrad was different—it was clear that the boy was physically weak and in pain. But other times it was something else entirely—perhaps the hunch that Conrad was far more dangerous than he appeared and posed some unnamed threat to Rory Ray and everyone else, too. A twisted herd instinct that dwelled in the deepest reaches of Rory Ray Miller was activated by the mere sight of Conrad.

"I done told you that you ain't wanted in these parts, Conrad No-name."

Conrad wouldn't tell anyone his true last name and so Rory Ray had taken to calling him "No-name." Rory Ray sauntered forward and his younger brothers flanked his every movement. "If I din't know better I'd start to think you liked these beatings."

Conrad watched the band of boys but said nothing. He made no movement to run away or preparations to fight. He was for all intents and purposes frozen, as though he knew what was about to happen next, but was unable to participate in it in any meaningful way.

"Maybe we didn't make ourselves clear," Jimmy Joe sneered.

"Maybe he ain't got the smarts to figure out exactly what our meaning is," added another brother.

Conrad couldn't think of what to say to this and so said nothing, giving Rory Ray the opportunity to lunge forward, smack him into the dirt, and force his face to taste muck. The four younger Miller brothers eagerly circled, Jo-Jo James getting a lick in with his strong right foot and Bobby Boo ripping Conrad's book bag away to scavenge through it.

Elbowing through the pack, Rory Ray grabbed Conrad's shirt in his beefy hand and yanked him up, eye level to dirty-sink teeth and stink breath. "We keep tellin' you and tellin' you that we don't like strangers none. Seems to me you must have some sort of learning disability, 'cause we can't seem to get the message through your thick head."

"Maybe we ain't talking right and he can't hear us none," a brother suggested helpfully.

"Or maybe we don't need to talk at all."

Conrad let himself fall limp like a helpless rag doll in the big boy's hands as Rory Ray Miller and his four brothers each took a turn. Even as he lay submitting to their blows Conrad considered how strange it was that he wasn't feeling any pain—or perhaps, he mused, that the pain had begun to feel good.

It would have gone on longer, but suddenly the leaves a few feet behind the boys scattered like they had been hit from above. Or like someone had dropped out of the sky on top of them. By the time the Miller boys turned around Piper McCloud was running full tilt at Rory Ray.

"Teacher's looking for you, Rory Ray." Piper squared

off directly in front of the big boy. Even though she had turned eleven in August, Piper only came up to the middle of Rory Ray's chest; heavy farm work had built his muscles and made him as strong as a bull.

"Outta my way!" Rory Ray reached to push Piper aside, but instead of flinching, Piper stepped forward and put her finger in the middle of his chest.

"I'll make you sorry." Her eyes blazed and her voice was low and threatening as she pushed her finger into Rory Ray's chest like it was a knife.

Something about the way Piper was standing gave Rory Ray pause. His mother had always said Piper wasn't right in the head. Then there was that strange Fourth of July picnic a few years back when she'd pulled some sort of weird flying stunt. After that strangers showed up and said that Piper had played a hoax on them. The strangers took Piper away, and when she'd finally returned, not that anyone in Lowland County had actually missed her a lick, this kid Conrad shows up out of the clear blue sky and moves in with the McClouds. No one knew who the heck Conrad was or where his kin was from, either. He wouldn't even tell anyone his last name, for heaven's sake. The boy stuck out like a sore thumb in Lowland County and it irked no one quite as much as Rory Ray Miller. Piper and Conrad were as thick as thieves, and while Conrad wouldn't lift a finger to protect himself, it seemed like Piper was itching for a fight. What was it about the small girl with her brown braids and flashing blue eyes that made Rory Ray think twice?

"If teacher's comin' we best scat, Rory Ray." His brothers shifted back and forth fretfully.

Piper waited for Rory Ray to back down, but the boy hated to walk away from easy pickings like Conrad.

"This boy needs a lesson." Rory Ray's voice hardened.

Piper got taller until she was eye level with the hulking farm boy and dealt him the full force of her stare.

"Show me what you got, Rory Ray."

Seeing Piper's feet rise up off the ground got Conrad's attention even if the Miller boys hadn't noticed it yet. "Piper, stop it."

Piper pointedly ignored Conrad. Her finger burned a hole in Rory Ray's chest, causing the fire in his eyes to flicker. He was not a smart boy, but he was smart enough not to tangle with a crazy girl.

"Likes of you ain't worth my notice, Piper McCloud." He laughed in a forced, hollow way and stepped back. "Like my mama says, something ain't right in your head."

Crumpled in the dirt, Conrad meekly looked away and let the boys pass, but Piper wouldn't give them the satisfaction of averting her gaze. She waited until they had crossed from the thicket of trees and back into the schoolyard before she stood down. Only then did she take a good look at Conrad.

"Oh, Conrad, you're bleeding."

Conrad clutched at the place on his stomach where a steel-toed boot had found purchase. Bending down, Piper used her sleeve to dab at the cut on his cheekbone.

"I'm fine."

"That's what you always say. Or 'I heal fast,' or 'Nothing I can't handle.'" Tears formed in Piper's eyes as she bent over him. "They've been beating on you more and more lately and you just let 'em. Why don't you fight back, or run away, or *do something*?"

Conrad tried to roll over and get on his knees, but without Piper's help he would have been stranded.

"I'm not gonna stand by and watch you do this, Conrad." Piper shook her head and took a deep breath. When Conrad didn't answer she pulled him toward home. "C'mon."

Conrad stumbled, but managed to keep up with Piper's marching gait. They walked most of the way home in silence, but by the time they reached the last hill Conrad noticed that Piper's hands were still balled into fists.

"I'm fine," Conrad said in an attempt to break Piper's stony silence.

"No, you ain't." Piper was fit to be tied. "It's like

you're sleepwalking. Snap out of it! I know you, Conrad, and I know what you are. You're not like most kids struggling over their math homework, and you never will be. You're a super genius."

"Not anymore," said Conrad, shaking his muddy head. "Besides, it's not like all my smarts ever did anyone any good."

"It's what you are. You can't not be what you are. What's the point of being able to if I don't fly? I've been blessed with flight, so I've gotta use it as a blessing. I don't want to hide anymore and I don't want to pretend to be what I'm not—and neither should you."

"It doesn't matter, Piper." Conrad pointed out to the world in general. *"We are not wanted!"* He emphasized every single word quietly and with conviction.

"Or maybe it's just *you* who aren't wanted," Piper snapped. "When are you going to stop punishing the rest of us 'cause your pa doesn't want you? Why do you even listen to him or care about him, anyway? What kind of father says his son is dead when he knows well and good that he's not? He's bad to the bone and mean and cruel, and you need to get his words out of your head. 'Cause he won't ever love you or want you back, and he probably never wanted you in the first place."

No sooner had the words escaped Piper's lips than she gasped and her hand flew to cover her mouth in horror. Conrad's eyes darted shamefully and he took a step back.

"I didn't mean it," Piper whispered urgently. She'd crossed the line and knew it. "I didn't mean it."

"Yes, you did. And it's true."

"I was mad and it slipped out."

Conrad turned away and Piper was glad she couldn't see his face. She didn't want to have to watch the way his pupils were going to have to fight to swim above the rising waterline in his eyes. The silence that fell between them was heavy.

Conrad put a muddy hand on his filthy head. He considered Piper to be his only friend. At his darkest hour, it was Piper McCloud who had helped him escape. But the same relentless optimism and unstoppable fervor that she had applied to that task she was now directing toward him, and it was that very thing that was going to destroy their friendship. She couldn't stop herself from trying to save him, but this time Conrad did not want to be saved. Conrad cared for Piper too much, and prized their friendship too highly, to allow anything to threaten it.

"I've been thinking that maybe it's time for a change," Conrad began slowly. "Your parents have been really kind to have me, and I appreciate it, but I've overstayed my welcome."

"What are you saying? My folks love having you. You're family!"

"Plus it's so quiet out here in the country, and I think it would be good for me to try the city for a while. It's easier to get lost and no one knows me there or what I am. It would be better . . . for me."

"You want to leave?" All of a sudden Piper felt desperate. "No! I said I'm sorry and I am. You don't hav'ta—"

"It's not good for us to fight like this, Piper."

"I'll stop. It won't happen again." Tears stung Piper's eyes. "You said this was your home. You said!"

"Things change; I've changed." Conrad shrugged. "Piper, you want to help people and fight, and . . ." He considered his words carefully and chose them with great thought. "I don't care the way you care."

Piper kept her mouth shut and did not ask Conrad if he would allow himself to care if he accepted that he was cared for.

"I'm sorry," Conrad offered, seeing the disappointment in Piper's face. "It's time for me to go."

CHAPTER

8

ON THAT WEDNESDAY IN APRIL, JOE GOT
up and went to work at the normal time. Like his
father before him and his father before that, and probably a great many fathers before that too, Joe McCloud
rose with the sun at five in the morning. Spring plant-
ing was serious business when you lived on a farm, and
Joe had his head full of chore lists.

By the time the chickens had been fed, the cattle
milked and turned out into the pasture, and the sheep
moved from the front field over to the north pasture,
Joe paused at the barn door to catch his breath. Somewhere between some harvest and the coming of its
following spring he had grown old without realizing it.
The dusting of gray hairs on his head had turned into a
forest of silver, and his thin shoulders, once rigidly straight,
had become bent. Holding on to the door, Joe was amazed
by how hard it was to draw breath into his lungs. He

considered the fact that he might have been walking too quickly, or that the morning wind had pushed too much against him, and waited for his body to right itself.

Absently he wondered where Conrad was. The boy had been with him so much over the last months. Before and after school, Conrad would just fall into step behind him and silently go about helping him with the various tasks of the farm. Not that morning, though, and Joe wondered, as he struggled for breath, where he might be. He knew that Conrad was a good boy, and Joe's heart was often saddened as he watched the terrible struggles going on inside one so young. There was nothing that the old man could do but stand next to him, as the boy's mind tossed and turned day after day. A steady man like Joe knew the power of faith and held firm to the knowledge that Conrad would find his own way in his own good time, and left him the space to do so.

From his bedroom window, Conrad had seen Joe walk to the barn that morning but he'd hung back in the shadows of his room with Fido at his side, gathering the last of his things in preparation for his departure. He wanted to leave without saying good-bye, but he couldn't do it. He knew that Joe would say little to nothing, but that wasn't what bothered him—it bothered him to not be with Joe, who was more to Conrad than his own father had ever been.

A mist clung to the fields as the heat of the rising sun hit the wet and cold morning air. When Conrad crossed the yard to the barn, he saw the sheep grazing in the pasture and knew the chickens would be sitting on their eggs in the henhouse after their morning breakfast had been pecked away.

It surprised Conrad to see Joe leaning against the barn door, swaying like an autumn leaf clinging to its branch—as though undecided whether or not to fall. Then Joe looked up to see Conrad and a smile touched the corner of his lips. Not more than a whisper later Joe crumpled, as though the earth was sucking him downward, and he fell on his knees and then down onto the ground.

Conrad ran to Joe's side, his arms scooping at him.

"Mr. McCloud? Where does it hurt?"

Joe's hand clutched at his chest and his breath came in labored gasps. With shaking fingers, Conrad pulled Joe's shirt back and quickly loosened the old scarf he kept around his neck. In front of him sacks of grain were stacked against the barn, waiting to be pulled to the feed room, and, just inside the barn, a pitchfork, shovel, and rake were hung. There was nothing within arm's reach that was going to help Joe at that moment.

Twisting away, Conrad gently laid Joe down on his back and rested his head on the floor. Joe was too heavy to lift and Conrad wouldn't risk trying it.

"Mr. McCloud, can you hear me?" Conrad held Joe's face and hovered over him, intently. Fido whined and nudged Joe tentatively with his horn as though to wake him.

Joe nodded, a fish out of water; gasping, gasping.

"Slow your breathing down as much as you can. Focus on relaxing and taking deep breaths." Taking Joe's hand, he placed it on his own chest and took a long, slow breath, all the while looking into Joe's eyes. "Like this. Long and slow. Long and slow."

Joe nodded again. His gasps became longer in duration but were gasps nonetheless.

"I'll be right back, right back," Conrad repeated. "Fido, stay."

Conrad crossed the yard and before the screen door had closed behind him, yelled, "PIPER!" The volume and pain in his voice startled even himself.

Betty immediately dropped the dish she was washing and turned around from the sink with dripping hands. "Lands' sakes, child, what's gotten into you this morning?"

"PIPER!"

Grabbing the wooden stool under the window, Conrad pulled it to the cupboard and climbed atop it, reaching back to where the medicinal powders were kept.

With her hair half braided and no shoes or socks yet on her feet, Piper landed at the bottom of the stairs with confusion and surprise written all over her face.

"Fly now," Conrad said. "Get Dr. Bell and bring him back here immediately. Go! GO!"

Looking from Conrad to Betty, and back to Conrad, Piper's confusion was apparent. "But why do we need Dr. Bell?" Suddenly looking out to the farmyard for her father and not seeing him, Piper answered her own question. "Pa . . ."

"Use the fastest route possible."

Piper's feet left the ground before the screen door bounced shut.

With Betty's help, Conrad was able to lift Joe onto a small cart and pull him to the house, where they carefully but gently laid him down on the couch. Before they even reached the house, Joe was slipping in and out of consciousness. When he was settled on the couch, Conrad began giving him small doses of aspirin. Joe perked up for a short while and then drifted away again.

Betty ran to gather anything that Conrad might need, but Conrad's mind was cloudy and rusted; he held his forehead as though trying to crank it into movement faster.

Doc Bell walked through the kitchen door right on Piper's heels to find Conrad leaning over Joe, with the heels of both hands over his heart. He pumped rhythmically on his chest with all his strength.

"He needs adrenaline," Conrad said to Doc Bell, who was temporarily rendered motionless by the scene before him. "STAT!"

Doc Bell roused himself to his task and moved in, pushing Conrad out of the way. "Step aside, son. I'll take over now."

Conrad followed behind Doc Bell, watching and scrutinizing his every decision. With red eyes, Piper held tightly to Betty's hand, her lips praying the same word over and over again in a silent chant. "Please," she said, "please, please, please, please . . ."

Betty, who had sat at her mother's and father's bedsides and at those of many other friends and neighbors in Lowland County at their time of passing, felt a creeping familiarity tickling up from her feet and into her legs. Her normal common-sense manner completely deserted her and she did not do one practical thing, but instead succumbed to every memory and moment that she had spent with Joe over their entire life together: the night of their wedding when he gently held her in his arms and fumbled across the dance floor; the spring when the rains came and the tractor got stuck and Joe spent three days and nights digging it out; the way Joe liked to eat apple pie—real slow, as though he could make it last forever. And the day Joe picked up Piper for the first time and his face lit up as though the sun were rising from inside his head, his hands trembling at her impossible littleness and the whiteness of her skin against his thick, fumbling mitts.

A cool breeze washed over them and Doc Bell said, "There's nothing more I can do."

Betty's hand came to her heart.

"But there has to be something," Conrad urged.

"He needs to be in a cardiac unit at a major medical facility."

"What about—" Conrad stuttered, trying to pull thoughts from his head, thoughts that were slow to come.

"He's been without oxygen for over ten minutes, Conrad. You got his heart started, but it can't maintain."

Doc Bell took off his stethoscope and wrapped it around his neck absently. Piper let go of her mother's hand and stepped between her father and Doc Bell, as though she were brokering a fight between them.

"But . . . can't you keep trying?" When Doc Bell looked down at his shoes, Piper looked to Conrad with wild eyes. "Conrad?"

Conrad turned away, grabbing hold of a chunk of his hair and pulling on it as if he could twist the answer out of his brains. "I need to think—think—"

Piper followed him with her eyes, hanging on his every motion, faithfully waiting for him to turn around and give a brilliant plan.

Conrad's mental tentacles reached and stretched, flailing wildly but finding no purchase.

When Piper witnessed Conrad's defeat she did the only thing she could think of. Bending down, she took Joe's hand in hers, and even though she was now eleven her fingers were still impossibly tiny and delicate against his. "Pa? Pa? I'm right here," Piper whispered to the still and crumpled face. "Don't go. I'm right here."

Betty came to Piper's side and put her hand over Piper's and the three hands were entwined. Piper's little hand between Betty's on one side and Joe's on the other.

"Shhh," Betty said.

Piper couldn't stop her pleas and so Betty repeated over and over again, "Shhh," until Piper's sobs prevented her from forming words.

And standing with his back against the wall, Conrad broke. He didn't sob or cry; indeed he was unable to move. It wasn't his cells but the atoms in his cells that separated and went riot over the pain of their existence. Conrad knew that if he moved even a fraction of a moment, he would disintegrate, and so he carefully kept from spilling out and shattering against the wood floor.

How, Conrad wondered to himself, could he live in a world that didn't hold Joe McCloud?

And the answer that Conrad had to that question was that he couldn't live without Joe. Joe McCloud was essential. Being a logical person, Conrad quickly realized that everyone was essential. And that included himself—he, Conrad, was essential and important and . . . not dead.

But if everyone was essential, Conrad understood, that changed everything. And suddenly, as though a dark cloud was blown free from the path of bright sunlight, his thoughts became brilliant and true again and then Conrad knew exactly what to do.

———◆———

THERE WAS NO RUSH NOW.

Conrad walked slowly to the barn, where his make-shift laboratory was coated in dust. Sitting on wood planks that he had made into a table was TiTI.

In a safe in the floor he'd locked away the eyedrop-per of plutonium. On the top of the egg was a place for him to insert his finger, and when his finger slid into it and his identity was verified, a compartment on the side opened. He carefully worked through the procedures and watched the plutonium settle into the receiving cham-ber at the core of the egg.

As he slid everything back into place, a small humming

sound vibrated out of TiTI. Conrad programmed a digital timer and then placed his hands on either side of the egg, gripping it lightly and making sure that all ten fingers made contact.

For many miles around, a strobing light could be seen detonating outward from the McCloud barn. That same light then hung suspended for an extended moment, as though time itself suddenly went into slow motion, and then a split second later the light was sucked back to its source, leaving everything in its wake strangely scrambled. The inhabitants of Lowland County were left to rearrange themselves back to their normal state and wonder if what had just happened was real or imagined. Most folks in Lowland County, being sensible people, chose to believe the latter.

ON THAT WEDNESDAY IN APRIL, PIPER woke feeling defeated after a fitful night. Today was the day that Conrad was leaving. She never would have thought that things would end like this and Conrad would just pack up and go away. As hard as she tried, she couldn't think of a way to persuade him to stay, and all her arguments fell on deaf ears. Once Conrad made a decision there was no swaying him.

Turning over in her bed, Piper almost jumped out of her skin. Sitting pressed up against her bed was Conrad! With shining eyes and a strangely joyful face, he was perched on her small wooden chair, waiting for her to wake up. As soon as he saw that she was awake, he leapt forward and seized her hand.

"Piper, you're right. You are absolutely right."

"What the heck, Conrad! You almost scared me half

to death." Piper's heart was jumping about like a terrified jackrabbit.

"Piper, I've got to start doing things differently!"

"What are you talking about?" Piper drew back from Conrad. He was acting weird and his clothes looked strange—as if he'd been wearing them for weeks and weeks. She saw that parts of them were ripped and stained with some strange substance. But last night when she had seen him in them, they were pressed and clean. What had he been up to for the last few hours?

"What I'm talking about is that we have incredible abilities and we've been wasting them! Look at you! You can fly! *Fly!* And what are you doing with it?" Conrad jumped to his feet and began pacing back and forth in a feverish excitement. "We can't waste any more time. Not one second!"

"Really?" Even though this was exactly what Piper wanted to hear, and how she felt, she never thought in a million years that she would hear it coming out of Conrad's mouth. Piper rationally knew that there was no possible way that Conrad could have changed so radically in the course of a few hours.

"What happened to you?" She monitored him closely.

"I can think again," Conrad said, holding his temples.

"I understand and I care. I care like you care. And I know what I have to do."

"You do?"

"Yes."

"Why?"

"Because, because it's the only rational thing to do!"

"But you said there was no point. You said—"

"You kept telling me that it was wrong not to use our blessings as a blessing. You said we had to help people in the ways that only we were able. I couldn't see the point until I could. I see it now."

Piper watched Conrad's frantic, excited pace as he went back and forth across her room. He was himself again, the amazing Conrad she knew and loved.

Conrad held up a file and dropped it next to Piper. She immediately recognized it as the one J. had given him on his birthday.

"And I read this," Conrad said. "My father has been keeping secrets from me for too long. And those secrets are my business, and I'm going to find out once and for all what they are."

Conrad pulled back the curtains and threw open Piper's window.

"My father wants me to stop thinking." He pointed to his head. "When I wouldn't stop he wanted me dead. But I get to decide what I'm going to do with my thoughts and my life, and he can't stop me. He thinks he can, but he's wrong—again. And I'm going to show him exactly how wrong he is."

A smile hit the corners of his mouth and then it turned into a laugh. Reeling around, Conrad grabbed Piper's hands, pulled her out of bed, and started to jump up and down.

"You've lost your mind."

"No, I've found it." Conrad couldn't stop laughing and, despite the fact that it was clear her dear friend had entirely lost his marbles, Piper started to laugh too.

"Let's do it!" Conrad yelled.

"Let's do it!" Piper repeated.

"Stop that racket, you two!" Betty called up from the kitchen. "Breakfast is on."

Conrad stopped dead and looked at Piper as if he were hearing Betty's voice for the first time.

"Where's your father?" Conrad said urgently.

"I don't know."

"I have to see him." Conrad rushed to the window and threw it open. He craned his neck to look out in the direction of the barn. "He should be on his way back for breakfast by now. I can't see him. Where is he?"

"Uh, I don't know," Piper repeated.

Conrad turned around and bolted from her room. Piper could hear him thunder down the stairs, and she dropped out the window and onto the porch. She opened the screen door and came into the kitchen at the same moment that Conrad came down from the stairs. She was in the perfect spot to see his face upon discovering Joe McCloud sitting quietly, as ever, in his chair and drinking his morning cup of coffee.

Piper could have sworn that tears came to Conrad's eyes. He walked with reverence to Joe and put his hand ever so softly on Joe's sleeve, as though to assure himself that Joe was really there.

Oblivious to the strangeness of the scene taking place in her kitchen that morning, Betty was consumed with the tasks before her. As was often the case at meal times, Fido was nosing about under her feet, hoping to catch any stray scraps that might fall. To keep him from pestering her further Betty tossed him a generous crust of bread, whereupon he happily flew to the top of the sideboard and sat munching on it loudly. Wiping the crumbs off her hands, Betty next gathered several prescription bottles off the window ledge and took them to the table, where she began doling out specific numbers of pills from each one.

Startled to see so much medication, Piper came to the table. "What's that for, Ma?"

"Oh, it's nothing." Betty waved away Piper's concern. "A few weeks back Doc Bell showed up out of the blue, saying that Conrad had told him to come and take a look at your pa's heart. Sure enough, just like Conrad said, there was a problem."

Piper noticed that Conrad was nodding as Betty spoke.

"But how come I didn't know?" Despite what Betty said, Piper was worried.

"I thought you did," Betty said evasively, as though she couldn't quite recall why Piper was not part of this. She shrugged and immediately dismissed the matter. "Of course, Doc Bell says that if we hadn't caught it in time, it could have been a nasty business."

Joe patted Piper's hand reassuringly.

"As long as he takes his pills, the doctors say that his heart is stronger than an eighteen-year-old's." Betty finished with the bottles and put them away to get to her next task. "We just thank our lucky stars that Doc Bell caught it in time. You know your pa, he'd as soon go to the doctor as a hen party. Can't say I even remember the last time he went to have Doc Bell take a look at him. It was providence, I tell you, providence plain and simple that Doc Bell came when he did."

As Piper looked between Conrad and her father, a shiver ran up and down the small hairs on her neck. Last night her father had looked tired—his shoulders were bent over and there was a gray tone to his skin—yet as she looked at him this morning, he looked as if he'd grown ten years younger overnight.

"Eggs are getting cold. Sit and eat," Betty commanded, getting Conrad to his chair and moving Piper about. "We've got lots to do today and there's no point standing around, gabbing about things that don't need our notice."

Conrad dug into his food and then asked for more. He sat up straight in his chair and his eyes were shining with excitement and plans and something else: something that Piper had never seen before in Conrad—joy. As long as she would live, Piper would never understand Conrad's miraculous transformation. While Conrad tucked into a huge breakfast, Piper couldn't eat a bite, maybe because she couldn't take her eyes off Conrad— afraid he was a mirage that might momentarily evaporate to reveal the sad, dispirited soul who had been shuffling about the farm for the last few months.

Breakfast was over, the plates were cleared away, and the new Conrad remained. He pulled Piper to the old bank barn.

"Conrad, are you sure you're feeling alright?"

"Never better." Conrad hurried over to one of his worktables, pulled apart a strange device, and quickly reshaped it into something else. Fido landed on the table next to him and began snuffling through the equipment, knocking things over.

"It's very strange is all." Piper sat on a bale of hay. "What happens now?"

"Now," said Conrad, "we call the others."

"Why?"

"Because you all want to change this world for the better. That's why. So, let's do it. If you want a leader, then here I am. It all starts here and now!"

S IT TURNS OUT, IF YOU REACH YOUR fourth birthday and have yet to utter your first word, people tend to get a bit jittery, particularly nervous and overambitious mothers, and this invariably leads to an enormous number of assessments. The purpose of these assessments is to determine exactly and specifically how dumb you are and why you are so dumb and then to hit upon just the right label for your particular brand of dumbness.

Aletha Harrington was exactly four and a half years old, and not a sound had ever been heard to come from her lips. She had her mother's long, curly dark hair, endlessly liquid brown eyes, and an utterly silent bow of a mouth.

Her mother, First Lady Abigail Churchill-Harrington, hovered like an agitated meerkat as Aletha underwent her second assessment that day. Silently, Abigail repeated the same words over and over again: *Say something. Anything. Please.*

"Aletha, babykins, can you purty please pick up the itty red block off the table?" For some reason that no one could fathom, the esteemed Dr. Dillweed spoke only in baby talk. In his dreams he was five feet tall (in daylight not a hair over four foot eight) and he perfectly fit into the toddler-size table in Aletha's playroom. Aletha sat opposite him on a Tinker Bell chair while Dr. Dillweed had to content himself with Fairy Mary.

"Reddy-weddy is such a pretty-witty color. I like reddy-weddy lots." Dr. Dillweed smiled and simpered.

Aletha stared at him and had nothing to say.

"She knows red. I'm sure of it," Abigail whispered over Dr. Dillweed's shoulder. "She understands; I know she understands."

"Does Aletha-kins like candy-mandy?" Dr. Dillweed held up a lollipop. "Would she likey this itty-bitty sweetie?"

Aletha looked at the lollipop; it was made of swirls of color and was larger than her head. Dr. Dillweed moved it inches from her face, either to tantalize her taste buds or tease her.

"If Aletha-weefa wants the yummy candy, she needs to talky-walky to Dr. Dillyweedy."

"Say you want it, Aletha." Abigail's voice came out

harsh and commanding. She bent down next to Dr. Dillweed and opened her mouth impossibly wide. Using her
fingers, she pointed to the movement of her lips. "Just
say 'yes.' Y-E-S."

Aletha folded her hands one on top of the other and
closed her lips tightly.

Suddenly President Harrington came striding into
the room. Abigail immediately jumped to her feet and
went to him.

"We're still in the middle of the assessment," Abigail whispered to her husband so as not to disturb
Dr. Dillweed. President Harrington looked at his watch
impatiently. He hadn't so much as set eyes on Aletha
in weeks, but Abigail had insisted—as in put her foot
down—that he show up to hear what the doctor had
to say.

"I don't have time for this. I have important things
to do," he snapped.

"And your daughter isn't important?" Abigail's whisper became harsh and accusing.

"She's fine." He dismissed Aletha with a wave of his
hand.

"She won't talk. That's *not* fine."

"It's a phase. It's not as if she's like—" President
Harrington stopped himself. He had few feelings for

other people, but he did have feelings for his own self-preservation, and there were certain things he couldn't say to his wife.

Abigail was not fooled. "Like who? Like Conrad? My boy was . . ." Tears came to her eyes and stopped her words.

"Conrad is gone now, and we shouldn't talk about him. Let the dead rest." President Harrington looked at his watch again. "I'm leaving. You deal with this."

When President Harrington looked to his wife again, her eyes were wide and her mouth had fallen open in astonishment. He turned on his heel to see what she was looking at, and there in the middle of the playroom stood Aletha.

Aletha was halfway between the table and where they stood. Both her feet were planted firmly and she was staring straight at her father as her index finger pointed at him. President Harrington stood still in astonishment, and the room was absolutely silent as all eyes rested on Aletha's serious and focused face.

With her finger pointed at her father, Aletha opened her mouth and spoke.

"Conjuror."

No one moved.

"Conjuror," she said again, as though shooting him.

The color drained from President Harrington's face and he took a step back. His eyes darted from side to side shamefully.

"Conjuror."

Aletha lowered her arm and turned back to the table. Taking the massive lollipop out of the hands of the ridiculous Dr. Dillweed, she sat on Tinker Bell and started to enjoy the strawberry swirl.

Unable to meet his wife's eyes, President Harrington backed out of the room. "I want her assessed again," he growled. "There's something wrong with her."

*P*IPER PUT THE WORD OUT AND IT DIDN'T take long for the farm to be overrun by all of their friends. Lily and Jasper, Kimber, Smitty, and the rest couldn't have been happier to see the change in Conrad at long last—for they had all been waiting for the day when Conrad would lead them and they could finally put their abilities to some greater use.

Immediately they transformed the old barn into a beehive of secret activity. The kids cleared away the hay and used the entire loft to suit their needs. In the middle was a raised area covered with mats for hand-to-hand training; around the edges were individual workstations.

"We need to sharpen our abilities and work as a team," Conrad warned the group after the initial excitement of gathering had settled down. "The sum of our talents is greater than our individual parts. Only as a team will we accomplish great change, and not until we work as a team, think as a team, and dream as a team will we be ready for the work before us. This means anticipating one another's strengths and weaknesses, it means communicating without speaking, it means being better than you ever thought you could be."

The kids were expected to be up and ready at sunrise, and by sunset they were often still at it. Conrad divided the day into three parts: the morning began with individual skill development, followed by team-building exercises, and by the afternoon, Conrad assigned the group mock missions. If anyone was still awake or able to stand after the mission Conrad would review results and performance, pointing out ways to improve.

"Precision, control, and discipline," Conrad repeated over and over again. "I want surgeons, not cowboys."

Conrad set Smitty the task of honing his X-ray vision as a lie detector. "When someone lies it affects their nervous system, creating subtle effects on their heart rate and blood flow," Conrad explained. "Learn to use your X-ray vision to detect those variations." And so every day Smitty was given a new target to study and test—trying to determine when they were lying and when they were telling the truth. It was exacting work that required great concentration, and at the end of the day he was spent and grumpy.

Of course, the Mustafa twins could whip up a tsunami that could take out an entire port town, but Conrad pushed them to control the movement of a single small cloud across the sky.

"We're sick of this," they complained after two weeks of working with small clouds. "Give us something fun to do!"

"Fun is what happens when you have control," Conrad snapped. "I don't want cowboys, I want surgeons. Move that cloud at exactly one mile an hour. When it reaches the sun make it hover for ten minutes. Then make it rain away. When you can do that, I'll show you fun."

Everyone was careful to keep a wide berth around Daisy's workstation, where she had to squeeze coal into diamonds (there was more than one incident of exploding coal shooting out willy-nilly across the place), and Kimber's—she had to learn how to channel electrical energy between her two hands until she was able to create light. Once the light was stabilized she had to vary its intensity. On the days she had to create a bright light, things could get a little unpredictable, and more than once a hole was ripped through the walls or roof of the barn.

"It looks like a little lightning b-b-bolt," Jasper commented one day.

"Exactly," Conrad agreed. "Next Kimber's going to learn to throw it." This information pleased Kimber to no end—she couldn't wait to get to the part of throwing lightning bolts about! Smitty lost more than one night's sleep contemplating the exact same scenario and mentally gauging exactly how painful a lightning bolt might be.

Lily complained endlessly about the difficulty of the "jelly bean torture," as she had coined her task. Conrad had devised an exercise for her whereby she had to telekinetically select one white jelly bean out of a bowl filled with red jelly beans. Once she successfully lifted the jelly bean from the bowl she had to move it through a glass maze without once touching the sides. After a solid month of working on this every single morning she completed the entire task flawlessly and turned to Conrad in triumph. Without missing a beat Conrad said, "Okay, do it again but this time blindfolded." At which point Lily picked up the entire bowl of jelly beans, telekinetically, of course, and dumped it over Conrad's head.

The only sore point in the entire operation was Fido, who proved to be absolutely untrainable. Conrad decided that Fido's training should start with learning how to fetch a stick, but Fido would have none of the stick fetching no matter what training method or inducement was offered, and the ground was littered with sticks that had been thrown but would forever remain un-fetched. Instead, Fido spent his days trailing around after Conrad and getting involved with whatever mischief he could find or invent. Once Violet took it in her mind to shrink down and go for a ride on Fido's back, but her first trip proved to be her last. "He flies like a maniac. It makes me feel sick," she complained. And so Fido was left to his own devices and was generally coddled and doted upon by all.

Once the kids had completed their individual train-ing agenda, they were paired up and given team tasks. As soon as Nalen and Ahmed successfully demonstrated their ability to control a small cloud, Piper had to learn to stay within the cloud while Nalen and Ahmed moved it across the sky.

As though that wasn't difficult enough, Lily was assigned the task of telekinetically moving Violet, who had shrunk down to the size of a small doll, through a specifically designed maze that was suspended from the ceiling. It was Violet's task to silently achieve certain goals while Lily moved her. These goals were ever-changing, but they usually involved picking a lock or rewiring a mock bomb or locating a hidden item. As Violet and Lily achieved some mastery, Conrad increased the level of difficulty by challenging Lily to telekinetically move more than one object at once. This proved too much for

Lily, and Conrad set her to juggling objects telekinetically, of course, for days on end until she could do it with
her eyes closed.

Daisy got herself into trouble when she added a ten-
ton boulder to the front-end loader she was holding
above her head and gave herself a sprained wrist. Then
Jasper's hands, which took on incredible heat and light
while healing, became overcharged after saving no less
than twenty-seven squirrels with mysterious stomach-
aches. His skin became burnt and started to peel away
and Conrad had him hold his hands in ice water for
the better part of an afternoon until his hands cooled
down.

Conrad did not hold himself exempt from this process, and challenged himself to create a Direct Brain Interface (DBI), which he then experimented with on his
own head. The device was the size of a quarter and had
the computing power of a mainframe. With the help of
Kimber's electrical precision and Jasper's healing hands
Conrad managed to hardwire it directly into his brain.
He then used the DBI in conjunction with specially designed glasses, which when worn appeared to be normal
glasses, but were actually computer screens in his line of
vision.

Piper was equal parts amazed and disgusted by the

device. "You mean you put a computer inside your brain?"

"No," Conrad corrected, showing her where the device was tucked discreetly behind his ear. "It's not inside, see? It's still outside my body, but I hardwired it into my brain so that I can't take it out."

"So your brain is now talking directly to the computer? It's like your brain's got its own computer." Piper poked at it gently with her face screwed up like she was worried it might explode. "Is that safe? And did *your* brain really need a computer in it?"

Conrad shrugged. "You can never think too fast or have too much information."

———

OF COURSE, THE FACT THAT THE MCCLOUD farm was suddenly bursting at the seams with kids had not gone unnoticed by Betty and Joe.

"We've got youngens comin' out of our ears, Mr. McCloud. Something's gotta be done!" Betty demanded soon after they arrived. She had kids bursting out of bedrooms and sleeping on floors and a crowd that wouldn't fit around the kitchen table jostling to be fed. So Joe got to work on converting the grainery into sleeping quarters for the girls and the upper loft for the boys. This kept the youngens close enough so that an eye could be put on them but far enough away that Betty didn't have to see all the antics they got up to. After all, there was only so much that a God-fearing woman such as Betty McCloud could take of their hijinks.

<hr />

ONE MORNING IN JUNE THE KIDS WOKE UP for training to find that everything had changed. During the night, Conrad had taken away the training mats and workstations and replaced them with a large table in the center of the floor. In front of the table stood a whiteboard and several huge monitors. The size of the new monitors elicited low whistles from Ahmed and Nalen, who appreciated the ever-growing number of electronic toys that were appearing daily, thanks to Conrad, who had hacked into a trust fund still in his name and used his sizable inheritance to fund their burgeoning hardware needs.

"Training is over," Conrad announced, turning on the monitors. "You're ready."

A jolt of excitement rippled through the air.

"This morning we prep; this afternoon will be our first mission."

When Conrad explained that their first mission entailed helping the Lowland County Feed Store locate a lost kitten, an audible groan arose from the group.

"Why waste our time on a stupid kitten?" complained Kimber. "We've got better things to do."

"The difficulty is not in the mission itself," Conrad explained to the disgruntled faces, "but in concealing that we have any involvement with it or, in fact, that we were ever even there. No one can ever see us. No one can know what we are doing. No one must know what we are capable of. We must be silent, work quickly, and then disappear."

"I could find a lost kitten if I was blind," Smitty complained.

"Let's get to work." Conrad turned to the monitors, flicking up real images of the terrain around the feed store and pictures of the lost kitten in question. He drew maps on the whiteboard and assigned tasks to teams so that at precisely half past one that afternoon the main street of Lowland County was the epicenter of something quite extraordinary. It was extraordinary because absolutely no one who happened to be walking the street or visiting the few stores was in the bit least aware of what was taking place.

First a single cloud, perhaps drifting a tad bit lower than normal, began hovering here and there above the street. Next, a boy with braces on his teeth climbed a tall oak tree and perched on an upper branch. This didn't catch anyone's attention and they certainly didn't notice the way he was scanning the area, his eyes squinting. No one felt a strong breeze whipping from place to place, and they certainly didn't see the girl who was running so fast that she created the breeze.

It was completely outside the imaginations of anyone in Lowland County, or anywhere else for that matter, to conceive of the idea that there was a flying girl hidden inside the cloud and that she was looking for a kitten. It was equally inconceivable that the boy in the tree had X-ray vision and that he was using it to direct the movements of a girl who could run at the speed of light. Of course, Lily's arrival at the feed store did raise a few eyebrows—there wasn't many a nine-year-old girl with an elegant silk green dress loitering in the dusty place on a normal weekday. But Lily settled herself in a corner quietly and soon no one gave her a second thought, even though she seemed to be looking at the pipes in a strange way. Never in a million years did they think that she was telekinetically moving another girl, who had shrunk down to the size of a tennis ball, through the pipes in search of a lost kitten who might have been stuck.

By two o'clock Smitty's X-ray vision had uncovered the kitten's location—she was stuck inside a small cavern at the side of a hill. Daisy moved in on the target without incident and removed several boulders without compromising the stability of the cavern. Jasper came next and made short work of healing the kitten's broken paw and damaged eardrum. Lily had just enough time to slip from the doors of the feed store as Myrtle deposited the kitten on the steps in plain view of Mr. Waynewright.

"Well, would you look at that? If it's not my little Meow," said Mr. Waynewright, scooping up the small ball of fluff. "I'd done gone and given you up for lost. But here you is. How'd you like a nice bowl of milk?"

Meow liked her bowl of milk very, very much, and that night there was a rip-roaring celebration at the Mc-Cloud farm. Despite the fact that the kids claimed the mission was entirely beneath them, when it was completed they felt an amazing amount of pride and an explosive sense of optimism.

SOON THEREAFTER IT GOT TO THE POINT where everyday miracles became the norm and folks in Lowland County started thinking of themselves as the luckiest people in the whole country. And the truth was, they were.

When a terrible drought hit and farmers couldn't keep their crops alive for anything, Lowland County got a full season of rain and crops that grew higher and better than any year before. Did anyone in Lowland County realize that Ahmed and Nalen Mustafa, adept weather changers, were responsible? You bet they didn't.

Or, just before the July Fourth barbecue, a truck full of high school kids got stuck on the old stone bridge over the river and it looked as though the bridge was going to collapse right then and there. But just as calamity was about to strike, it didn't, and everyone slept soundly in their beds that night. Not only that, but when the bridge was checked the next day it was stronger than the day it was first built. Could anyone in Lowland County have guessed that it was Lily who telekinetically lifted the car off the bridge in just such a way that it appeared to be rolling of its own accord, or that Smitty had used his X-ray vision to report the crack to the foundations of the bridge, or that Daisy had used her super strength to shore it up with new rocks and concrete? Of course no one thought to think that, because to imagine such a complicated and impossible set of circumstances would be completely insane.

And once the kids had whetted their appetites in Lowland County, their hunger began to grow. Small miracles and happy accidents turned into major relief efforts. The bigger the scale and more complex the job, the more Conrad worked overtime to keep a handle on every single tiny little detail. And he liked the challenge of it. It was a task worthy of his ridiculous abilities. He wasn't the only one—they all got good. They worked as a team and they figured out how to do things better, faster, cleaner.

As the summer days passed and fall took hold it seemed as though nothing could stop them and nothing could ever go wrong. They were on a roll and the sky was the limit.

CHAPTER

12

A WHISPER SWEPT ACROSS THE NATION, through playgrounds and parks, toy stores, Girl Scout meetings, during Little League practice and soccer tryouts. One kid would lean in to another and in a voice hardly audible would tell what they knew or heard: just snippets—never more than that.

Because the truth was that no one knew much, but everyone was hungry to hear more. Some kids were more hungry than others; they had to know *now*, wanted to know *everything*. They searched and listened and waited impatiently.

They called themselves "the Seekers."

On a farm outside of San Francisco, Bella Lovely charged home from her art class with a dirty piece of paper the size of an eraser clutched in her hand. She got to her computer, feverishly praying she was in time: twice before she'd been too late. Her fingers shook so much that she had to type the address in four times before she finally got it right.

www.LookToTheSky.org

Bella gasped as a simple Web site, consisting of a single page, filled her computer screen. Success! She ate the small piece of paper and read her screen quickly, her lips moving to form the words but careful not to let any sound escape.

Beware—this information is dangerous.

If you are reading this it is because you have heard and want to become part of what is happening. There are a lot of rumors and stories, but not all of them are true. We will tell you the whole story and the whole truth and then you can decide for yourself.

There is a girl who can fly. We have seen her.

There are others like her and they have started to affect change and help. They do this silently.

They cover their tracks so that no one will find them. They are very, very smart.

They are led by a boy who knows everything—

Suddenly sparks flew off her computer and her screen went black. Bella screamed and jolted backward. She was not scared, but disappointed. She had been so close—everything she had wanted to know had been right in front of her.

She leaned back in her chair, allowing her knobby eleven-year-old knees to kick back and forth while she considered what had just happened. These whispers she was hearing were awakening something inside of Bella, something she couldn't quite place her finger on. Sometimes she felt like she could almost remember, but in the next moment it was gone, like a shadow following you but always out of sight. The more she discovered the more she needed to know. What she wanted to find out exactly she couldn't precisely place a name on, but the feeling of that discovery was undeniable, the longing was palpable, and the need burned inside her.

As the wiring in her computer softly sizzled, her resolve found new strength. Tomorrow she would see what else she could find out. Maybe next week or next month there would be a better lead. Bella wasn't going to give up. Not now, not ever. . . .

A T THE START OF THE SCHOOL YEAR THAT autumn the number of new students at the Lowland County Schoolhouse swelled by an unprecedented amount. Betty McCloud had to do some fancy footwork to explain why she had such a bevy of foreign children suddenly living on the farm, a fact that had not gone unnoticed by the watchful eye of Millie Mae Miller.

"Don't know what them McClouds is up to," Millie Mae sniffed to her sewing circle. "Got youngens comin' out of the woodwork from heaven knows where, doing heaven knows what. Something's goin' on is all I'm saying. I don't know what but it's something. I for one am keeping my eye on 'em, I'll tell you that much!"

Conrad was more than aware that despite his best efforts the activities at the farm were not completely covert. He was also keenly sensitive to the fact that they couldn't afford to have their base of operations threatened by whistle-blowing neighbors, and he therefore strategically determined that the best way to squelch gossip was by hiding in plain sight: namely, in school. Like it or not (and the kids definitely did *not* like it) Conrad had Betty enroll every single one of them in school and then made sure they arrived on time and ready to learn. As Conrad predicted, the folks in Lowland County grew slightly less suspicious, while not particularly friendly, when they saw that they were just normal kids. The fact that they weren't normal kids, not normal by a long shot, was a detail that required Conrad's constant attention.

On the first day of school Lily had to abandon her silk dresses and wear a serviceable cotton gingham. This was tantamount to death as far as Lily was concerned.

"It itches. I can't stop scratching," she complained, her face going red and her hands pulling at the material as though it were on fire.

They were trudging down the road to the school-house and even though it was a perfectly pleasant morning the looks on the kids' faces would have convinced any unknowing onlooker that they were on a death march. Lily happened to be the most passionate and vocal, but if the others weren't voicing their unhappiness, they were loudly thinking it.

"Lily, none of the kids in Lowland County are

flouncing about in silk dresses from Paris," Conrad explained. Again. "We have to fit in."

"Ugh. How does anyone wear this? It's torture!" Lily fussed.

When they arrived at the schoolyard things did not improve. Rory Ray Miller and the rest of the Lowland County kids stopped what they were doing and stood staring at them. In the schoolroom it was a new teacher's first day, and without any prior information to prepare him for how to deal with this strange and divided community, he assigned seating. Thankfully Piper was placed next to Violet, but Conrad was forced to share a desk with Rory Ray Miller, a situation neither was happy with.

One of the unexpected consequences of starting school again was that the new teacher immediately saw that Piper was exceptional. Unfortunately it wasn't the sort of exceptionality she was accustomed to.

Piper had never been one for math—everyone knew that. Unlike their other teacher, who hadn't paid much attention to anything, Mr. Finley was fresh out of teacher's college and up on all the newest learning methods and testing assessments, which he was eager to employ. He discovered at once that Piper's faculties for numbers and mathematics was more than just limited; Piper was unable to recite any of her multiplication tables, had difficulty with long division of even the most rudimentary kind, and couldn't make heads or tails of decimals or fractions.

"Ugh, my brain hurts when I look at these," Piper complained. "It's like they're angry ants on the page."

"I'm sorry to say," Mr. Finley told her, "that you have dyscalculia."

Somehow Mr. Finley did not seem in the least bit sorry, but quite pleased with himself. He was, just as he suspected, a great teacher, and his ability to diagnose Piper McCloud's learning disability was, in his opinion, further proof of this. Without delay he promptly sent a very clinical note home to Betty and Joe McCloud detailing Piper's condition. Needless to say, Betty was fit to be tied.

"There'll be no more gallivanting for you 'less you sits yourself down and learns your lessons." Betty waved the spoon she was using to stir the soup at Piper.

It was Piper's turn to be appalled. "But Ma . . ."

"There'll be no buts." Betty had planted herself firmly and there was no budging her. "Flying is all well and good but schoolwork comes first. And if you don't learn these math lessons like Mr. Finley says, then these goings-on about this farm will stop once and for all."

With that last comment Betty had Conrad's full attention too. Conrad had long suspected that Piper's mathematical sense was not normal but had never felt the need to place a label on it. As it was, they had an urgent situation that very evening to attend to and Conrad couldn't do without Piper's flying.

"I can help, Piper," Conrad offered Betty. "I'll make sure she catches up."

Betty eyed Conrad. "She don't need you doing her lessons for her. Ain't no way that'll teach her anything."

"No, ma'am," Conrad agreed. "She needs teaching. I can help do that."

Betty sniffed suspiciously. "Well, see that you do, or mark my words, all you youngens can stay put."

True to his word, Conrad immediately got to it. A mine had collapsed in Tennessee, and while they worked through the night saving the miners Piper had more than flying to worry about.

"There were thirty miners down in the shaft to begin with, isn't that right, Smitty?" Conrad asked over the comm.

"That's right," Smitty grunted, trudging through dirt to get a better view of the terrain.

"So, Piper, we've rescued half of them; how many are left?"

Piper was flying a miner up through the center of a rock that Daisy had busted through. The miner was a heavy guy and unconscious. To make matters worse it was pouring with rain, she was tired, and it was late. "Uh, I don't know."

"Think about it," Conrad pressed. "We started with thirty and now half are safe. What is thirty divided by two?"

"Ten?"

"You're guessing. Picture the numbers in your mind."

"My mind doesn't like the numbers, Conrad," Piper huffed. The guy she was lugging up to the surface was 210 pounds easy.

"What number multiplied by two equals thirty?"

"I don't know."

"Sure you do."

Piper reached the surface and the miner's eyes fluttered open. "You're going to be okay," she told him.

"Piper, I mean it, answer the question. What is thirty divided by two?"

"Fifteen," the miner whispered to her.

Piper smiled. "It's fifteen," she repeated.

"I heard that," Conrad said.

While salvaging a plane from the Pacific Ocean, Piper practiced her multiplication tables, and as they rescued a pod of beached whales in San Francisco Bay, she worked through word problems.

"I don't get it," she fussed. "If he picks an apple every mile and walks ten miles why doesn't he have ten apples?"

Piper got out of Jasper's way as he placed his healing hands on the whale she was attending to. Daisy was using her super strength to move the whales into the water and Nalen and Ahmed were causing the tide to rise to make the job easier.

"Because he started with an apple, Piper." Conrad manipulated his sensors and spoke into the comm. "Myrtle and Smitty, I have an incoming pedestrian on the west side of the beach."

"Copy that, I have a visual," came Smitty's response.

"Maybe it's the apples that are confusing me," Piper said pathetically. "Can he have something else besides apples?"

"Go home, Piper," Conrad said. "We're almost done here and it'll give you more time to finish up your homework before you go to sleep."

Piper was relieved. With school and their rescue efforts she had more than enough on her plate. "See y'all back at the farm." Piper flew away for home.

Daisy, Jasper, and Lily guided the last whale into the water. The team stood together watching them swim away as Conrad monitored their progress with sonar.

"They'll clear the bay in thirty minutes," Conrad reported. "Well done, team. Pack up, move out."

Five minutes later the beach was empty, with no evidence that they had ever been there. As Conrad surveyed the scene one last time he noticed a strange red pebble in the sand. Leaning down, he picked it up and held it between his fingers, watching the way the moonlight made it shimmer and glow. Although he had an encyclopedic knowledge of geology, this specimen was like none he had ever seen before. Strangely enough, he'd found two others just like it in the last three weeks: one by the entrance to the collapsed coal mine and the other near a bomb site. Wrapping his fingers tightly around the stone, he held it in his fist and disappeared into the night.

CHAPTER 14

9T WAS THE MIDDLE OF THE NIGHT AND J., as only J. could, had silently gathered Piper and Conrad to the barn without rousing another soul on the farm. Conrad immediately noticed that J. was more agitated than he'd ever seen him, his skin gaunt and pale, as though he'd been without sunlight for months.

After shedding his backpack, J. had drawn them close together and hunkered down, his face inches from Piper and Conrad, his voice low and urgent.

"There is a place that is hidden and no one can get to. Only those who live there know about it. I have learned that in this place everyone is like us and yet everyone is completely unique. In this place you can be exactly as you were meant to be—your specialness is deeply cele-brated. The people know true peace and happiness, sur-rounded by beauty and contentment. It's paradise; no one wants for anything and everyone is given everything that they could ever need. Your days are filled doing the things that your heart yearns to do; if you need to learn something a teacher will help you; if you want to try something different every new opportunity is given to you. No one will ever hurt you again. No one will make fun of you and you will not have to hide. You will be safe and free. And not just free for a while, but free forever."

J. paused. Piper's blue eyes were as large as saucers as she drank in the wonder of such a place. Conrad, on the other hand, had skepticism knitted tightly into his eyebrows.

"We should go there." J. got to his feet and reached for his backpack as though it was already decided. "We should go tonight."

"And where, pray tell, is this *paradise*?" Conrad's voice dripped with sarcasm.

"I don't know," J. admitted. "Well, not specifically, anyway. But I've narrowed it down and with all of your help we could get there in no time."

"This is ridiculous. We're not going," Conrad said firmly.

"Why not?" Piper turned on him.

"Tell me this, J., where did you find out about this 'paradise'? Hmm?"

"I have my sources."

"That's not an answer. I want a name. Who told you?" Conrad planted his feet.

J. shook his head. "It doesn't matter who—"

"Answer my question!"

"You wouldn't understand—"

"I understand more than you know. *Who?*"

"Letitia Hellion." J.'s eyes were on fire. He was in the business of exposing secrets, not revealing them. "She is my sister."

Piper gasped.

The air around them turned dense and charged with electricity.

Conrad shook his head, then snorted as though he had suspected something like this, or worse, all along. Turning to Piper, he gestured with his hands as though to say, *See! Just like I told you. This guy is crazy.*

"Dr. Hellion is alive?" Piper was in shock.

"After you saw Letitia fall from the sky, Piper, someone saved her. She can't remember who. She has memories of this place—she says that she lived there and she wants to go home." J. confessed this information in a pleading voice. He needed Piper and Conrad; he needed to help them and save them, and now he needed them to help his sister. He wanted Piper to understand.

"Where is Dr. Hellion now?" Conrad demanded, suddenly concerned that she might be close by.

J. hesitated, not wanting to tell but knowing that Conrad would accept nothing but the truth. "Area 63. It's a secret government prison for the criminally insane."

Conrad let out a low whistle. "Wow. Why am I not surprised? She sounds like . . . a credible source."

"She's different now," he said quietly.

J. had not fully appreciated what horror the name Letitia Hellion struck in Piper McCloud's heart, and the rest of the kids too. They had suffered under her control at her evil school and she had done them all great harm, which was not easily forgotten. Piper turned her back on J. and walked away. J. felt the sting of her rejection in his core.

Seeing that Piper was unreachable, J. turned back to Conrad. "Conrad, Conrad, listen to me. First of all, my name is Jeston. And I have more information for you." He scrambled to pull a file out of his backpack, placing it in Conrad's unwilling hands. "This is about your father." J. opened it quickly and flipped through the pages. "Did you know that your father was abandoned when he was twelve? It's true. Look. The police found him wandering by the side of the road. He carried no identification and had no memory of who he was. They placed him in foster care and no one ever claimed him. Then when he was sixteen he ran away and they were never able to trace him again. Not that they tried very hard."

J. flipped through the pages and Conrad's brow furrowed as he looked at the police reports and foster home evaluations.

"He hired people to pretend to be his family, and he has a mysterious benefactor who has been guiding his political career." J. pointed to specific passages and photographs excitedly.

With a tremor in his hands Conrad absorbed this strange twist. "But . . ." He looked to J. "When did you get this information?"

J. paused. "A year ago."

"And you're only telling me now?" Conrad slammed the file shut. "What other information are you withholding? What else do you know?"

"But I already gave you good intel on your father. You have to understand—"

"I understand all too well."

"This is so big, there is so much—"

"*Stop.* Stop treating us like children. We are not going with you to this place and we will not help you. I can speak for all of us when I say that we aren't going to be put back into another prison, even if this one has been given the name 'paradise.'" Conrad crossed his arms over his chest. "You should leave, J. You aren't welcome here anymore."

J.'s shoulders deflated. He glanced toward Piper, but

her back was still turned away from him and she couldn't or wouldn't face him. With great reluctance, he swung his backpack over his shoulders, and it suddenly felt so heavy his body heaved with the effort it took to hold it up. He turned to go.

"If you won't come with me, you should know this." J. paused at the door. "You are all in the greatest danger. Your father knows where you are, Conrad, and he knows what you are doing. You are interfering with his plans and he will use every means at his disposal to stop you. All of you. Under no circumstances can you continue with these missions or . . . you will not like what will happen next. That is all I can tell you because it is all I know."

J. turned himself invisible and walked out the door.

Piper swung around to face Conrad, her eyes flashing with fear.

"What are we going to do, Conrad?"

Conrad ran his fingers through his hair and exhaled in a long, measured blow. "We're going to embrace our fears," he said simply. "Let's get some sleep."

ON THE THIRD DAY TRAPPED INSIDE THE attic of their house, the Kaiser family had finished the last of their food and water. By ten in the morning temperatures were hovering above one hundred degrees and the two children lay on the floor quietly, too hungry and tired to play or even talk. Mr. Kaiser had stopped listening for helicopters or boats; none were coming.

When the dam above Shady Grove mysteriously broke open they were among the very few lucky ones. Their house was on a small hill at the edge of town and they had just enough time to run up the stairs, and were fortunate enough to have an attic. On that first day they sat in a state of euphoria, cataloging the various ways, both large and small, that fate had smiled down on them and saved their family; like how they happened to all be at home; how Katy skipped soccer practice to go to a birthday party; how Timmy spent the morning in bed because he wasn't feeling well instead of going over to his friend Jack's house.

What luck, they said to one another. What incredible luck.

On the second day inside the attic restlessness set in and conversation revolved around the rescue efforts. Would they be sending food soon? Would there be rescue boats or helicopters? How much longer would it take? Mr. Kaiser had been trained for situations like this in the police academy, but without the proper tools he was unable to break a hole through the roof and they were trapped. At noon the two protein bars that Mrs. Kaiser had kept in her purse were finished, and the bottle of water from Katy's gym bag was drained. There was nothing left.

When she thought the children were sleeping Mrs. Kaiser whispered urgently to her husband.

"Why's it taking so long? Where's FEMA and the Red Cross? The kids need food and water now. We can't last much longer. . . ."

Mr. Kaiser didn't dare share the thoughts that ran through his mind. After all, the government knew that the dam was old and crumbling. Hadn't their local paper printed a story just the week before about the dire engineering reports? The same reports that the government, even the president himself, consistently refuted and denied.

Mr. Kaiser wondered silently if perhaps the government was purposely slow. And maybe not just slow— maybe they wouldn't come at all.

It was when the children stopped complaining that Mr. Kaiser got scared. They were so young and didn't have the strength for this. He didn't allow himself to consider that they might not last too much longer.

On the morning of the fourth day all hope was gone. When Mrs. Kaiser tried to wake Timmy it took a long time to rouse him and then he'd only moaned and gone right back to sleep. She exchanged a long look with Mr. Kaiser—they both knew what was coming next. Even though the attic was like an oven they moved the family close together, in case there might be some small gesture or comfort they could give to the children or each other. Katy reached out and held her father's hand and Mrs. Kaiser gently stroked Timmy's hair.

MR. KAISER WAS THE ONLY ONE WHO WAS awake to hear a small set of footsteps on the roof of the house. Next he heard a clunk that was followed by the crash of wood. As though he was dreaming, he watched as a hole was punched into his roof. Wood splintered and shattered around them but didn't touch them.

Moments later a young girl flew—but how could

that be? He squinted his eyes to refocus and yet still the girl was flying. . . . *Flying?*

She flew through the hole in the roof into the attic and across to where the Kaiser family was huddled. Her long brown hair was caught up in a braid and she wore a pair of jeans and a blue T-shirt that said SECOND STAR TO THE RIGHT AND STRAIGHT ON TIL MORNING. A smattering of freckles dotted her nose and cheeks. When her feet touched down she crouched next to Mr. Kaiser, and he was able to see that she was as ordinary as any girl he might have seen walking up and down Main Street. Ordinary, that is, except for her blue eyes. Her eyes were made from the sky and held a depth and understanding that was almost impossible for such a young girl to have. She was ordinary and at the same time utterly extraordinary.

"Me and my friends are here to help you," the girl said.

Mr. Kaiser nodded. He had no words.

She called out and another child suddenly jumped down through the hole in the roof and onto the attic floor. She was a big girl, perhaps fourteen years old, and she lumbered toward them. Mr. Kaiser could feel the already feeble house shaking under her weight. She nodded to him and without a word picked up the two children with a disarming gentleness. Holding Katy and Timmy in one arm, she picked up Mrs. Kaiser in the other and made her way back to the hole in the roof, where she handed them up to waiting arms. Their combined weight was well over 250 pounds, but this girl handled them as though they were feathers.

With a small amount of help, Mr. Kaiser was able to follow behind, and once he was hoisted up onto the roof what met his eyes was alarming and seemingly impossible. There were no relief workers, no medical personnel, or police officers of any kind. There were three boats and each boat held two or three kids. They were moving from house to house. At one house that leaned at a particularly precarious angle, a dark girl shrank down to the size of a Barbie doll so that she could fit through a chimney and save trapped parrots. One kid, a scrawny boy with black hair, looked at a house and knew if someone was inside as though he had X-ray vision. A delicate Asian girl (in a spotless white silk dress, no less) was telekinetically moving debris out of the way. The big girl who had lifted his family was busting up roofs or cars or anything else that prevented them from getting to the wounded and waiting. And the flying girl was moving above it all, landing on houses, hovering between boats, rising out of sight and then back again.

And yet they were ordinary kids. Take them and

stick them in any classroom and you wouldn't give them a second glance.

When the boats were full they returned to two large black transport trucks. Like the boats, the trucks were large and unmarked.

According to need, each survivor was led to the first transport truck in turn. When Mr. Kaiser was finally invited forward he was not surprised to find the truck equipped with an array of medical equipment and devices. What he was surprised to find was that not a single needle or swab was used. When he was sitting on the examining table, a boy, slight, thin, and very pale, approached him.

"P-p-p-please don't m-m-move," said the boy.

He reminded Mr. Kaiser of his Timmy. He was maybe six years old and uncomfortable in his own skin. It made Mr. Kaiser yearn for his own son.

The boy then began to rub his hands together until they glowed. The light they gave off was like a klieg light; it hurt to look at it directly and Mr. Kaiser squinted and looked away, glancing back as much as he could. As the light grew the boy began to blow into his hands and the light changed from bright white to red. Softly the boy stepped forward and placed his hands on Mr. Kaiser and the light leapt off his hands and into his belly.

Mr. Kaiser jumped, not because the light hurt but because it felt so good. Every muscle that was knotted, every cut and bruise, every part of him that was sore or hurt released the pain and anguish of the last four days in an instant and was replaced with a warm feeling of contentment and health. Mr. Kaiser sighed deeply as the healing took hold.

Before he could thank the small boy, he scuttled away like a scared fish and Mr. Kaiser let himself out. He found his family laughing and eating under a tent as though the last four days had never happened.

In another few hours, all who could be helped were safe. Mr. Kaiser watched the recovery efforts with a keen eye. His training and his experience as a police officer made him appreciate as few could what an extraordinary effort this was in terms of the way the entire operation was run. *But how?* he thought over and over again. It would have taken any other workers days or weeks to accomplish what he counted as ten kids did in a few hours. It was nothing short of a miracle.

"Mr. Kaiser?" The flying girl was at his side, surprising him from his thoughts.

"Yes?"

"Are you the same Mr. Kaiser who is chief of police?"

"I am."

"Well, that's just grand. You think you'd be able to come with me for a moment, sir?" The girl was polite but not formal.

Mr. Kaiser got to his feet and followed the girl to the second transport truck. He had yet to see anyone enter or leave that particular truck. As they walked he could hear the girl mumbling multiplication tables under her breath.

The girl flew up the steps and opened the door. Mr. Kaiser used the stairs and arrived not long behind her.

Inside the trailer it was dark but for the glow of computer lights.

"Conrad?" she said.

"Right with you," came the reply.

Mr. Kaiser let his eyes adjust and finally caught a glimpse of the missing link of the entire operation: the piece of the puzzle he had been looking for—the central command. It consisted of a single boy: Conrad, as the girl had called him. He was a serious-looking kid with blond hair. He looked like he'd sprouted up recently, like he wasn't used to being so lanky but was growing into himself just fine.

Conrad was standing in the middle of the room. Surrounding him were three-dimensional images, which he manipulated with his hands like an orchestra conductor. Before his face was a 3-D house; it looked like the

Jenkins house on Avon Street. Conrad turned the image of the Jenkins's house this way and that. On his left were files containing faces and information on families. As he touched the house and turned it with one hand, he opened files with the other that instantly responded to his touch, turning into images of people next to which were their stats: age, height, medical conditions, etc. Over his shoulder were more files with weather stats, satellite images, and topographical information.

Like all the other kids, Conrad had a small silver device the size of a toothpick coming from his right ear.

"Smitty, check that last house in the fourth quadrant. I'm showing movement," Conrad said. With quick motions Conrad closed down and organized the images into a row and turned his attention to his guest.

"Chief Kaiser, thank you for joining me. My name is Conrad." Conrad extended his hand and Mr. Kaiser took it.

"Will Kaiser." They shook briefly and Mr. Kaiser took note of the fact that the boy's hand felt small in his but there was strength in it all the same.

"Please, walk with me." Conrad indicated the door and allowed Mr. Kaiser first passage.

Outside, the sun was starting to set and Mr. Kaiser saw that the boats had been packed away and pretty much everything else had too.

A blur of movement stopped abruptly in front of them and it took Mr. Kaiser a moment to realize that the movement was actually created by a girl. She was rather thin and scruffy looking with dark hair that fell over her face.

"Piper, we need your help with those parrots," the scruffy girl said. "Smitty wanted to look at them but Kimber said no and they got into a fight. The parrots got away and now we can't find 'em. And there's a lady over there who's upset about her parrots being missing."

Piper shook her head. "I'll take care of it. Excuse me, Mr. Kaiser." A moment later she flew off and the scruffy girl darted away so quickly it created the illusion that she had disappeared into thin air. Both Conrad and Mr. Kaiser watched Piper flying up past the trees.

"Who the heck are you kids?" Mr. Kaiser couldn't take his eyes off Piper.

"No one."

When Mr. Kaiser gave Conrad a look, Conrad shrugged. "No one that matters, at least. We aren't mutants, we aren't superheroes; we're just kids who happen to be able to fly or have X-ray vision or shrink. It's just who we are."

Conrad walked and Mr. Kaiser matched his stride. They were close to the water's edge and between them and the setting sun was the landscape of the lost town. The church steeple and a few other buildings peeped up through the water, but for the most part the water was filled with floating pieces of debris.

"But how come I've never heard of you before?" Mr. Kaiser couldn't imagine how all of this could logistically take place. "How in the heck can you keep stuff like *this* secret?"

"With great difficulty. And at great cost to us. There are those who would like us to be like everyone else. In the past they went to great extremes to see to it that we conformed." Conrad fell silent. He didn't want to go into details with Mr. Kaiser; he had more important things to discuss with him.

"Chief Kaiser, I realize this is so strange that it's hard not to ask questions, but there is more to tell and I don't have time." Conrad took a small envelope from his pocket and handed it to the man. "In here is a cell phone. You will also find the numbers of local and national relief offices as well as the news media. I would encourage you to call them all. In addition there is an electronic file of information regarding the facts surrounding the events that led up to the breaking of the dam over your town, as well as the ways it was covered up by certain people in the government."

Will Kaiser turned the envelope over, considering what the boy was telling him. "You're . . . leaving?"

"We're leaving in the next few minutes." Conrad

stopped and faced the older man. "We've helped all we can. I'm sorry that we weren't able to come sooner."

Mr. Kaiser shook his head. "So, what? You're just going to walk off and that's it."

"That's it." Conrad smiled.

"And we don't even get to thank you?"

"It was our privilege to help."

"It doesn't seem right." The older man looked at his shoes for a moment, embarrassed.

"Well, maybe one day things will be different and we won't have to be so . . . mysterious and secretive."

Conrad held out his hand one last time and Will Kaiser took it. He held on to the boy's hand with deep emotion. He didn't have a lot of words but that didn't mean he didn't have a lot of feelings.

"I'm sorry you won't remember me, Chief Kaiser. I would have liked to have known you better."

Mr. Kaiser wasn't particularly surprised when he saw a silver cylinder the size of an asthma inhaler in the boy's hand. He could have guessed something like this was coming, so he stood still and didn't resist as the boy placed the cylinder on his wrist.

"It won't hurt," Conrad said. "Your memories of the last few hours will be gone but you'll have everything else."

Mr. Kaiser nodded. Looking at Conrad, Mr. Kaiser

said the nicest thing he could think of—the thing he knew every boy yearned to hear. "If your father could see you now, he'd be very proud of you, son."

Conrad stopped, startled.

"My father?" Conrad thought about his father and considered Mr. Kaiser's words. "Somehow, I think my father's reaction to this would be . . . let's just say, not thrilled. And the truth is, I don't have a father. I'm an orphan."

Before Mr. Kaiser could respond Conrad pressed the cylinder to his skin. Mr. Kaiser didn't flinch when it bit into him, but soon thereafter he swayed ever so slightly and sank to his knees. Conrad guided him down and laid him gently on the ground.

Ten minutes later Mr. Kaiser woke to find a cell phone in his hand and the sun setting over what had once been the town of Shady Grove.

"MY FELLOW AMERICANS," PRESIDENT Harrington began. His hair was slicked back and his white shirt crisp against his navy jacket. Under the bright lights and the watchful eyes of a room full of staffers he addressed his message into the network cameras with practiced composure.

"As many of you are aware, there has been a disaster of tragic proportions that has befallen the town of Shady Grove." President Harrington spoke with authority but allowed himself a meaningful break, as though his sadness required a moment of quiet.

"Like you, I mourn the loss of life that our fellow Americans in Shady Grove have had to endure. And like you, I have many questions." Harrington's features now turned from concerned to angry, but not too angry. "How could such a tragedy occur in this day and age and remain unnoticed for so long? Who among us is responsible? As your president I demanded answers to these questions, and as your president I wish to share with you what I now know to be true."

Harrington looked sternly into the camera. His message was carefully crafted to address all Americans, but the truth was that Harrington was only speaking to one: his son. There was no doubt in Harrington's mind that Conrad was staring into his own eyes at that very moment, albeit separated by a television screen. Harrington imagined that he could see Conrad looking back at him, and the thought of his son made his blood rage. A painful headache immediately broke out in the back of his head and he could feel it knocking wildly against his skull.

Hadn't he warned Conrad that things happen for a reason and not to interfere? Hadn't he told him to stop his infernal thinking? And now this. . . .

"We currently have verified and credible information on a group of approximately eleven individuals who played a significant role in this disaster. We have reason to believe that these individuals are very dangerous and that they do not have the best interests of our country at heart. Based on the lives lost to innocent families in Shady Grove we now know that they will stop at nothing. For the safety of our country and the well-being of our citizens we will use all the resources at our disposal to find these individuals and bring them to justice."

President Harrington dropped his chin a quarter of an inch because he knew it gave his jaw a stronger, firmer line, and brought his index finger forward.

"I hereby declare them public enemy number one."

$\mathcal{I}$F THERE COULD HAVE BEEN A WORSE day for the Lowland County Fall Festival, Conrad and Piper would have been hard pressed to think of one. Shaken by the presidential press conference, they felt like doing anything but celebrating the harvest or pretending that everything was hunky-dory. Conrad calmly insisted that the best way to deal with the situation was a "business as usual" approach. He'd given the rest of the kids the day off for much-needed rest and relaxation, while it was necessary for Piper and him to attend the Fall Festival with Betty and Joe, just as the McClouds had attended every year for generations without interruption.

The Fall Festival in Lowland County was not only a celebration of the harvest but a chance for those in the community to recognize the best among them. The long hours and backbreaking work of farming were for the most part wholly unrecognized, but once a year Lowland

County let loose and put all to rights in one overwhelming burst of prize-giving at the Fall Festival. One and all, both young and old, were greedy for blue ribbons.

While a flimsy bit of blue ribbon might seem to be a small acknowledgment, it made a difference to the winners, and every category was hotly contested. Techniques and recipes, like vegetable growing or cattle raising, were passed down and perfected through generations. To have the best raspberry preserves or milking cow reflected not only on your ability but on your family as a whole. It spoke of the work of generations and it honored not only a particular farmer but their parents, grandparents, and great-grandparents, at the very least.

Most folks in Lowland County spent hot summer days mentally preparing their strategies to win the Fall Festival prize, and often secretly worked into the night as the days grew shorter and cooler.

It seemed as though there was a category for everything imaginable: best pig, best cow, fastest horse, best apple pie, largest pumpkin, jams and jellies of every variety, picklings, butter, and butter sculpting. There was a plowing competition, a tug-of-war, a milking competition, a fiddle-off, a square dance–off; and quilting, crocheting, and knitting displays, with a blue ribbon fixed on those deemed superior. For the small fries of Lowland County, besides the apple bobbing, three-legged races, and greased-pig run, there was an essay contest and a science competition.

As the sun reached the middle of the sky on the last Saturday of October, every last soul of Lowland County could be found gathered around the old water tower next to the mill, where long tents were erected for displays and the large mill doors were opened so that its floor could be turned into a stage.

By the time the McClouds arrived and Conrad and Piper had settled into seats next to Betty and Joe, the talent competition was in full swing.

"I believe I can fly," sang Sally Sue Miller, "I believe I can touch the sky . . ."

The sound of Sally Sue's singing voice called to mind the tones of a cat in heat. Sally Sue's large cheering section consisted of everyone, as long as their last name was Miller, and was boisterous, but none was quite so loud as her mother, Millie Mae.

"Sally Sue has the voice of an angel," Millie Mae said loudly, temporarily drowning out Sally Sue mid-squall. This unbiased appraisal was quickly followed by another equally loud remark. "She's got a voice so beautiful she'd make a stone cry."

"Yeah, cry out in pain." Piper snorted.

Conrad gave her a quick elbow in the ribs. "Shhhh."

"It's the truth," Piper quibbled.

Conrad gave her the eye and Piper slouched back into her seat.

When Sally Sue completed her song the Millers clapped wildly and endlessly. Sally Sue took bow after bow.

The minister's wife was sitting in front of Piper and Conrad and noticed Piper's dour face. "Piper, ain't we gonna see you perform in the talent competition?"

Piper shot a glance at Conrad and then shook her head. "No, ma'am, I didn't sign up."

She smiled encouragingly. "Ah, now, you must have something special that you do. The good Lord doesn't leave anyone out when he hands out talents. I'd like to see what you got."

"Is that so?" Despite everything, the minister's wife spoke to the place in Piper that yearned to stop hiding, and she couldn't stop herself from imagining a talent competition that would include her flying. Conrad's elbow in her side jolted Piper back to reality.

"Thank ya, ma'am, but I'm not . . . I mean I don't have a talent."

"You just keep at it and you'll find it. Next year I'll be looking for you. Y'hear?"

Piper smiled and nodded.

"And that goes double for you, Conrad!"

"Yes, ma'am," Conrad said earnestly, as though he was seriously considering the matter.

When the Straighern boys started up a rousing fiddle-and-banjo number, Conrad's DBI clicked on and alerted his brain of an emergency, and he was quick to pull out his glasses to see what was going on.

"What's the matter now?" Piper saw Conrad's special glasses perched on his nose and recognized the intense concentrated look on his face, both telltale signs that he was in the middle of something important.

"There's been activity. Unusual activity. And . . ." Conrad's forehead knit itself into knots. "Ahmed and Nalen have gone missing."

"What?" Piper's eyes went wide.

"Shhh," Conrad hissed.

"Missing how? Where?" Piper whispered back urgently.

"I don't know yet. Myrtle said that they went out to the Grand Canyon to have some fun. She was supposed to meet them, but when she arrived all she could find was one of their boots. Smitty is on his way to investigate." Thanks to the wonder of his device, Conrad dashed out text messages and sent them to Kimber and Smitty without anyone else being aware he was doing anything other than enjoying the music.

"This is just what J. said was going to happen. It could be a ploy to distract us," Piper pointed out.

"Distract us from what?"

"From whatever it is your father is planning to do to us—unless, of course, his plan is to snatch us up one by one. You heard what he said at that press conference!"

As Piper considered this, Conrad sent out messages to all the members of the team. When the music abruptly ended they had to participate in loud rounds of enthusiastic applause.

"Well, hi there, Conrad." Amy Anne Halloway smiled breathlessly as she inserted herself on the bench next to him. She wore a soft pink dress that was tightly fitted, and she was often described by Millie Mae, with a strong sniff and a knowing eye, as being an "early bloomer."

Conrad distractedly angled his glasses. "Hi, Amy Anne."

Over the last several months things had changed a lot at the Lowland County Schoolhouse. Conrad had transformed from a sickly target for bullies into a strong young man lit from within by the unmistakable aura of ascendancy. This change had not gone unnoticed, definitely not by Rory Ray Miller, who somehow instinctively knew not to try his luck on another mud-racking episode, or by another unexpected classmate: Amy Anne Halloway. For reasons that remained unfathomable to both Piper and Conrad, Amy Anne often flitted about Conrad, giggling uncontrollably in the strangest manner. For the most part they dealt with this uncomfortable and peculiar circumstance by walking away whenever possible. Of course, in situations where Amy Anne shoehorned herself in and refused to be ignored, there was little to do but grin and bear it.

"That sure was some nice fiddling." Amy Anne smiled in such a way that she was able to show every single one of her teeth. If Piper hadn't been so irritated that their conversation had been interrupted she actually would have been impressed by Amy Anne's smiling skill.

"Nothing that they haven't played a hundred times before." Piper cut her off quickly, hoping that she'd get the message. She wanted to hear more about Ahmed and Nalen.

"My ma says they're the best in four counties." Amy Anne shared this information in such a way that meant Conrad should appreciate how vital it was and how fortunate he should consider himself for now knowing it.

"I see," was all Conrad could manage as he darted quick looks from Amy Anne to the messages being projected onto his glasses. Smitty was already at the scene and was texting him information on the disappearance.

"I told my ma that you're almost the smartest boy in the class," Amy Anne continued.

Piper snorted in a decidedly unladylike way. "Almost? Who's smarter than Conrad?"

"Rory Ray did win that last science quiz." Amy Anne didn't take her eyes from Conrad.

"Rory Ray didn't win." Piper rolled her eyes. "Conrad wasn't in class that day."

"Rory Ray says that he woulda won anyhow." Amy Anne smiled. "'Course, I ain't sure that's true."

Piper snorted. *Is this girl an idiot?*

"Rory Ray is very smart, Amy Anne. You're quite right," Conrad said, nodding. "You know, I think that Rory Ray might like you."

Amy Anne giggled hysterically and slapped her knee, thrilled that Conrad had noticed such a detail. "He done tells me so all the time," she said, grinning.

Conrad texted and, oblivious to the multiple conversations he was conducting with various points about the globe, Amy Anne glowed, confident of Conrad's undivided attention.

"Of course, Rory Ray's gonna get the twenty acres of land his father promised him," Amy Anne said wistfully. "But I told him that I won't have any old dumb boy." Amy Anne's logic was somehow lost on Piper. Perhaps the fact that Amy Anne's father's mathematical abilities were severely challenged by the most rudimentary sums, and that all of Lowland County knew he was regularly cheated by his hired hands and scorned by his wife, played a role in Amy Anne's sudden interest in the intellectual capabilities of any future mates—a subject she had lately taken a lot of time to ponder and felt the need to be proactive about.

Smitty texted Conrad: *No traces. No clues. They've vanished!*

Conrad quietly and discreetly whispered the news to Piper, who let out a gasp.

Amy Anne leaned toward Conrad. "I'm bettin' you're a wee bit smarter than Rory Ray." She smiled winningly and gently laughed.

"Amy Anne!" a loud voice called gruffly from the end of the benches. Rory Ray stood glaring at Conrad and Piper.

"Well, I guess I'll see what he wants," said Amy Anne, as though it was her duty and a bit of an imposition besides. Of course, the twinkle in her eyes said it was anything but, and she rushed to Rory Ray like the wind, giggling wildly and loudly the entire way.

The science competition was announced and everyone scattered; Betty wanted to make sure her apple pie was properly displayed before judging started, and Joe went to check on the tractor pull. Conrad and Piper ended up getting separated, and by the time Conrad made his way to the water tower, where the tables were set up for the judging of the science competition, the crowd was already tightly gathered and the judging was half over. Conrad took a moment to look at the potato fertilizer experiment before moving on to Rory Ray's science project, which sat in the middle and dominated the rest of the projects for its sheer size and flash quality. Rory Ray had trapped a barn owl in a large cage. At the bottom of the cage he had placed six plump field mice. By removing the screens that protected the mice from the owl Rory Ray demonstrated how the owl would quickly swoop down and gobble up the mice one by one. According to Rory Ray, his experiment unequivocally proved that owls do not tire of their staple diet, namely mice.

In actuality, of course, the project proved precisely nothing, but the shock value was fantastic. The poor owl, having been starved for several days, quickly ravaged each presented mouse. Young girls squealed and women covered their eyes to keep from seeing the cute little mice live their last. None carried on as loudly as Amy Anne, who was delighted to show that her delicate sensibilities were quite overcome by such a gruesome demonstration. This, in turn, pleased no one quite so much as Rory Ray, who not only had successfully and very publicly demonstrated his superior scientific smarts, but now had the opportunity to step forward and settle Amy Anne's feminine hysteria. Truly, it was his bumper day.

That is, until Piper McCloud ruined everything.

"What the heck!" Piper spoke in a cadence of such horror that all eyes were immediately riveted on her and away from Rory Ray's opus.

Piper was standing in front of the last table in the row of science experiments, where the judge was currently examining the final entry. Except for Piper and Timmy Todd, the town runt, no one else much bothered with that experiment because it looked pathetic. Sitting on the table was one simple instruction card, next to which sat a small box.

Conrad squeezed around to see what the matter was. With eyes the size of two moons, Piper pointed at the box on the table. Just at that moment the judge was reaching inside the box and he pulled out of it a white egg-shaped cylinder. Holding it up in the light for all to see, he inspected it closely. As it shone in the sun Conrad recognized it immediately—

The judge was holding TiTI—Conrad's time machine!

Conrad bolted forward, pulling his glasses from his face, and quickly assessed the damage. The table had two typed cards on it. The first card stated, *Time Travel*

Dial. Created by Conrad Harrington III. A set of instructions indicated how it worked. A second sheet of paper was filled with mathematical equations and diagrams indicating how it was possible to travel in time.

Conrad's face turned white.

"Everyone's watching," Piper whispered. There was no graceful way to handle this situation. They had to stand there and do what damage control they could.

"That looks real fancy, Conrad," Amy Anne cooed. Conrad's dramatic reaction had caught her attention and drawn her away from Rory Ray's experiment. "You can make people travel through time?"

"It don't work," Rory Ray said, and snorted loudly.

"He's right," Conrad quickly agreed. "It's a prototype, nothing more."

"You know how to make a prototype?" Somehow Amy Anne was even more impressed, perhaps because she had no idea what a prototype actually was.

"It's a piece of junk," Rory Ray continued.

"It's true," Conrad concurred again, even more loudly. "I got the idea out of a comic book and I just made something that looked like the picture."

There was no mistaking the fact that the judge was absolutely impressed. He kept nodding his head as he turned Conrad's time machine over and jotted down notes. With each nod, Rory Ray's face grew redder and redder. When the judge finally walked away to tabulate the scores, Rory Ray was fit to be tied.

"Betch'a you'll win, Conrad." Amy Anne smiled.

Unable to contain himself any longer, Rory Ray swiped the dial off the table. "It's a hunk of junk. Any idiot can see that."

Before Conrad could do anything, Rory Ray haphazardly shook it.

Conrad threw himself at Rory Ray, bracing for the worst.

Absolutely nothing happened.

Rory Ray looked down to find Conrad dangling off his muscular torso, and laughed. "Get the heck off me!" He kicked Conrad away and Conrad landed in the dirt.

Suddenly a loud hum began to rumble out of the egg in Rory Ray's hands. Shocked, Rory Ray stood still.

"Drop it!" Conrad begged. "Throw it to me!"

But Rory Ray was looking at the egg as though mesmerized. Then a blinding light flashed out of its core and Rory Ray disintegrated into light particles right before their very eyes. The light particles swirled and whipped away, leaving nothing behind.

The look of horror on all the gathered faces was unmistakable. No one moved, no one could do anything.

"Holy Mother of God," a woman breathed, and her

words carried outward, echoing the sentiments of all watching.

Piper, her mouth agape in shock, looked to Conrad, who didn't know where to look.

Suddenly Millie Mae Miller broke through the crowd and grabbed Conrad by his shirt, shaking him. "What'd ya do to my boy? Where'd you put him?"

"I-I-I don't know," Conrad stuttered, partly because Millie Mae was shaking him so violently and partly because he was amazed that the dial had powered up. Had someone put plutonium inside? Who had set the time dial?

"Mrs. Miller? Mrs. Miller, ma'am?"

Millie Mae was in such a state she was insensible. Piper had to grab her arms to stop her from shaking Conrad.

Millie Mae wailed, "That thing's got the devil in it."

"No, no, it doesn't work that way," Conrad assured her, but a buzz was gathering among the waiting crowd. "It's science," Conrad said loudly. "It works by bending the space-time continuum around a single object: in this case, Rory Ray. It's not about the devil or anything else."

Blank faces met Conrad's explanation.

"What the boy say?"

"He's making up nonsense, is what."

Conrad shook his head and held his breath. If Rory Ray didn't materialize in another ten seconds he was going to have a whole new set of problems on his hands.

"THERE HE IS!" someone shouted.

Everyone looked up, way up, to the plank that ran around the girth of the old water tower. Confused and frightened, Rory Ray stumbled and lurched about.

"Ahhh!" Rory Ray screamed.

"My baby!" Millie Mae sobbed.

Disoriented, Rory Ray threw himself against the water tower, bounced off, and fell against the fragile wooden railing. The force with which he hit the railing, combined with his heft, proved too much for the tired old piece of wood, and it gave way with a *crack*.

The water tower was fifty feet if it was an inch, and hadn't been repaired at any time that anyone could actually remember. As he fell over the edge, Rory Ray reflexively caught hold of the gangplank and dangled off of it, with only three fingers separating him from the air.

The crowd below gasped in unison. He swayed back and forth, attempting to throw his other arm up to anchor himself onto the plank of wood. On his first try, his arm swung up uselessly and missed. The second time, his fingers grabbed for the wood and slid off, but the third time he held firm.

A sigh of relief washed over the onlookers as Rory Ray began to pull himself up and angle his body back onto the board. When he finally came to a sitting position, grateful applause swept through the crowd.

Getting to his feet, Rory Ray turned to walk to the ladder when a loud *crack* emanated from beneath his heel. Rory Ray froze and looked down. No sooner had his eyes traced the long fracture running through the center of the board than it gave way beneath him completely and Rory Ray fell.

"Ahhhhh!" Rory Ray screamed for a second time.

Everyone froze to the spot they were standing on, unable to look away as their worst fears were realized and Rory Ray's big body tumbled through the air.

Of course, no one saw the actual moment when Piper took flight, but everyone saw the moment when she flew up and caught Rory Ray in her arms.

For the second or third time (or was it by this point the tenth time?) in as many minutes, the folks of Lowland County were transported by a vision of shock and horror. At first Rory Ray's weight and the speed with which he was traveling almost knocked Piper out of the air. Buckling beneath him, she redoubled her efforts and slowed and then stopped his free fall until she was hovering fifteen feet above the ground.

Rory Ray's shocked eyes met Piper's struggling features as she used all her energy to keep him aloft.

His shock quickly morphed into anger. "Git yer hands off me! Freak!"

"Ever heard the word 'gratitude'?" Piper wheezed between gritted teeth. It was hard enough to land with Rory Ray in her arms, but having the boy fighting against her made it impossible. At two feet up, Rory Ray got his wish and tumbled free, landing on his backside.

A circle formed around Rory Ray and Piper, who landed next to him. As a show of helpfulness, she offered her hand to help him up. Rory Ray would have none of it and scrambled backward and away from her. Millie Mae ran over and hugged him tightly, which left Piper alone in the center of the circle. Conrad quickly squeezed through and came to Piper's side. They stood close together and waited for what was coming next.

No one spoke but instead watched Piper and Conrad with hangdog expressions and something between fear and revulsion in their eyes.

Mr. Andrews shook his head and looked away.

Mrs. Corkoran pressed little Sarah Sue behind her back so that she was hidden and protected.

It was probably one of the kids at the back who threw the first rock. It was a big one, though, and it hit Piper on the shoulder.

Piper grabbed her shoulder in pain as a second rock hit Conrad on the knee, causing him to crumple. From where he crouched in the dirt, Conrad jammed his hand into his pocket and pulled out three purple pebble-shaped capsules. He threw them onto the dirt with a wild swing, and the capsules broke open, releasing a thick violet gas.

"What the heck is that?" someone had just enough time to say before they lost consciousness. Like an ocean wave hitting the shore, the good folks of Lowland County sank to the ground, struck by the gentle sleep of the purple mist. Piper and Conrad, who had both been inoculated against its power during training, stumbled to their feet.

"They'll only be out for three minutes," Conrad explained, clutching where his knee hurt. "The last ten minutes of their memory will be erased, too."

"Jeez Louise," Piper groaned, moving her shoulder.

"You can say that again. We'd better get home."

They helped each other up and started walking, carefully picking their way through the sleeping townsfolk. Piper walked painfully for a moment until finally she could not stop herself from blurting out, "I just don't understand why you put your time gadget in the science competition. Did you really want a blue ribbon so bad?"

Conrad stopped in midstride. "What?"

"'Course you'd win. You know that. No one'd stand a chance against you. But why? It don't make sense." Piper searched Conrad's face for answers and found confusion.

"Piper, I never—I never, I mean I *never* entered my work. Never." Conrad was affronted by the very idea.

"I saw you," Piper said.

"What are you talking about?"

"You know! When you were walking to the water tower with the box and those sheets."

"What?"

"C'mon, Conrad, I was there. I yelled to you and you said, 'Hi, Piper,' and kept walking. Remember? So I followed behind you and that's when you told me that Nalen and Ahmed were okay and I didn't need to worry anymore."

Conrad took Piper's hands and very calmly but clearly said, "Piper, listen to me now and believe me: I never did that. It wasn't me."

"What?"

"I don't know who you were talking to, but it wasn't me. I didn't say those things and I never put my time machine in the Lowland County Fall Festival science competition."

"But if it wasn't you, then who was it?" Piper's voice was edged with panic. "Conrad, what is going on?"

"Someone's sending us a message," Conrad breathed. It was just as J. had warned them: they were in danger and that danger was closing in fast.

$\mathcal{T}$HE KIDS HUDDLED AROUND THE GATH-
ering table in a state of fear and anxiety, painfully
aware of the empty seats that Ahmed and Nalen should
have occupied. Conrad had turned the barn into a war
room with maps and terrain information on the monitors.

"It's like they vanished into thin air," Myrtle pointed
out, even though Kimber had already said just the same
thing not more than one minute before. They'd been at
it all night and nerves were starting to fray; Piper was in
such a high state of anxiety that she couldn't sit or keep
her feet on the ground and had taken to flying about in
circles while Smitty paced back and forth beneath her
while Fido flew in and out of the barn and crashed into
things at inappropriate moments.

"But I couldn't see a single clue at the site," Smitty
argued, "except this muddy boot."

Lily angrily squashed an errant tear. "It's like when Dr. Hellion took us away to that school."

"Well, we don't have to worry about Dr. Hellion anymore," Kimber pointed out confidently. "She's dead."

Piper's alarmed eyes instantly connected with Conrad's, but Conrad shook his head. "This wasn't Dr. Hellion's style. She lured her prey, and Nalen and Ahmed would have put up too much of a fight for her."

Conrad manipulated a three-dimensional terrain map from side to side, studying the landscape where Nalen and Ahmed were last seen. "Obviously it was a trap."

"But what about that guy who was posing as Conrad at the fair?" Piper pushed. "Aren't these two things connected?"

"Yeah," Kimber agreed. "And who else even knew about TiTI? And how did they get to it?"

"Or look so much like Conrad?"

"It's like someone is out to get us."

"Someone really p-p-powerful and smart," Jasper added.

Conrad held out up his hand to stop the rapid patter and draw the focus to what was at hand. "Smitty, pass that boot to me."

Smitty slid the boot down the table into Conrad's expectant hand. Conrad turned it over and examined it closely. Slipping a penknife out of his pocket, he used the blade to jam free some debris in the ridge of the treads. With each thrust, dirt scattered across the table until Conrad gave one last push and a red pebble was pried loose from a tread and fell before them. Conrad did not seem surprised to see it, and he held it up to the light. It shone blood red.

"What's that?"

"This"—Conrad carefully placed the rock on the table in front of them—"is a mystery. Without the proper tools it's difficult to say conclusively what it is made of, but I'm willing to bet it's beryllium and lanthanum. To meld those two metals at a molecular level you'd need temperatures greater than a thousand degrees Celsius." He whistled softly in appreciation, allowing himself a moment to wonder at the genius of whoever created it. "Whoever did this knew what they were doing."

Lily used her telekinesis to move the rock into her hand for a closer look. Even at point-blank range she couldn't make head or tail of it. "But why bother? What is it supposed to do?"

Smitty used his X-ray vision to scan it. "I've never seen anything like it."

"I have." Conrad pulled ten more rocks just like it out of his pocket, scattering them across the table. "At every disaster site we've been to in the last month I've found one."

Hitting a button, Conrad pulled up a map diagramming exactly where the rocks were found and when.

"The boot was left behind because someone wanted us to find it and know. Whoever has created these rocks has been everywhere we have. Why? Do they simply like to watch, or is it more than that? Are these accidents really accidents?"

The kids hung on Conrad's words.

"The data isn't conclusive, but there is a distinct pattern and it's definitely not random," Conrad said meaningfully. "What I'm saying is that someone out there is behind these disasters."

A shiver passed through the room.

"Who could do that?" Violet shrank at the thought.

"Who would do it?" agreed Piper. "And why?"

"Exactly." Conrad's brain sank its teeth into the matter. "What is the motive? Who has the means? Those are the questions that we are going to find answers to. Next steps—we need to return to the site where Ahmed and Nalen went missing to gather more evidence. I've created a grid and assigned search teams. Each team takes one section."

Conrad was pointing to the grids when a distant thumping sound caused a hush at the table. Turning their ears, they tracked the direction of the noise. Conrad activated his surveillance program and quickly identified an incoming helicopter heading straight for the Mc-Cloud farm. With deft hand movements he manipulated the image. "It's a Nighthawk."

The next moment the pounding of the blades in the air above them caused the timbers of the barn to quiver.

Myrtle prepared to bolt. "Let's make a run for it."

"No, wait!" Conrad pointed to the image of the helicopter. "Look!"

Piper squinted at the insignia on the door of the helicopter where Conrad was pointing.

"It's Marine One." Conrad could see that Piper didn't comprehend the full importance of what he was trying to communicate. "That's the insignia for the President of the United States."

Now Piper's eyes went wide. "Your father is coming to snatch us, too."

"In broad daylight with one helicopter? Not likely."

"So, what then?"

Conrad headed for the door. "We're about to find out."

THE BLADES OF THE NIGHTHAWK HELICOPTER swirled dust and dried leaves about the farmyard. Betty came outside, her baking apron smudged with cookie dough, and shielded her face with her hand. The other kids came to Betty's side and Joe emerged from the tractor shed as Marine One landed expertly between the barn and the house. The engine of the helicopter went from a roar to a terrible whine, the blades slowed, and then a marine threw open the door and lowered a set of steps.

All eyes watched the helicopter doorway, waiting. Finally a woman in a beautifully tailored blue skirt and jacket appeared. She stepped carefully down from the helicopter and the marine assisted her on the last step, where she paused to wave at the McClouds as though she were performing at a charity event or arriving at a grand function.

With one hand holding a fashionable hat atop her head and the other gripping her clutch purse, she trotted across the yard until she reached the house.

"So sorry I had to drop in unannounced," she said to Betty and Joe. "Allow me to introduce myself; I'm Abigail Churchill-Harrington."

She held out her hand to Betty.

Betty and Joe had, of course, seen the First Lady on television and in the newspapers and so they knew exactly who she was. The only thing they didn't know was what she was doing at their farm, in a helicopter no less. Seeing the confusion in Betty's face, Abigail got right to the point.

"Conrad's full legal name is Conrad Henry William Churchill Harrington III," she said. "He is my son."

Betty's mouth flew open and she looked between Conrad and the First Lady.

An extremely awkward pause followed. It was exactly the sort of pause that generally crops up when a person discovers that the child she has been caring for is actually the son of the President of the United States, who, in turn, has been lying about the fact that said child is dead.

———✦———

IT DIDN'T TAKE LONG FOR ABIGAIL CHURCHILL-Harrington to be seated comfortably in the parlor, sipping a cup of tea and nibbling on a chewy molasses cookie while a flustered Betty and a speechless Joe sat on the edge of their seats.

"It's such lovely fall weather this time of year." Abigail smiled, enjoying a second cookie. Despite the most extraordinary nature of her visit, Abigail was more than equipped to engage Betty in the most mundane conversation imaginable. Meanwhile Conrad hung at the back of the room with the other kids and glared at his mother.

"Do you think she's here to snatch us, too?" Piper whispered to him.

"It's not likely," Conrad whispered back.

"Maybe she's here to negotiate our surrender," Lily suggested.

"We don't negotiate with terrorists," Kimber spat.

"Shhh," Conrad warned. "Listen."

"Mr. McCloud thinks we'll have our first frost in another week or so," Betty said politely. "We're awful glad we managed to get the garden up."

"This is a lovely room. The furniture is really quite unique. You must tell me where you bought it."

"Mr. McCloud made it hisself. He's real handy with the wood."

"Well, I am amazed." Abigail smiled at Joe. "Your work is splendid, Mr. McCloud. Really. The carving is quite intricate."

Color rose to Joe's cheeks.

"He don't like to brag about it none but he's got a knack for it. I tell him he could sell his carvings if he'd put his mind to it. He gets so attached to 'em, though, he don't never want to let 'em go."

"Then we are all the sorrier for that, Mr. McCloud. I am quite sure your work would delight many people if they ever had the chance to see it."

With that, the conversation hit a dead end; neither woman was able to conjure another topic, and Betty, who was never one to not speak her mind, could not contain herself anymore.

"We didn't kidnap him or nothing. Conrad came to us of his own free will. He could'a gone anytime he wanted. And we love Conrad—love him like he's our own flesh and blood. If we'd known, we would'a told you where he was, but we didn't know. He never said nothing about having a ma and pa." Betty shook her head at the thought. "He needed a home and we gave it to him, is all. He's a good boy, real helpful. He's got a kindness to him, but I don't think many folks know that. They get so caught up with all his smarts they don't see that he's still just a boy and has a heart and soul like any other child."

Emotion was bubbling in Betty, who did not possess polished manners or the ability to act like nothing whatsoever was odd or extraordinary when there certainly was. "We didn't do nothing wrong," she finished.

"Please understand," Abigail said, "the president—I mean, my husband and I know that. We don't think that you are kidnappers."

Betty breathed a deep sigh of relief. "Well, that's a mercy. If I was sitting in your shoes and my Piper went missing, I'd tear my hair out till she came home to me. Can't imagine how you must feel."

"Yes, well, he's here and so no harm done." Abigail shrugged her delicate shoulders as though it was too small a matter to even quibble over. Then, for the first time, she turned her full attention to Conrad and took a good look at him.

"You've grown, Conrad. But of course you still look exactly like your father." For a moment Abigail's facade vanished and a true mother's caring face emerged. "You were seven when you went away to school. The last time I saw you, you were quite small still."

Conrad remained absolutely still, watching his mother as if he were studying an alien species for traces of intelligence—or hostility.

"I've missed you," Abigail said, reaching out to Conrad.

Conrad pulled back. "When?"

Abigail was confused by the question. "I beg your pardon?"

"When, specifically, did you miss me? When I was away at that 'school,' which wasn't really a school? Did you miss me when Dr. Letitia Hellion was torturing me day after day? Or did you miss me most when I got out and you refused to have me back and I was homeless and alone? Or was it just recently that you missed me, when the McClouds, the only good and decent people I've ever known, showed me how to be a happy person?" Years of neglect and anger shot through Conrad's eyes and into Abigail's face.

Abigail blinked several times. "I wonder," she said, turning to Betty, "if I might have a word with my son in private?"

Betty, who was deeply uncomfortable with the entire

situation, got to her feet like a shot, and Joe was not far behind. Betty shooed the other children out of the room with her, but Conrad grabbed Piper's hand and pulled her down next to him.

"Piper stays. Anything you have to say to me she can hear."

When the three were left alone, an electrified quietness crackled through the room and Abigail uncrossed and re-crossed her legs. "I don't know what to say."

"In that case, we have to go." Conrad looked at his watch. "Piper and I have important things to do."

"You're just like your father."

Conrad jumped to his feet. "Don't ever say that. I'm nothing like him."

"You don't understand. He's changed. He wasn't like this before, or at least he wasn't as bad as this." Abigail got lost in her thoughts as she considered it. "He frightens me."

Conrad exchanged glances with Piper.

"He's having these secret meetings all the time. He used to tell me everything; and now he keeps things from me. He hides things, important things—like you." Abigail walked to the window. "He convinced me that you were dead and it wasn't until recently that I discovered the truth."

"I'm really not interested," Conrad said.

"Yeah, me neither," Piper agreed. "What have you done with our friends? Where've you taken them?"

Abigail looked from Piper to Conrad. "What friends? What are you talking about?"

"The ones you snatched up," Piper challenged, her eyes flashing.

"But I know nothing about this." Abigail appeared genuinely confused. "You mean there are other children who have gone missing?"

Conrad noticed his mother's hands were shaking. He believed her when she said that she knew nothing about the disappearance of Ahmed and Nalen, but there was something else she wasn't telling them. Something, Conrad knew, that was important.

"Who else is missing?" he asked pointedly.

"Excuse me?" Abigail appeared flustered.

"You just said that 'there are other children who have gone missing,' which implies that you know of another child who is missing."

Abigail adjusted her expression. "Children go missing every day, all over the country. It's most unfortunate, but it simply can't be helped. Accidents happen."

"Sometimes accidents happen and sometimes they're not accidents at all," Conrad said. "You chose today to visit me. Why?"

"Conrad, you are my son."

"A fact that has never particularly troubled you in the past." Conrad took a step forward, bearing down on Abigail. "What do you want?"

"I should go." She collected her gloves and purse, smoothing her features into even, sensible lines. "I wanted to see for myself that you are well, and I have. It's time for me to leave." She walked to the door.

"It's my sister. She's gone missing, hasn't she?"

Abigail froze in her tracks.

"And you came to ask me for help. You think that I can find her." Conrad was saying it not so much as an accusation but as the pieces of information formed a puzzle in his brain and he caught a glimpse of the entire picture.

Abigail turned around, her face quivering with barely contained fear and suffering.

"Aletha went missing three days ago. Your father doesn't want anyone to know she's gone, he says for national security reasons. Everyone is looking for her but no one can find her. You could, though. I know that you could find her, Conrad."

The tears coming down Abigail's face were a direct contrast to her outward composure. "I know I've failed you. I did so many things wrong, which was why I swore that with Aletha it would be different."

Conrad shook his head, looked away, and considered many things before turning back to the woman who was his mother. "Why would you think that I would help you?"

"I don't think you'll do it for me," Abigail admitted. "You'll do it for her. You are her only hope."

19

"WE NEED TO SPLIT UP. PIPER WILL come with me to the White House to look for my sister. In the meantime the rest of you will return to the scene and continue the search for Nalen and Ahmed as planned." Conrad had reconvened the team in the barn away from Abigail as he quickly prepared to depart. "Lily, Jasper, and Myrtle will be on team one; Smitty and Kimber on team two; and Daisy and Violet on the third. We'll meet back here this evening and go over the findings."

Conrad's news was met with shocked silence. Jasper in particular was shaken that Conrad and Piper wouldn't be joining them.

"But what if we n-n-need you?" Jasper worried.

"You'll have each other; you're a team." Conrad's attention was on downloading pertinent information from the mainframe onto his DBI.

While Conrad was oblivious, Piper clearly saw the uneasy looks of concern on the kids' faces and a trembling creeping up Jasper's legs.

"Conrad?" Piper tugged at his shoulder.

"We need to move out." Conrad didn't look up.

Turning her back so that the others couldn't see her, Piper poked Conrad's shoulder hard. "Conrad," she whispered, "you can't just tell 'em like that. They're freaking out. You gotta give them more direction or something."

"Huh?" Conrad looked up from his computer and saw what Piper saw: Lily fidgeting nervously with her sash, Violet at half her normal size, and random sparks flying from Kimber's fingers. Despite the fact that they were under a time crunch, Conrad took a deep breath and came out from behind his computer. Jasper was the youngest and the smallest, and Conrad bent down to his level and looked him in the eye. "Am I a good leader?"

"Y-yes. You're the b-b-best, C-Conrad."

"Well, I trained you all to be leaders, not followers, and you are ready. All of you. But on this mission, since I'm not going to be with you, I am assigning a new leader. That leader is going to be you, Jasper."

"M-m-me?"

"Absolutely. Take over until I get back."

"You th-think I can l-lead?"

"I don't think, I know."

Jasper's reed-thin body grew a half inch with the honor. His mouth found strength he didn't know he had and pulled itself into a proud line. "Okay," he said. "Okay."

Turning to face his team, Jasper's voice suddenly became strong and louder than anyone had ever heard it. "We move out in five. Smitty, prepare the necessary equipment. Myrtle, you're in charge of packing."

So it was that in five short minutes Piper was pressing her face against the window of the helicopter and waving good-bye to her parents and the other kids, who, by Jasper's orders, would depart for their own mission as soon as the helicopter was on its way. Piper waved back to Betty and Joe and noticed that Jasper stood slightly in front of the others, his back ramrod straight. Betty was having a hard time containing Fido in her arms as he struggled madly to follow after Conrad.

"Hush now," Betty chided the strange creature. "There's no point carrying on because you can't go. Simple as that."

Poor Fido hated to be left behind. Sometimes Conrad let him come on missions, but not this one, and Fido didn't understand. He whined and snarfled but Betty held him firmly.

"They always come back," Betty told Fido. "We just have to wait for them. But they always come home eventually."

Soon the farm was out of sight and Piper availed herself of the multitude of snacks in the luxurious interior while Conrad consumed the thick file Abigail had given him.

"So Aletha's been missing for seventy-four hours and twenty-two minutes?" He flipped quickly through the pages.

"That's right," Abigail confirmed.

Conrad paused on various pages, reading quickly. "No evidence of forced entry. No evidence of anyone coming or going from her room. She went to bed late that night. Why?"

"She's only four years old. Her normal bedtime is seven o'clock, but there was a garden party that afternoon and it went late."

"I'm going to need to see her room."

"Yes, I planned for that." Abigail briefly consulted her watch. "The president is in Ottawa until nine o'clock this evening and is expected to return to the White House after midnight. By the time we land, you'll have a few hours." Abigail hesitated and started fiddling with the hem on her skirt. "Of course you'll have to leave before he returns."

Piper watched as Conrad quickly looked up from the file to his mother. A slight flush rose up the side of his cheeks and his jaw clenched.

"I suppose it's best to keep the dead dead," Conrad remarked.

"He was wrong to say that about you." Abigail kept her eyes firmly on her hem. "I believed him."

"People believe anything he says," Conrad said with some amount of kindness.

They arrived in Washington, D.C., as the sun was setting and the lights of the city were coming up. The Capitol building and the Lincoln Memorial caught Piper's eye and she made a mental note to herself that, if the opportunity presented itself, she would have her own private flight that evening to explore the city.

The helicopter landed on the South Lawn, and the marines escorted Abigail and the kids from the helicopter. An assistant was waiting on the lawn and quickly guided them in through a side door and then down the hall and into the private quarters.

Aletha's room was in the east bedroom on the second floor. The bedroom that the president shared with the First Lady was at the end of the hall on the opposite side. As soon as they walked into Aletha's room they saw a fireplace on the far wall flanked on either side by bookshelves.

Piper was not surprised to find that the little girl's room was nothing short of a designer's paradise: antique dolls lined the bookshelves and a large dollhouse, complete with detailed furniture, curtains, and functioning lights, sat on a table in front of the fireplace. Bright and colorful learning toys were stocked on the shelves next to every imaginable children's book. Next to the only window in the room was a puppet theater with a cast of puppets neatly arranged on it and ready to take the stage. The canopy bed was opposite the fireplace and was covered in sparkling butterflies and fairies floating above a thick comforter.

"I feel like I'm in a toy store," Piper said.

The assistant was handing each of them a pair of surgical gloves and cloth boots to place on their feet.

"Nothing has been touched, of course," Abigail said. "You need to keep these on and be careful not to move anything, touch anything, or leave anything behind."

"Fine." Conrad held on to the file and the tablet. "We've got it from here. We'll call you if we need you."

The assistant looked to Abigail, alarmed. "I'd be happy to stay—" she began.

"That won't be necessary," Conrad cut her short. "We have a lot of work to do." He didn't want anyone getting in the way.

The assistant glanced again at Abigail, who waved

her hand. "Fine. Nothing must be disturbed. Bernice will wait outside while you investigate. If you need anything, or me, just call her and she'll see to it."

"Understood."

"You have ninety minutes." Abigail checked her watch again as she left the room.

Bernice glared at them before closing the door and locking Piper and Conrad inside. Conrad immediately set about his investigation.

"I think your ma feels bad."

"I think she should feel bad." Conrad carefully opened the closet door and peeked inside. It was lined by row after row of outfits.

After Piper circled the room five or ten times and carefully poked through a few things she wasn't sure what to do next, and so she took to looking out the window. It was nighttime but the street was busy below with traffic and pedestrians. Meanwhile, after taking a quick tour of the attached bathroom, Conrad lay the file on the floor, spreading the photos all around and carefully looking from one to the next, and then back at the room. After a full hour passed, Piper grew antsy.

"So, call me crazy, but someone musta snuck in here and snatched her."

"Nope, that didn't happen." Conrad spoke with certainty.

"Well, she didn't just disappear."

"You're right about that."

"So, if no one took her and she didn't disappear, where is she?" Piper worried that Bernice or Abigail was going to come through the door at any moment.

"I don't specifically know."

"Great. So she's just going to stay missing forever."

"No." Conrad snatched up a few pictures. "She was never missing. Look at this."

He handed the pictures to Piper and she looked at them. "What do you see?" he pressed her.

Piper shrugged, flipping through the pictures. "Aletha's room. Her stuff, her bed, her dollhouse."

"Look more closely. Start with the dollhouse." Conrad pulled out the dollhouse picture and handed it back to Piper. "Look," he said, pointing.

Piper looked again, and then looked back to Conrad, shrugging. "It's the dollhouse."

"Come closer." Conrad pulled her to the dollhouse. "No one's touched anything, right? The room's been sealed and these were taken as soon as they found her missing. But look here." He pointed to the dollhouse. "The curtains in the dollhouse are closed. But they're not closed now; they've been opened."

Piper looked from the picture to the dollhouse, and a shiver ran up and down her neck.

"Now look at this." Conrad handed Piper a picture of the bookshelf. This time Piper was careful to look more closely, but she still couldn't see what he saw.

"Two books are missing, and this book here . . ." He pulled out a copy of *Angelina Ballerina*. "This one was replaced. Someone's been reading the books."

Piper felt creepy crawlies tingling across her back. "What is going on?" she whispered.

"Aletha is hiding," Conrad said in a low voice. "When she feels it's safe, she comes out. She gets bored and plays with her toys."

"Hiding?" Piper looked around. "Where?"

"No." Conrad squinted for a moment. "The question is not where but why. Why is she hiding? And from whom? And what is making her so afraid?"

Piper edged closer to Conrad, fear seeping into her as she imagined what could have driven Aletha to such an extreme measure. "If she's in danger, then we're in danger."

"Yes," Conrad agreed. "My father wants to get her before anyone else does. She knows something. . . ."

Suddenly the door to the room swung open.

Piper gasped.

Bernice glared at them from the doorway. "Twenty minutes," Bernice said, her eyebrows raised as though she expected them to defy her.

"Thank you," Conrad said, waiting for her to leave. Finally she did.

As soon as the door was closed, Conrad spun around and faced Piper, whispering in her ear. "Do exactly as I say, when I say it. We don't have a second to spare."

Twenty minutes later on the dot, the door to Aletha's room was flung open for a second time. "Time's up," Bernice said.

When she saw the room was empty, her heart rate shot up. As she carefully checked the room her hands were shaking, and she noticed that her breath was catching in her throat.

She had to be careful when she walked down the hall to the First Lady's sitting room. She couldn't show how alarmed she was, or there would be questions. Abigail was waiting for her.

"They're gone," Bernice stammered. "I went in and they were gone. I checked the room. They've disappeared . . . just like Aletha."

"No." The color drained from Abigail's face. "I don't believe it."

20

*C*ONSTRUCTION OF THE WHITE HOUSE began in 1792. The whole place was burned in 1814 and rebuilt from the ground up. For the next 200 years every president who set foot in the place proceeded to make their own changes both large and small. Thomas Jefferson wanted toilets, Ulysses S. Grant had a penchant for Victorian decoration and electric lights. Other presidents not only renovated but added significantly. In all those years of change and evolution small things were forgotten with the passage of time and tenants. Alcoves that had been temporarily boarded up were lost altogether and cupboards and crawlspaces got concealed behind walls until no one even knew they were there anymore.

The fireplace in Aletha's bedroom was originally built in 1792, and even when the White House was burned down it was one of the few things to remain. The bricks were old and the space was wide and ample and full of long-buried secrets.

Piper flew up the chimney but Conrad had to climb it. From his position on the floor he had seen telltale signs that the chimney had been in use and he climbed it with care, following the small handprints that showed him exactly where he could go. Piper held up his flashlight device on his PDA so that they could use that light as a torch.

"There is no way she climbed up here. She's how old?"

"Four." Conrad grunted, clinging on.

Hovering up above, Piper studied the brick patterns. "And you think she climbed up here to get away?"

"She's been coming up and down here a lot the last three or four days. Look at this." Conrad pointed to the wall. Flying downward, Piper peered over his shoulder to see fingerprints in the soot.

"Amazing. But where was she going? There's no way out, unless you're smoke."

"We'll see about that." Conrad pulled himself up bit by bit. It took all his strength to hoist his body upward and he had to pull on the bricks to do so. Suddenly the brick he was holding gave out and he only just managed to wedge himself in place by throwing his legs out and pushing his back into the wall. Piper quickly flew down to him and picked up the brick off his stomach, where it had thankfully come to rest instead of crashing into the fireplace below.

As Conrad panted they both heard voices below. Bernice and Abigail had figured out that they were missing. Conrad placed his finger on his lips.

"Shhh."

With the greatest care Piper quietly and gently pulled Conrad up and helped him to find his footing again. Once he was in place they both pushed themselves into the hole that now gaped in the chimney.

"There's a room on the other side," Piper whispered. Conrad nodded and pointed to the other bricks. One by one they worked together to carefully and silently slide bricks from their place until at last there was a hole just big enough to squeeze through. Piper helped Conrad through first and hovered patiently until he had scrambled safely over to the other side. Wiggling past the hole, she found herself in a small cramped passageway. This time Conrad was using the light from his PDA to discover any clues he could. He didn't have to look hard because he soon found crumpled food wrappers. Holding up a shiny silver one, he turned it over and both Piper and Conrad studied what remained of a cereal bar.

Conrad smelled it. "It's fresh."

From that point on it was a matter of following the

trail of debris along the passage: a peanut pack, mini Cheerios boxes, Goldfish Crackers, almonds, two juice boxes, and finally a fun-size Milky Way all led to a cracked panel of wood. Piper traced the seam of the crack until she could determine that it formed a one-foot-by-two-foot opening.

Conrad grabbed hold of the bottom of it. Piper wedged a finger into a crevice in the wood to gain traction and together they silently coordinated their efforts, easing the wood from its hole. Once free they propped it up against the wall and peeked into the darkness.

As their eyes adjusted it became clear to them that they were in a storage area that rested high above the East Portico. It was a large chamber lined with wooden shelves, each one holding carefully labeled boxes. Conrad slid through the opening and crouched down in the room. He felt Piper crouch next to him. Once in position neither of them moved a muscle. Slowly their eyes adjusted to the dark and Piper was able to make out a blanket in the corner of the floor, next to which were several bags and some scattered toys. She poked Conrad and pointed to it but Conrad already had his eye on it.

Taking out his light, Conrad directed it at the clutch of debris bundled in the corner.

"Where is she?" Piper mouthed to him. Both of them craned their necks and scanned the area but could see nothing. Conrad scooted forward and began to pick through the remains. More wrappers crinkled and fell like confetti about the floor. In the blanket was also a small doll no bigger than a finger. Picking it up, Conrad saw that it was clothed in a little pair of blue shorts and was missing a shoe.

"She's here somewhere," Conrad whispered back to Piper.

In the distance the sound of helicopter blades pumped the air but they ignored them.

"She's small and she could hide anywhere."

Conrad agreed and suddenly sat down, leaning his back against the wall. He took several deep breaths and put the light on the floor so that it lit them from below.

"What are you doing?"

"The easiest way to find someone is to make them want to be found," Conrad explained.

"How are you going to make Aletha want to be found?" Piper sat down opposite Conrad in the dark.

"Talk," Conrad said simply.

Piper's confusion mounted. She was sitting in a dark, dirty secret nook in the White House looking for Conrad's sister, whom he'd never met, but who was hiding—and all he wanted to do was . . . talk?

"Uh, okay."

"Did I ever tell you about the day I found out I had a

sister?" Conrad said in a normal voice. They had been whispering since they began the journey up the fireplace and his voice seemed inordinately loud.

"No," Piper replied in her normal voice.

"It was after Letitia Hellion took me away to I.N.S.A.N.E. I kept trying to call my father, but he wouldn't take any of my calls."

The sound of the approaching helicopter was growing closer. Beads of sweat burst upon Piper's forehead. She looked upward toward the sound, but Conrad's gaze drew her back to the conversation. "You called your father?"

"Not often," Conrad admitted. "Only when I could sneak to an empty office and manage to get to the phone. One day I called and my father had just gotten a new assistant, and when I told him that I was the senator's son, he told me that the senator only had one child, a baby girl, who had been born the week before. He told me that they had named her Aletha." Conrad repeated the name, tasting it in his mouth. "A-letha. And that is how I found out I had a baby sister."

Piper quietly listened.

"I used to think about her all the time. I would look at the calendar and know that she was crawling or had probably started to walk. I would imagine her first word and think about what it would be like to be a big brother to her. I imagined what my name would sound like when she said it. I wanted to show her things like how to do fractions and how to figure out quantum mechanics."

"Quantum mechanics?" Piper raised her eyebrow.

"There's nothing like figuring out your first real problem."

"If you say so."

"Mostly I just wanted to be a brother and have family. To have someone who I could always be there for and who would always be there for me. Blood. Family. That's what I wanted."

"Me too," Piper said softly.

"But I guess she never even knew about me. And even if she did she probably doesn't want a brother."

The darkness against the far wall was quietly moving. Piper was tempted to react but Conrad squinted his eyes at her and almost imperceptibly shook his head. They both remained still and tried to watch out of the corners of their eyes without watching.

"You would be a great brother," Piper offered up.

"I would try my best," Conrad affirmed. "I would do my best and do everything I could for her. And if we were ever to meet, I'd never leave her again."

The shadow crept closer and closer until it breached the light.

Making no sudden movements and careful to keep

neutral expressions on their faces so as not to frighten her away, Piper and Conrad turned toward a delicate waif covered from head to toe in soot. Her clothes had become rags over the last three days and she had lost weight too. She was tiny to begin with, hardly more than thirty pounds, but she appeared to have become thinner. Her skin was so dirty that the only part of her that flashed white was her eyes. She kept those eyes on Conrad.

"Aletha," said Conrad quietly. "I am your brother. My name is Conrad."

Slowly and with the utmost tenderness, Conrad took her small hand in his.

"Smart," said Aletha, looking at her brother.

Conrad smiled and nodded. "This is my best friend. Her name is Piper McCloud."

Piper broke into a mile-wide smile and was only just able to restrain herself from seizing the child and covering her in a massive bear hug.

Aletha returned Piper's smile. "Flyer," she said simply.

The helicopter was directly over them and could no longer be ignored. Piper shot Conrad a look and Conrad worried that Aletha might flee in alarm, so he remained gentle and unruffled.

"We have to leave now. All of us." Conrad pointed to all of them, including Aletha in the group. "I'm going to take you somewhere safe where you won't have to hide. Okay?"

Aletha nodded.

Conrad's first brotherly act was to take Aletha's hand and help her escape from their parents.

CHAPTER

21

*W*HAT WOULD CONRAD DO? JASPER thought over and over again, holding his head.

A windstorm was blowing in the Grand Canyon at the site where Nalen and Ahmed had disappeared. The wind made it tough for the teams; they had diligently worked their way through Conrad's search grids to no avail. Just as Smitty had said, there weren't any clues to be found. High hopes had turned to despair, and the kids hung about aimlessly, wondering what they should do next and waiting for Jasper to set out a plan.

"Maybe we should go home and wait for Conrad," Smitty said over the wind.

"Yeah, it's not like we're doing anything here." Kimber was slumped on a rock, tired from all the work.

"N-n-no," Jasper said adamantly. "Conrad said we have to f-find clues."

"But there aren't any," Myrtle offered quietly. "We looked."

"No." Jasper shook his head. "We must find a clue."

What would Conrad do? Conrad had said that Jasper was ready. He said that he was a leader, and Conrad was the smartest person in the world.

The swirling wind picked up small rocks and pebbles and pelted them at the kids as they waited for Jasper. Lily, in particular, was bothered by the dust.

"Yuck! Can we just go home and get out of this wind?" For the millionth time Lily smoothed her skirt and fixed her hair, but it was a losing battle; she was covered in filth—her dress was ruined and her hair was a disaster. "Ugh! I'm moving over there."

Lily picked herself up, marched thirty feet away, and plopped herself down on a rock out of the wind. This seemed like the only sensible plan going, and the others followed in her footsteps and huddled around her. Jasper remained where he was, pacing back and forth.

"Ugh!" Lily suddenly shrieked. The wind had started up around them once again and she was being pelted with shale. "You've got to be kidding me!!!"

"Can't we just go?" Smitty called out to Jasper, an unmistakable note of frustration in his voice.

Jasper stopped pacing and stood very still, looking at his friends as they covered their eyes and braced against the force of the wind. It was then that he noticed the wind was no longer blowing where he was standing. Goose bumps rose on Jasper's arms.

"Listen to me!" Jasper yelled. "Come here!"

"Why?" Violet wanted to know.

"Just do it!" Jasper spoke with an authority that got not only their attention, but also their immediate action. When they rejoined Jasper, questioning looks on their faces, Jasper raised his hands as though to say "be quiet and watch." They did as directed—but saw nothing. Then suddenly the wind started again.

"Really?" Lily moaned.

"Don't you see?" Jasper said with quiet intensity.

They didn't.

"The wind. It's following us. When you moved over there it went with you. But now that you've come back here it's with us again." Jasper swung around to Smitty. "When you were here yesterday was it windy?"

Smitty's face transformed. "Yes! Yes, it was. Really windy."

"The wind is the clue." Jasper felt his body exploding into fireworks.

"I get it." Kimber jumped up and down. "It's Nalen and Ahmed. They're creating the wind."

"Exactly." Jasper pointed to her. "They're sending us a message. They want us to find them."

"But where are they?" Smitty looked around. "I can't see them."

"They have to be able to see us," Jasper reasoned, "or they wouldn't know how to direct the wind. They are watching us right now."

"Jasper, you're brilliant!" Lily squealed.

Jasper swelled—he was a leader, just like Conrad said he was. Once again Conrad had been right.

"So what do we do next?" The kids hung on his every word now.

"Where haven't you looked?" Jasper directed his question to Smitty.

"I've looked everywhere!" Smitty threw his hands up in despair. "I checked in the caves, I looked through the rocks, I—I looked everywhere."

Jasper imagined he was Smitty and looked as he had looked. He walked a few paces and the kids followed behind him, matching his movements. When he stopped, they stopped. "But you were only looking down," Jasper pointed out.

"Of course." Smitty shrugged. "Why would I look up?"

The moment he said it they all looked up. Way up. Immediately Smitty's vision located a strange propeller in the clouds. Hanging from the propeller, bound and gagged, were Nalen and Ahmed.

"I see them! I see them! They're right over us!" Smitty pointed to them, but no one else could see what he saw.

If Piper had been there, of course, she would have found them right away and made short work of returning them to the ground. As it was, it took great time and attention for Smitty to give Lily specific directions so that she could use her telekinesis to pull them down.

When Nalen and Ahmed finally came into view the team cheered. Lily carefully set them on the ground and Daisy snapped their chains while Myrtle took the gags from their mouths.

Ahmed and Nalen were shaking and cold.

"Cover them," Jasper said.

Immediately sweaters and vests were stripped off their own bodies and laid over Nalen and Ahmed, who coughed and spluttered.

"C-Cunrd," Ahmed began.

"What did he say?" Violet whispered.

The effort Ahmed put into speaking was so extreme that it was causing him to gag.

"It's okay," Kimber said. "Relax."

He shook his head violently. "No. No."

"Where—" Nalen got the word out.

"Where what?" Myrtle prompted.

"Where," Ahmed said again, "Piper? Conrad?"

"Oh," said Kimber, understanding. "We had to split up. They've gone to the White House. By the time we get back they'll be waiting for us at the farm."

Once again Nalen and Ahmed shook their heads violently.

"No," said Ahmed.

"Danger," said Nalen.

"Piper—Conrad . . . walking into trap," they said together.

CHAPTER

22

BY THE TIME PRESIDENT HARRINGTON'S helicopter touched down on the west lawn of the White House, his knuckles were white from clenching his fists; his jaw was tight and twitching with fury. Of course the Secret Service had informed him the moment his son set foot in the White House and, of course, he had immediately left the state event and flown home. He planned to catch him unaware and ensure that he was never seen or heard from again.

As much satisfaction as this plan gave to Harrington, the mere thought of Conrad—particularly now that he was causing so many problems—infuriated him so much that it manifested in a physical burning inside his head, like part of his brain was threatening to erupt. Recently he'd begun to feel that way around Aletha, too, the little brat. Their mother would forgive them anything, but not him. Not now.

Inside the west portico he was met by a security detail that directed him to the roof over the family's private quarters. Before springing up the stairs he briskly turned on Special Agent Norris and barked, "I'll take care of this. You hear me?"

"Yes, Mr. President."

"Everyone off the roof. Now!" yelled Harrington.

"Copy that, Mr. President." Special Agent Norris began speaking into the communication device on his sleeve, giving firm orders to evacuate the roof area.

The stairs curved up to the second floor. As he raced upward he spotted Abigail pacing at the other end of the hall, but said nothing to her and kept moving toward his mark.

The roof was dark, the cold night air crisp, but not harsh. A strong wind whipped around Harrington, who silently searched the area. He wanted to catch them by surprise. They were children, but children like these could never be underestimated.

He found them huddled by one side, peering over the edge. Aletha was holding on to Conrad's hand, looking up at him with a trusting expression on her face. It was the same expression he'd seen on Conrad's face when he was a very small boy. It triggered a memory in Harrington, and he stayed in the shadows watching them as he recalled Conrad's second birthday. Abigail had thrown a fancy shindig to celebrate the big day and had chosen a superhero theme. She'd arranged for Harrington to be in a Superman costume and had found a matching Superman costume for two-year-old Conrad. All afternoon Harrington had carried his son around in his arms while guests cooed over how much alike they were and how proud he must be to have such an adorable child. At one point little Conrad was overcome by all the activity, and he had taken his son inside.

Harrington had sat down on the nursery floor and quietly played a game of snap with Conrad. Sounds of the party wafted up from below, but they just sat, the two of them together in their own little world, needing nothing else but each other's company. Conrad won the first hand and the second. Harrington had never felt so proud of his son or so close to him. He felt as though he would watch over Conrad and protect him with all his might and with everything that he was. He would see to it that his son had a different life—a better life—and he would give Conrad the best of himself.

As Harrington was sitting lost in thought, Conrad had pulled out an electronic alphabet toy. It was designed to ask the child a simple question to which the child could respond by pressing a button. Conrad did this a few times and quickly grew bored. Turning the machine over, he opened the back access panel and began pulling wires off the main control panel. The intensity of the expression on Conrad's face caught Harrington's full attention. He watched as his young son quickly reprogrammed the machine, replaced the panel, and turned it over.

"Hello," the toy said.

"Hello," Conrad responded. "I want to talk to someone in South America."

"I can help you with that," the toy affirmed. "Dialing now." A dial tone was heard and then the sound of a phone ringing somewhere in the distance.

"*Hola,*" said a voice.

"*Hola,*" Conrad responded. "*¿Cómo estás?*"

For the first time in his life Harrington felt a pain detonate in the back of his skull. It was so strong he crumpled, gasping his way through it until the pain transmuted from pain into an intense horror—a horror of his son. With the urgency of a mortal danger he felt compelled—

"*Hang up!*" he barked.

Conrad turned to his father, surprised and confused. "It's a new friend."

"*Estoy bien,*" the friend was saying. "*¿Y tu?*"

"Hang up *now!*" Harrington hit the toy with murderous intent: he would kill that voice inside it. He smashed it savagely against a table until the voice from South America was gone and pieces were shattered everywhere across the floor. He stopped when there was nothing left and he was breathless and his Superman outfit was ripped.

"Don't ever let me catch you doing anything like that again," he growled. He couldn't look at his son now.

"But I made it better," Conrad explained.

Harrington stormed out of the room and Conrad trailed after him on his tiny legs, his Superman cape fluttering. "Dad," he pleaded. "Dad."

And now a full ten years later, the exact same disgust and anger mixed with physical pain was coursing wildly through Harrington as he watched Conrad, except this time Conrad was with Aletha and that made it worse. He pushed against the back of his skull uselessly with a shaking hand, beads of sweat popping from his forehead until he could contain himself no longer. Lunging forward, he burst from the shadows and snatched hold of Aletha's small arm. She jumped in fright, wincing.

Piper screamed.

Conrad hadn't been expecting his father, but he wasn't surprised to see him, either. He regarded him—saw the way his tie had been roughly pulled apart and dangled about his neck and the way his top button had been torn off in frustration. He saw the evening suit and his polished shoes, but mainly he saw the way Harrington's eyes shone with manic rage.

"Hello, Father," he said calmly.

"Don't call me that," Harrington snapped. "You aren't welcome here."

Angry heat rose on Conrad's cheeks. "Aletha doesn't want to stay with you. I'm taking her with me."

"You aren't going anywhere." Harrington twisted Aletha's arm and she whimpered, her face contorting with pain.

"Let her go," Piper demanded, rising into the air and thrusting forward.

Harrington lashed out with his free hand, capturing Piper.

Piper bucked and revolted but Harrington held tight. When Piper's arm was bent behind her back he twisted it away from her socket.

"Stop! You're breaking her arm." Furious, Conrad charged at Harrington, hitting him at a precise angle to knock him off balance. Harrington lurched backward toward the edge of the roof. Piper yanked herself free but in doing so tugged at Harrington, changing his trajectory. Harrington crashed into the railing, and before Conrad's horrified eyes, the force of his fall sent Aletha soaring into the air and over the railing.

Even as she fell, Aletha was silent.

Piper shot down like an arrow. The child was moving fast but she was small and light and Piper scooped her out of the night before she was halfway to the ground.

Aletha wound her arms around Piper's neck and held tight.

"I won't let you fall," Piper whispered.

"Fly away, Piper," Conrad called, leaning over the railing, weak with relief to see that Aletha was safe. "Get Aletha out of here!"

Piper could see that Harrington was back on his feet and bearing down on Conrad, but there was no time to argue. She ascended and flew fast. Conrad could only track her path for a few seconds before his father grabbed his shoulder and spun him around. His father was at least twice his size but Conrad was too furious to feel fear.

"How unfortunate there aren't any more toddlers and girls here for you to pick on," Conrad spat.

"Shut your mouth," Harrington growled.

"So you're going to throw me off the roof now too?" Conrad jeered. And indeed, Harrington was bending him dangerously over the railing, his hands shaking with rage. "This is really presidential, Dad."

"Stop talking. Don't call me *Dad*." Harrington shook Conrad. "You are forcing me to do this. I told you to stop. *Stop*. Stop it. There is a reason. But you won't stop and now this. *I must make you stop*."

Harrington had pushed Conrad so far over the edge that the only thing that was preventing him from falling was his crushing grip on the boy's shoulders.

"Tell me this. What happened to your heart, Dad?" Conrad held his father's gaze fearlessly. "Who took it away from you?"

Harrington's breath came in choked gasps. "You stupid, stupid child. You understand nothing."

"I understand that you want to throw me off this roof."

Harrington's face contorted, a reflection of the war being fought inside his head. He let out several angry puffs and wrestled with himself. When dominance was established he acted, pushing Conrad out the remaining inch, and released him.

Time turned strangely slow. It was not more than a second, but in that time Conrad was aware of the way the vein in his father's forehead bulged and considered the pain in his shoulders. Conrad was falling when he saw his father's head violently jerk to the side like someone had hit him hard. In the next moment his father's body collapsed, his eyes rolling back as he fell to the ground unconscious.

How strange, Conrad thought. And then something grabbed him—

Conrad was no longer falling; his shirt was being pulled and held him firmly in place. Conrad looked but saw nothing and nobody around him.

"J.," Conrad said with relief.

J. materialized, panting like he'd been running or climbing or both. He had grabbed a handful of Conrad's shirt and was pulling him back onto the roof. Taking J.'s forearm, Conrad steadied himself, regained his feet.

"You can call me Jeston," J. said, leaning over, gulping for breath.

"J.'s a good name." Conrad shrugged, also breathless. "It suits you."

J. snorted. "You're full of surprises."

"Coming from you that means something."

Conrad took a moment to gather himself—his heart felt violent and his breath came out in steam-engine puffs. It wasn't every day that your father tries to throw you off the roof of the White House, and it was a lot to process, even for Conrad.

"How did you know that we'd be here?"

J. shrugged. "Like I said, I look out for you and Piper."

"So you were spying on us." Conrad spoke without anger.

J. smiled. "Spying is . . . a good word for it. Yes. I like to spy."

Conrad smiled and shook his head. "Just as long as we have that clear. Well, I guess you saved my life."

"You're welcome," J. said briskly. "But if we don't get out of here now I may have to save it again."

Conrad nodded his agreement and saw that his father

was still lying motionless. J. had hit him on the side of the head and he had fallen in a limp puddle. In the moonlight, Conrad thought that his father looked peaceful, for once.

"Is he going to be alright?"

"Check his breathing." J. pulled rope from his backpack. "We've got to get out of here."

With effort Conrad swallowed his rage and bent over his father's body, feeling his chest.

"His breathing is shallow," Conrad reported. "And his heartbeat is irregular."

Conrad's hand caught on something hard outlined by Harrington's starched white shirt. When he pressed against it, it slid free, falling between the buttons.

"What's that?" J. leaned in.

Conrad held a dark metal medallion in the shape of a star on a necklace. The workmanship was distinctive and the fine metal was twisted around a stone that sat in the center of the piece. Holding it up so that it caught the moonlight, Conrad saw that the stone glowed red.

"It's a bloodstone!" He yanked the chain, breaking it free from his father's neck, and studied it hastily. At the center of the bloodstone was a throbbing glow, like a tiny heartbeat. "It's alive. The stone is alive."

Harrington began to gasp loudly.

Conrad looked past the bloodstone to Harrington,

his mouth open, his chest bucking with each strangled breath. Conrad saw that his father was breathing in synchronicity with the beating heart of the bloodstone. As the bloodstone began to grow dim and the heartbeat lost its rhythm Harrington took fewer and fewer breaths.

"They're connected." Conrad showed J. "Look!"

If the light in the bloodstone was dying J. understood that Harrington was in danger. "Your father's heart is going to stop." J. had no particularly good feelings for Harrington, but didn't want to see the man die, either. "What do we do?"

Conrad made quick calculations and then suddenly swung the chain around, slamming the medallion to the ground. In the next moment he stomped with all his might on the stone, crushing it. An explosion of red light erupted from beneath his foot, throwing him backward.

At the same time Harrington's whole body jerked, and his eyes popped open and locked hold on Conrad's face. He sucked air as though emerging from the depths of the ocean.

"Save me," he begged.

CHAPTER

23

*H*ARRINGTON COULDN'T GET TO HIS FEET, but his body rocked with frustrated effort. He appeared to be delirious.

"Don't take me away," he moaned. "Don't make me leave my home. I want to stay with Mother." He was holding himself like a helpless child. "Where is my mother? What have you done to her? I must find her— save her."

J. and Conrad remained still, riveted; whatever was happening, they didn't wish to disturb it in any way.

"Mother told me about the prophecy," this strange new Harrington said. "I know about the girl who can fly and the boy who knows everything, and they will save me." His face, suddenly boyish, turned defiant with hope. "They will save us all."

As quickly as the mood had come over him it melted away and he collapsed into himself. After a brief stillness his body jolted several times as though rebooting. They watched as his muscles regained tension and he came into himself once more.

"Owww," Harrington moaned, struggling to sit. His hand went to his head where J. had hit him. "What—?" Harrington looked around, blinking as the floodgates of memory opened wide. "It's like—" His palm pressed against his head as though something inside of it was seeping out. "It's all coming back to me. The memories are so fast—so bright. My mother sacrificed everything for me. There is a sword in the sun. My mother is trapped in the sword in the sun. She called me Peter. My name is Peter. Yes, I remember now."

He looked at Conrad. "You are?" The moment he asked the question pieces of his brain snapped together like Legos; old pathways long dormant lit up.

"You are my son. Conrad." A softness covered his face. "I've missed you so much. I'm so glad you've come home."

With glistening eyes Harrington reached out his arms to his son, gasping at the pain the movement caused. "Conrad!"

Conrad stiffened and made no move to come closer. "Uh, Dad, you just tried to kill me, so I'm not really feeling this whole father-son thing at the moment."

"Y-you don't understand."

"That's an understatement."

"You were right; I had s-secrets," Harrington admitted, his face growing pale. "I remember now. I had secrets from everyone—s-secrets from myself. But this is what you need to know, son: the problem was the secrets, not you. You were never the p-problem."

Hearing his father's words made Conrad's breath catch.

"You were never the problem," Harrington repeated, his voice dropping to a whisper. "D-do you hear me? You would make any father proud. I see you, I see what you are, and I am so proud."

The words settled over Conrad like a balm, and his whole being started to vibrate. His brain was critical of his reaction, but there was some other part of him, a part that needed the words like a drowning man needs air. Conrad was filled by the words, transformed and released by their power.

"You are my son. You are my heart. . . ." Harrington didn't take his eyes from his child. "I-I would do anything for you. You need to hear that and know that."

Conrad didn't know what to do. He had longed his whole life to hear his father say those words, but the sound of them made him feel pain, too. His longing and pain kept him rooted to the spot.

Suddenly Harrington sat bolt upright, holding his

head. "You are . . . the boy who knows everything. You are Conrad. I was waiting for you but you were here all the time but I—no, *He* wanted me to destroy you." The realization made Harrington's eyes grow wide with fear. "Conrad, you are in great danger. You have to get out of here!"

"Danger from what?" J. prepared himself for anything.

Harrington looked hunted. "*He* is coming for you."

"Who is?"

A door slammed loudly behind them, but President Harrington didn't react, keeping his eyes on Conrad.

"He planned all this to trap you. Listen to me, you are the only one . . ."

Conrad heard footsteps.

"He gave me power so he could use me. He'll try to use you, too."

"*Who?*" Conrad demanded.

"He is . . ." Harrington struggled for words to remember. "He is—the Dark One. He is—"

Bang!

Conrad saw J. react, falling down, clutching his chest. By the time he turned from him, there was a dark figure emerging from the shadows holding a smoking gun and it was now pointed squarely at his chest.

"NO!" screamed Harrington.

Bang!

Harrington dove in front of Conrad, crumpling as the bullet pierced his heart. Something bit Conrad's shoulder and he was thrown to the ground. He was surprised when he heard Piper scream. His arm dangled limply.

"You've been shot. Oh, Conrad!" Piper's wild face was in front of him.

It was all so strange.

"I was flying back when I heard the first gunshot. We have to get you out of here!"

Piper hoisted Conrad up, and in that position it was possible for him to see that the dark figure had grabbed hold of Harrington and thrown him over his shoulder and was fleeing the scene.

"Dad!" Conrad called. "Dad!"

J. tore away his Kevlar vest, which now had a bullet hole in it. He jumped to his feet and chased after the dark figure, who jumped off the roof using a hidden zip line, still carrying Harrington with him.

Piper shot through the air, quickly closing the gap as she joined J. at the edge of the roof.

"I'll follow them from the ground," J. told her. "You track them from the air." J. grabbed hold of the zip line and was gone.

Instead of following Piper turned around and went back for Conrad.

"Go!" Conrad panted. "They'll get away."

"I'm not leaving you behind." Piper was resolute. She threw her arms around his torso and picked him up.

"Aww," Conrad groaned. "I'll slow you down."

"I'm not leaving without you."

Piper flew off the side of the White House. She kept her eyes firmly fixed on her target as she disappeared into the night.

24

THE WAVES OFF THE ATLANTIC COAST were rolling mountains of water that crashed against the shore with blasting sprays. A punishing rain shot from the sky, got caught in the wind, and pelted the ground in slanting whips. J. waited by a large group of gray rocks crusted with barnacles and seaweed, his back to the ocean and his eyes scanning the shoreline. It had been a long night and a hard chase. Piper had tried valiantly to keep up, but the weight of Conrad held her back and she fell behind. J. would have stayed with her, but she insisted that he go on ahead and he had.

Then the news had broken throughout the nation announcing the death of President Harrington. Conrad and Piper had been identified as the culprits with pictures taken from a White House security camera; the images were splashed across every news channel. A manhunt was under way to apprehend them and the entire resources of a nation were dedicated to their capture. If they were still alive and on the run, they'd endured a hard night and J. knew that their odds of survival were slim.

Meanwhile, J. had kept himself invisible and doggedly chased the mysterious stranger, who led him to remote cliffs by the ocean. Lugging Harrington's body, the stranger escaped into a hidden cliff, going deeper and deeper into its passageways. Invisible and silent, J. followed with his heart beating so loudly he thought it might give him away. When they reached an underground river the stranger loaded Harrington into a waiting boat and got in after him. With a willpower J. hardly knew he possessed, he'd halted his pursuit and returned to the beach in the hopes that Conrad and Piper would join him. And so, as the morning dawned, J. continued to watch and wait and hope.

Most of the morning had passed before J.'s patience was finally rewarded with the sound of a scream blowing to him on the wind.

"Ahhhhhh!"

J.'s head twitched and he bent his ear, listening carefully to a sound higher than the roar of the ocean and with a different beat than the rain.

"Ahhhhhh!"

J. immediately turned himself invisible, jumped to

his feet, and ran to the center of the beach, where he craned his neck, listening. He saw it before he heard it. Falling from the sky came Piper with Conrad in her arms, her face contorted from the weight of her cargo.

The thump of a helicopter was close, and despite the danger, J. became visible and threw open his arms and screamed.

"Here! Here!"

Piper was beyond seeing or steering. With the last of her energy she managed to drop onto the beach. Sand exploded upward from where the two bodies landed and tumbled into a giant heap.

J. ran to the mess of them and began to untangle limbs away from heads and torsos. Piper was at the bottom and when J. got to her she blinked at him curiously, finally realizing exactly who it was hovering anxiously over her.

"J." Her eyes traced the lines of his face and then down to his chest. "You're all wet."

J. smiled at the absurdity of such an everyday remark in such extraordinary circumstances. "You are too," he pointed out.

Piper considered this and looked down at herself. "Yes," she agreed sadly. "I'm wet."

Then she remembered. "Where is Harrington? Did you follow him?"

"Yes, I was waiting for you," J. assured her. "I'll show you the way."

Piper sighed with relief but the effort of this exchange wholly consumed the last of her energy, and her head fell back on the sand.

Hearing a low groan coming from Conrad, J. darted to him next to find that his shirt was drenched with blood and he had lost consciousness. J. felt for his pulse and listened to his breathing. The boy was weak and his shoulder had a bullet wound. J. surmised that the bullet that hit Harrington had passed through his body and lodged itself in Conrad's shoulder.

The beating of helicopter blades grew ever closer, and when J. looked up he caught sight of a Black Hawk dropping out of a large cloud toward their position on the beach. A moment later that Black Hawk was joined by another, which was followed by a third. J. didn't wait to count the final number; he grabbed Conrad and threw him over his shoulder, then pulled Piper up into his other arm.

Leaning into the wind and rain, J. ran at full tilt toward the wall of rock that surrounded the beach.

Helicopters touched down on the sand, creating a triangulation pattern to cut them off and keep them contained. As marines started to pour onto the beach, J. ran into the mouth of the cave. He needed a distance of thirty yards from the opening to make it safe and he counted those yards off under his breath.

At the thirty-yard mark he brought his load down as gently as he could and swung his backpack off his shoulder. It took him two quick movements to pull an explosive out of its seemingly bottomless depths. Without hesitation he pressed the button on its side.

"One, two—" Before he said "three," J. tossed the explosive back at the mouth of the cave and used his body to shield the children.

BOOM!

The entire rock structure groaned and threw off debris. Large boulders fell and the mouth of the cave pulled itself closed with a resolute thud. It was impassable but not for long. The marines would have their own explosives and they would act quickly.

Before the dust settled J. pulled a flashlight from his backpack. It had an attachment that secured around his head and he lashed it on quickly. He pulled light sticks from his pack and threw them into the cave.

J. hoisted Conrad and Piper back into his arms. From that point on it was a matter of retracing the path he'd followed; farther and farther into the darkness of the cliff, down one cave, up another, and through unmarked passages with hairpin turns. After a solid hour of walking, the sound of water dripping led J. to the underground stream. This was as far as he'd watched the stranger go last time, and now it was up to him to figure out the rest of the way.

Laying Piper and Conrad at the side of the stream, J. shone his flashlight to the right and then the left until he caught sight of a little piece of reflective tape. He grabbed it and discovered it was attached to an inflated raft.

He tested the raft for safety before he lifted Piper and Conrad aboard. He sat at the back and used a plastic paddle to push off. The current of the stream and J.'s paddling soon had them traveling at a fast clip. Piper stirred and sat up weakly. J. threw her a flask of water and an energy bar, after which she was much revived. Conrad showed no signs of consciousness and Piper hovered over him, worried.

"He's lost a lot of blood," she whispered to J.

"I can see a light ahead. We'll be out of here soon." J. nodded to the growing light at the end of the tunnel. When they emerged Piper and J. shielded their eyes against brilliant sunshine.

They were on a cliff about halfway down a mountain. J. pushed the boat to the side and jumped out, securing it to a waiting post where another boat, a twin to theirs, was tethered. J. helped Piper and Conrad to a safe perch on the side of the mountain, laying Conrad on a soft bed of leaves.

When Conrad was comfortable, Piper and J. had a moment to look at their new surroundings. What they saw startled and amazed them.

"Holy moly, would you look at this!" Piper said.

The word "paradise" seemed inappropriate. It was more beautiful than anything Piper could ever have imagined or J. had ever seen. Bright sunlight showered over a valley populated by brilliant plants and trees and strange creatures. Surrounding the valley on all sides were towering mountains that reached into the clouds.

Piper pointed to large pink flowers the size of trucks growing out of the mountain off to her right. They swayed gently in the breeze and filled the air with perfume.

"Look," she said in amazement, inhaling deeply. No sooner had she pointed than her eyes were drawn to a fantastic rainbow made up of diamond-like stones floating across the valley. Reflecting light of colors that Piper had never seen before, it began to vibrate, creating a harmonic hum. Not only was there a hyper-brilliance to this strange place, a clarity of color and light that placed everything into a sharper focus, but there was a distinct feeling to it as well. A relaxing calm washed over Piper's entire body, making her feel weightless, as though the breeze was rejuvenating her being. At the same time, her mind snapped awake, her thoughts sharp and succinct. Everything suddenly made sense, while all that had come before in her life felt like it had been a silly dream mired in confusion and darkness.

"Where are we?"

"I knew it. I knew it existed." J. spoke quietly. "It's exactly the way my sister described it."

Piper's face was flushed and glowing. "And this is where Harrington was taken?"

"Yes."

Abruptly J. stopped talking and shielded his eyes from the sun, watching some point in the distance. Piper followed his gaze, squinting to see something coming toward them across the valley. It appeared to be a boat floating in the air. But not really a boat—more like a canoe composed of some sort of shimmering energy. As it came closer they could see that a girl about Piper's age was standing in it. She was using a long stick to paddle through the air, which propelled it forward. Clad in robes made of a material that floated more than hung, her hair was woven with beads and flowers and she held herself with a simple, innocent grace.

In awed silence J. and Piper stepped back to allow the floating canoe enough space to dock on the mountain. When it came to a stop the girl stepped out of the canoe and stood before them. Piper noticed that her cheeks were flushed and her hands shook, as though she was collecting herself for the task before her. After a painful silence in which J. and Piper had no idea what they should do, the girl finally thrust her hand forward awkwardly.

"Hello," she said, "my name is AnnA. Welcome."

Piper realized that the girl meant for her to shake hands, and she did so. Then J. did the same.

"We have been expecting you," AnnA said, looking at Piper.

"You have?" Piper shared a startled look with J.

"Yes. At the beginning of the growing season the Guardian told us to prepare for newcomers."

Piper thought about this. No doubt AnnA was referring to the late spring or early summer when she said "the beginning of the growing season." It was currently late in the fall, so how could this Guardian have known that they would be coming when they didn't know themselves?

"I am to be your guide," AnnA said, interrupting Piper's thoughts.

"What is this place called?" J. asked eagerly.

"This is Xanthia, home to the Chosen Ones." AnnA glanced at Conrad and her face visibly paled. "Your friend is hurt."

"He was shot."

"Shot?" Confusion rippled across AnnA's brow.

"Do you have medicine?" J. cut to the point. "A healer?"

"Yes. Come." She pointed to her boat and looked like she wanted to go to Conrad, but then wasn't able to actually make herself do so. Instead J. and Piper lifted Conrad up gently and laid him in the place where she pointed.

When the task was complete AnnA took a flower out of her hair and handed it to J. "This is for you."

J. received the flower graciously. "Thank you." It was unlike any flower he had ever seen, with a purple center and green and red petals. Lifting it to his nose, he inhaled its scent and no sooner had his breath hit his lungs than his face turned white and still—deathly still.

"J.?" Piper watched him closely. "J., are you okay?"

J.'s face looked to Xanthia in the distance, his eyes open and fixed. With mounting concern, Piper approached him. "J.?" When he didn't respond she reached for his hand. It was as cold and heavy as stone.

"Oh no!" Piper gasped. "J.? J.! Can you hear me?" Piper shook him frantically to no avail.

"What happened to him?"

AnnA seemed neither surprised nor moved by his plight. "Do not be . . . sad. He is still. I gave him a Sooon flower."

Piper kicked the flower away angrily. "Why would you do that?"

"He was not chosen," AnnA said. "Only you two were chosen, and so only you two may stay."

"But why us and not him?"

AnnA appeared not to know how to answer this question, and after many shadows of half-formed thoughts passed over her face she gave up and looked at Piper.

Anger rose in Piper with a big hot blast, and she jumped to her feet and rushed at AnnA, who threw up her hands as though to shield herself.

"That's not fair!" Piper yelled. "J. deserves to be here just as much as we do. You can't turn him away after he got this far. If it wasn't for him we wouldn't have made it. He wanted to be here so, so bad. It was all he ever talked about."

AnnA whimpered, and the fear in her voice took the edge off Piper's fury.

"I cannot bring him. I am not allowed," AnnA replied.

"Then forget it, I'm not going either."

AnnA had not expected Piper to say this, and she looked around as though she might find a solution to the predicament in the mountains surrounding them. Conrad moaned in pain, distracting Piper and providing AnnA with the answer she was looking for.

"If you do not come, your friend will not receive healing. He will die."

"But . . ." Piper looked from Conrad, who was bloody and curled in pain, to J., whose eyes were frozen on the promised land he longed for. "Couldn't you please bring J.? Please! It's not right to leave him behind."

AnnA sighed. "I cannot. He has not been chosen."

Conrad moaned again and the remaining fight in Piper melted into fear. Tears prickled her eyes. "You promise J. won't be hurt?"

"They will return him to the Outsiders. We have no need of him." AnnA spoke in a simple and straight-forward tone, as though the answers should have been obvious.

Going to J. one last time, Piper settled his backpack by his feet and placed her hand on his cold cheek, whispering, "Thank you." Then quickly, before she changed her mind, she got into the canoe next to Conrad and didn't look back.

Stepping in carefully and positioning herself as far as possible away from Piper and Conrad within the confines of the raft, AnnA grasped the oar and paddled through the air. Soon they were soaring over the valley, charting a course to a distant mountain. If Piper hadn't been so worried about Conrad, the journey would have taken her breath away.

"Don't worry," she whispered to Conrad. "Everything's going to be okay. Nothing will hurt us now."

CHAPTER

25

$\mathcal{T}$HEY WERE ALWAYS ONE STEP BEHIND.

As they arrived at the White House, the news of Harrington's death broke and the capital was locked down. Fortunately, Piper had activated a beacon, which was another one of Conrad's useful inventions, and placed it in the Lincoln Memorial. Myrtle ran to the beacon and found Aletha safely stashed away there. With the help of Violet, who shrank down to Aletha's size and whose gentle nature made her feel most comfortable, they coaxed the terrified child out.

After that the chase was on.

Jasper did his best, but Piper and Conrad were moving fast in a pattern that was unpredictable and appeared random. To make matters worse, the kids had to keep their distance from the military, as well as help Ahmed and Nalen, who were not in the best shape. On top of which, they now had a young child to take care of. Aletha was still very small and didn't have their training or strength, which meant they each had to take turns keeping an eye on her. Smitty had suggested that they send Aletha back to the farm for Betty and Joe to take care of, but as the appointed leader, Jasper felt personally responsible for her safety—and to him, that meant keeping her close.

By the time they arrived on the beach it was high noon and the marines had cordoned off the area. Smitty located a rock perch where they could watch the activity below without being seen. Myrtle scavenged food, water, and some blankets and they set up camp, waiting and watching.

"There will be another clue," Jasper said, and the kids believed him.

"Whoever did this used Nalen and Ahmed as decoys to split us up," Kimber reasoned. "Divide and conquer."

"Y-yes," agreed Jasper. As they looked back on the series of events, it seemed plain to all of them now that it was a trap. But Jasper didn't have the intellectual capacity to think his way through this situation. Not like Conrad. Conrad had said he was a leader, not a genius.

That night the kids huddled together under the blankets and let exhaustion take them. In the small hours of the morning Jasper woke with a start—someone was approaching their position. Noiselessly, he woke Daisy and motioned to the sound. She immediately understood and the two of them crept from under the blankets to investigate.

The night was bitterly dark and cold but a cloud blew away from the moon and they could see a bush thrashing about for unknown reasons.

"Maybe an animal?" Daisy whispered in Jasper's ear.

Jasper didn't think it was an animal. The bush was being hacked at and pushed aside from the top.

"Umph."

They both distinctly heard the sound. It was the sort of sound that you make when you bump into something and hurt yourself.

Then, almost as though the moonlight was playing tricks with their eyes, the air around the bush shimmered.

The shimmer became J. He was clutching his elbow.

"J.!"

J. immediately took a defensive posture until he recognized Jasper and Daisy, at which point he sagged with relief.

"W-what are you doing here?" Jasper was elated to see him.

J. was strangely disoriented and frightened. "Where are we?"

"It's a beach," Jasper explained. "We followed Piper and Conrad here."

"Piper! Conrad!" J. looked past Jasper urgently. "Where are they now?"

"We don't know. We can't find them. Do you know where they are?"

J. threw his knapsack down in frustration, clenched his fists, and screamed. Jasper took a step away from him and toward Daisy. Daisy prepared herself for anything because by all appearances J. had clearly lost his mind.

It took J. more than several minutes before he calmed down enough to speak. "I was right there. Right there and they . . . Ugh. They didn't want me. They turned me away." He kicked the ground. "I have to get back. I have to . . ."

"Do you know where Piper and Conrad are?" Jasper repeated timidly, trying to focus him.

"I—I . . ." J. clutched his head. "They took the memory. But it doesn't matter. I'll find my way back."

"We have to find Piper and Conrad."

J. looked at Jasper and Daisy as though seeing them for the first time clearly and not as merely part of a throng of kids who didn't require his attention. He noticed that they looked small and helpless.

"Where are the rest of you?" J. asked.

"Sleeping, just over there." Jasper pointed.

J. nodded as a plan formed quickly in his mind. "Good. Yes. I'll take you with me. We'll go together. It'll be better that way. What about the kid with the X-ray eyes? Is he here?"

"Smitty? Yes."

"We'll need him. And the strong girl?" J. had never bothered to learn their names.

Daisy glared at J.'s rudeness. "That's me."

"Right. At daybreak the marines will move out and that's when we'll move in." J.'s mind was going a mile a minute and he started plucking things out of his bag. "We'll need—"

Jasper planted his feet. "N-n-no."

J. was astonished by the little boy's nerve. "No?"

"Conrad said I was the leader until he got back. I make the plan. C-Conrad said."

J. took a deep breath. "What's your name again?"

"Jasper."

"Jasper." J. practiced his patience. "Okay, Jasper. If that's the way it's gotta be, then what's the plan?"

Jasper paused, lifting his chin decisively. "At daybreak when the beach is empty we'll start looking for them."

J. nodded seriously. "Good plan."

"And we don't stop until we find them!"

"That works for me."

Part II

CHAPTER

26

CONRAD WOKE GAGGING, GASPING, AND flailing his arms. He was vaguely aware that Piper was standing over him and trying to restrain him.

"Get down!" he yelled, pulling Piper wildly. "He has a gun!"

"Conrad, you're safe."

Her words struck him as nonsensical. He clutched at where the bullet had ripped through his shoulder, but his hand came down upon a bandage, causing him further confusion.

"Where's my father?"

"He needs to remain calm," a strange voice said.

Conrad jerked his head around to discover an old man looming over him. He had snow-white hair and was dressed in a red cloth that was fashioned like a toga but wrapped intricately in a way that Conrad had never seen before.

"Get away!" Conrad scrambled off the bed, knocking Piper in his mad efforts to escape.

Piper spoke in a low voice, asking the strange man to leave, which he did quickly and without another word. After he was gone Piper turned to find Conrad cowering against the wall like a hurt wild animal.

"Shhhhh. Conrad, it's okay. I'm here. It's me, Piper."

Her soothing voice calmed his breathing until he could relax his body.

"No one's gonna hurt you. Your shoulder's still healing and you gotta take it easy. Honest. You're safe. Be calm now."

The White House and his father and the stranger with the gun began to dissipate in Conrad's mind like a fog being blown away by the wind.

How strange, he thought as he looked around. The walls and floor were all made of stone that had waves of detailing through it as though some master craftsman had sculptured it into delightful motion. Crystals hung across the ceiling, creating an iridescent glow. On the far side of the room was an arched opening leading out to a balcony, where Conrad caught a glimpse of a waterfall and a valley dense with rich vegetation.

Piper was also wound in a robe made of a material no more substantial than a summer breeze. Gathered around the waist, it hung in soft folds to her knees. She watched him with concern knitting her forehead.

"This isn't . . ." Conrad made quick mental leaps. His voice was hoarse from lack of use and he swallowed hard. "I'm not in a hospital. That man was . . ." Conrad's eyes suddenly went wide with surprise. "J. was right. This is the place he was talking about."

"It's called Xanthia. Oh, Conrad, it's so beautiful here."

"But my father?"

"We followed him here."

He ran his hands through his hair. "Have you seen him?"

Piper shook her head. "As soon as I knew you were safe I asked for him, but no one knows who I'm talking about. They say that we are the only Outsiders."

"Outsiders?"

"That's what they call us and anyone else who isn't from Xanthia. We're the only Outsiders who've ever been here."

"Where's J.?"

Piper sighed deeply, shame dusting her cheeks. "They wouldn't let him come with us. I had to leave him behind."

"Why?" Conrad was startled to discover that he was disappointed that J. wasn't there with them.

"J. wasn't invited. Only us."

Conrad thought about this, looking closely at the room.

"C'mon," Piper urged, noticing his interest and anxious to change the subject. "Wait until you see!"

Piper led Conrad across the room to the balcony, where he caught his first glimpse of a whole city that had been carved into the side of the mountain in a horseshoe shape. There were four tiers that reached above a large plateau, and falling through the center of it all was a waterfall that pooled before pushing forward as a river into the valley.

The air was soaked with perfume and there wasn't a place that Conrad could set his eyes that wasn't its own prayer of beauty. A vine of purple flowers danced through graceful stone archways and the waterfall had lights within that made it shimmer.

"Isn't it something?" Piper gushed. "And not one person has asked me to solve a math problem!"

"How long have I been here?"

"Two days. By the time we got here you were more dead than alive, but Irgo, he's the healer, has been doing all he can. 'Course he had no idea how to heal a gunshot wound and he's not as good as Jasper, but he did his best. Isn't that waterfall something? I think it's even more grand than J. said it would be." Piper pulled her gaze from the beauty to see Conrad's reaction and was disappointed to see he was distant and unengaged. "What?"

"When I was with my father he was different. He changed." Conrad was engrossed by the memory of him. "And he talked about a Dark One."

Piper wasn't interested in hearing about Harrington. "You've gotta rest."

"I really need to find my father and talk to him."

"Conrad." Piper swallowed hard, bracing herself. "Maybe your dad didn't make it."

"Why would you say that?"

"He was shot through the heart." Piper had seen Harrington hit when she was flying back to the roof. "I saw it with my own eyes."

"Then you saw," Conrad retorted passionately, "that my father saved me. You saw that if it wasn't for him . . . I would be dead right now."

"He never moved after he was shot. I never once saw him move when we were chasing him." Piper could feel herself getting heated. "There's no way he's alive."

Anger hung heavily in the pause that followed her words.

"All I'm saying," Piper continued gently, reining herself in and preventing this from turning into a fight, "is that he was never much of a father to you. Sure, maybe he was nice for a few minutes, but it might not be such a bad thing if he wasn't part of your life anymore. It might be . . . easier. Better. For you."

"I don't believe that, either," Conrad replied bitterly. "My father is alive and I will find him. And if you don't want to help or join me then you can just fly away and I'll do it myself."

Shocked by the anger and hurt in his voice, Piper became aware of the painful dark circles that lined Conrad's eyes and the sadness that was etched into his forehead and tugging at his mouth.

"We're a team, Conrad. You know that. We stay together, we work together, I have your back."

A bottomless sigh escaped Conrad's lips in a measured exhalation, releasing his anger. "Good. I want to start searching for him right away."

By this point Conrad's shoulder was throbbing wildly and he was dizzy. He slumped over without warning and Piper eased him to the bed.

"You're as weak as a newborn foal."

Conrad didn't resist Piper's help. When she had him settled he curled himself into a ball and closed his eyes. For the next twenty-four hours straight he slept without moving as Piper watched over him.

27

*A*T DAWN THE SOUND OF SINGING DREW Conrad from his bed. He found Piper sitting on the balcony with her knees curled up to her chest looking down to the plateau. Conrad followed her gaze to where an old man was standing at the very edge of the precipice. He had a shock of white hair and his arms were raised upward as he sang.

Sitting himself down next to Piper, Conrad arranged his shoulder into a comfortable position and listened.

"His name is Aldo," Piper said, breaking the quiet between them. "He is called the singer of Xanthia. Every morning at dawn he sings to Mother Mountain."

"Mother Mountain?"

"Mother Mountain is the spirit inside the mountain. AnnA told me all about it. Thousands of years ago the Chosen Ones had to wander below with the Outsiders.

At long last the Guardian of the Chosen Ones led them to this hidden valley and the singer woke the spirit inside the mountain with her song. She asked the spirit if the Chosen Ones could live here and Mother Mountain wrapped her rock arms around them and never let them go."

"They don't seriously believe that?"

"AnnA told me that Mother Mountain let her rocks tumble away to create all of these rooms and meeting places." Piper shrugged. "She gives the Chosen Ones everything they need. She even made the waterfall on the plateau for them."

"Who's AnnA?"

"She's our guide. She's gonna show us around and teach us about Xanthia."

"Asanti," Aldo sang. "A–SAN–TI." Aldo stretched the sounds of the word out, his voice rising and reverberating with the assistance of the perfect acoustics.

"Asanti," Piper repeated. The word melted on her tongue. "They use that word a lot. AnnA told me it means great blessing. Gratitude. Joy. They use the word to honor the day and the life in all things. Asanti."

"A–strange."

Piper fixed Conrad with a look.

"I'm just pointing out that the word 'Asanti' is strange. But it doesn't matter because all I want to do is find my father and get out of here. We've got to get back to the others."

"Then I'll call AnnA," Piper said, getting to her feet.

By the time Conrad was dressed in a robe that he deemed equally strange, they were joined by AnnA.

"Asanti," AnnA greeted Conrad nervously, looking more at his feet than his face. She looked to be about eleven years old, and had trusting eyes and skin so clear it was like a blank sheet of paper waiting for someone to write on it. Her long auburn hair curled about her shoulders and she fiddled with it so that she would have something to do with her hands. Conrad had the distinct impression that AnnA would melt into the shadows if she could.

"We are glad that you are well," AnnA said quietly. "Equilla wishes to welcome you in person. She is the leader of our council of elders."

"I'd like to find my father first," Conrad said bluntly. "President Harrington."

AnnA looked to Piper, folding her chin down. "I have told Piper that we do not know this man. There is not one among us by that name."

Conrad exchanged a loaded glance with Piper, quietly deciding to bide his time and not press the issue with AnnA, who seemed genuinely confused by the matter. "We'd be happy to meet Equilla."

"Please follow me." AnnA bowed, guiding them from their chamber.

With AnnA in the lead, Piper and Conrad walked to the outdoor passage that was carved along the entire second level. Outside, the activity of a normal day was under way and Conrad noticed that the Xanthian people were calmly attending to their daily tasks in unhurried grace; no one was rushing, no one was angry. Dotted about the side of the mountain, wrapped in their colorful robes, they looked like strange, beautiful flowers.

A woman was spinning a web into a sculpture with delicate spidery movements, using a silk-type substance that she was shooting out of her fingertips. Not far from her two men worked together on a cloud that they had tussled to a rock with a silver rope. The cloud was pulling against the rope but the men were carefully shaping it before releasing it back up to the sky. An old woman was talking to a gathering of purple ducks that were respectfully quacking at her and wagging their tail feathers.

Curious eyes followed Piper and Conrad wherever they went, but no one approached them or addressed them directly, and all kept a careful distance. Except, of course, AnnA, who was technically with them but at the same time maintained a calculated buffer space, as though she might catch something from them, or they might suddenly strike her.

AnnA led them down the main staircase and past the waterfall. "Over there is the garden," AnnA said, pointing to a small plateau tucked off to the side.

Conrad saw a woman walking through the garden. As she moved, the plants leaned toward her as though yearning for her attention. He was surprised to notice that he could not identify any of the trees or plants. One of the trees was a bright orange color with black fruit the size of basketballs hanging from its branches. Next to the tree was a rippling blue bush with leaves that subtly changed color.

As they passed the waterfall's pool, Conrad's attention was caught by small shiny things moving at the bottom of it. Their movement was so peculiar that Conrad leaned over the edge to get a closer look. Tiny fish-shaped coins, which had both fins and legs, darted about in the water, often twirling and doing something that appeared like a jig.

"Those are called Jangles," AnnA explained helpfully, noting Conrad's interest. "They are lucky, if you can catch them. They are very fast, though."

"They look more coin than fish."

"Yes. They say that the Jangles were once coins that

were thrown into fountains and wished upon. But the fish in the fountains swallowed the wishing coins, and when those fish had babies they came out looking more coin than fish."

"I've never seen them before." Nor had Conrad ever read anything about them.

AnnA was not surprised. "The Guardian brought them here because he said they would die off if we didn't protect them; the Outsiders trapped and killed them. Almost everything here has not survived in the world below because the Guardian says the Outsiders are killers."

Conrad sharply turned to AnnA, who seemed wholly innocent of the inflammatory nature of her last statement. Determined to carry out her task, she resumed leading them across the plateau.

"And when will I meet this Guardian?" Conrad pressed.

"The Guardian is often busy," AnnA said vaguely. "This is called the Celebration Center. At the age of four or five a child is called to join."

AnnA nodded to the side of the plateau where an arched roof was held up by rows of pillars. A set of steps led up to it and Piper was immediately intrigued. "Are we allowed to see inside?"

"Of course. But Equilla is waiting for us and we must

not linger." AnnA guided her two guests up the steps and through the columns.

Inside the Celebration Center, Conrad saw different platform levels with views of the valley from every perspective. He counted eighteen kids at work, focusing with steady concentration on their own individual tasks. One girl with golden hair had no less than thirty bees and other insects flying around her. A thin, awkward boy was creating miniature wind worms in his hands next to where a very small girl was coaxing carrot seeds to grow into full-size carrots.

"I wish I'd had this place to teach me to fly!" Piper remarked with longing.

Conrad silently admitted to himself that it was an impressive setup.

"Each morning the young ones gather here to explore and celebrate their abilities."

"You mean like school?"

"School?" repeated AnnA.

"Yes," Conrad said. "A place of learning where children are taught math, history, and to read and write."

"No, no, it is not like school." AnnA shook her head, disturbed by the notion of such a place. "No, we do not wish to learn new things. The goal is to merely uncover that which is already inside of us and celebrate it into a blossoming."

"Hmm." Conrad watched the children's efforts.

AnnA led him past a boy who was causing the air around him to turn from pink to blue to yellow, around a fountain that was somehow suspended in the middle of the air with no seeming intake or outlet, to a circular space that hovered several feet above the ground. Five children played on top of it.

AnnA stopped before they actually approached so that Conrad could watch. All the children appeared to be between the ages of four and six, and one of them, a curly-haired boy, had a blindfold over his eyes. He was reaching out to catch the other children, who were giggling wildly and darting away from him.

"Oh, I know this game." Piper smiled. "We play it back at home. It's called blindman's bluff."

AnnA cocked her head. "You have a game like this?"

"Sure. If you're 'it' you've gotta catch someone and guess who it is."

The little boy darted forward and grabbed hold of a little girl. Suddenly the two children merged into one, creating a new creature comprised of both their parts.

Piper and Conrad gasped.

"Wait," AnnA warned.

After about ten seconds the merged entity tore apart and the two children returned to their normal shapes. A moment later they laughed uproariously.

"This game is called Habatet," AnnA explained quickly, to quell the shock on both Conrad's and Piper's faces. "The children become one so that they can feel what it is like to be someone else. It awakens their natural empathy and acceptance of differences."

"Oh," Piper said, finding that she could breathe again. "Yeah, that's not so much like blindman's bluff."

Suddenly, a fat, glossy-brown squirrel jumped up on a railing next to where they stood.

"Equilla wishes to welcome the Outsiders now," the squirrel chucked. His voice was strangely feminine and throaty. He then bobbed up and down until AnnA fed him a nut that she pulled discreetly from a pocket of her robe. The squirrel snatched the nut up and ate it greedily.

Conrad watched the squirrel with fascination.

"This is Nuttle," AnnA explained. "The squirrels deliver messages for us. It is very . . . convenient. They keep us all connected."

"Like the internet."

"But super cute." Piper reached out her hand to pet him. "Hey, little fella."

Suddenly the squirrel lunged forward, baring his teeth and making an alarmingly loud screeching noise. AnnA threw herself between the two, protecting Piper from the squirrel's wrath.

"Go, Nuttle." Throwing out another nut, AnnA pointed firmly away from the Celebration Center. "Your message has been heard. Go!"

Nuttle glared at Piper before huffily scampering away.

"What was that?" Piper was entirely unsettled by the squirrel's viciousness.

"They are proud creatures. It is best not to pet them. Or get too close to them. Or look them in the eye. They will not like it."

"No kidding."

"We must not delay," AnnA told her guests. "I will take you to Equilla now."

CHAPTER

28

$\mathcal{A}$NNA DEFTLY WOVE THROUGH PAS-
sages and stairways until she led Piper and
Conrad to the very top of the mountain. "The elders watch
over Xanthia and ensure our safety," AnnA explained as
she went. "Equilla is the leader among the elders."

AnnA's journey ended at a chamber with high ceil-
ings and a spectacular view of the valley below. As they
waited, Conrad and Piper nervously looked out at the
valley, catching fleeting glimpses of a strange creature
that looked strikingly like a dragon and a swarm of flies
that picked up a tree and carried it off.

"I wonder what you think of Xanthia?" a throaty
voice asked, interrupting the quiet.

Conrad and Piper turned to find Equilla watching
them. She was a regal woman with careful eyes and a
dove-gray robe that draped so perfectly about her that

when she stood still, which was almost always, she appeared to be a statue. AnnA had told them that Equilla was 153 years old, but the wisdom of those years had lightened her frame instead of weighing it down.

"It's beautiful," Piper said, smiling. "I'm Piper."

"Yes, I know." Equilla returned Piper's smile. "And you are Conrad." A nod of her head sent AnnA away, and all her attention fell on Piper and Conrad.

"We welcome you." She smiled. "Asanti."

Conrad returned her nod politely. "A—thank you."

"In all our time in Xanthia you are the first newcomers to be welcomed among us. I hope that AnnA is explaining our ways to you so that there is no confusion."

"Yes, thank you." Conrad was about to bring up the subject of Harrington, but before he could Equilla continued.

"That pleases me to hear." Equilla's eyes considered the details of Conrad's wound. "I want you to know that the elders are here to help you with anything that might trouble you. We live in peace on Mother Mountain and our people know no lack for anything. We are happy to share all that we have and all that we are with you. From now on you will be considered one of us: a Chosen One."

"Thank you. I wanted—" Conrad started to ask about his father when Equilla cut him off once more.

"Our history with the Outsiders is a long one. When you are settled we must take the opportunity to explain the journey of the Chosen Ones. In Xanthia we encourage you to fully embrace all that you are and experience it in every way possible, but we do not wish for you to introduce any Outsider ways that would disrupt the happiness of others. Of course AnnA will help you with that."

"My father is here too," Conrad blurted out. "I would like to see him. Now."

Equilla pursed her lips. "AnnA has spoken to me of this. I know nothing of your father, nor does anyone in Xanthia. He is not here. You are mistaken."

Conrad bit his tongue. The persistent calm of Equilla was irritating, but not as much as her all-knowing condescension.

"He is hurt," Conrad tried again. "He would need medical care."

Equilla turned and took a few steps away before facing them again. "I understand that Outsiders often trade in untruths, but it is not our way here. If your father were in Xanthia I would know of it, and if I knew I would tell you so. I cannot speak more truly than I am."

"But—" Conrad argued. "If everyone was to look—"

Equilla paused meaningfully. "There are those among us who do not think that an Outsider can live with the

Chosen Ones peacefully. They think our ways will be too strange for you. They wish for you to be returned to the Outside."

"What?" Piper was suddenly confused. "You want us to leave?"

Conrad understood not only the meaning of Equilla's message but the unspoken meanings, too. If he was going to get anywhere then he was going to have to change his tactics immediately and play by their rules.

"You're right." Conrad shrugged good-naturedly and smiled, making his expression calm and relaxed. "If you say that my father's not here, then he's not here."

Piper's head swung toward Conrad in shock. "But Conrad—"

Conrad raised his hand to silence her. "It's a great opportunity for us to join you in Xanthia, and we appreciate the welcome. I'm sorry I got carried away about all of this, but, as you say, it's different on the Outside. It's a good thing that we're young and we'll learn your ways easily."

Conrad nudged Piper pointedly. She shot him a dirty look.

Pleased that the matter was resolved, Equilla bowed her head. "We are happy to have you and eager that you are settled. We will be having a Celebration in a few days' time. I hope that you will join us."

"We wouldn't miss it!" Conrad chirped. "We want to see everything."

Conrad didn't give Piper the chance to utter another syllable until they were alone on the balcony after being dismissed by Equilla. AnnA was waiting for them a short distance away, and the moment she spotted them she trotted in their direction.

"What was that about?" Piper hissed. "You're going to give up on your father just like that?"

"Don't be ridiculous!" Conrad scoffed, talking quickly before AnnA reached them. "Either Equilla doesn't know if my dad is here, or she's hiding him. If she doesn't know, then she can't help us, and if she's hiding him, she won't. Either way we have to find him, and if we don't act peacefully they're going to kick us out and we'll never find him and get back to the others."

Piper could see the logic in this. "So your dad is here?"

"Maybe. Or maybe not. It's up to us to find out for sure."

"How?"

"The first thing we need to do is not cause problems. If they trust us we'll get the run of the place and that will make it easier for us to search. Obviously if he is here, he's being hidden, and so we're going to have to dig around."

"But what about the others? They'll be worried sick."

"The faster we work, the faster we can return. Now shhhhh."

AnnA walked up to them and bowed. "Asanti." She smiled.

"Asanti." Conrad smiled and bowed back.

29

*A*S A PARTING GIFT, THE MARINES detonated enough explosives to implode the entrance to the cave—if they couldn't learn the secrets to the place, they decided, then no one else would, either.

This wasn't a problem. Indeed, there really wasn't a problem until there was, and then it wasn't a problem— it was an insurmountable obstacle.

It took Daisy a few days to clear away the rocks and punch through, and soon enough they were standing in the caves. It was then up to Smitty to identify invisible clues that would lead them through to the secret passage. Once again, this didn't turn out to present too much of a challenge even though the military efforts had mucked up the terrain. Smitty was able to isolate the blood that had fallen from Conrad's shoulder and combine that trail with random strands of Piper's hair that had fallen along their way. Progress was quick, and a few days after they had first started, J., Jasper, and all the other kids stood on the cliff where Piper had caught her first glimpses of Xanthia.

"Ahhh." J. inhaled deeply, soaking it all in. Seeing the view made his brain feel like it was being tickled. Even though he couldn't remember it, his body knew that he'd been here before.

Lily was captivated by a flock of seagulls that flew in circular patterns and decorated the sky with flower designs. "It's . . . soooo magical."

"Look!" Violet pointed to a group of migrating bushes.

Next to where they stood, some rocks began to hum and bounce. "What is this place?" Daisy asked as Aletha moved behind her, the small girl's hand snaking up to grasp hold of Daisy's shirt as though seeking protection. Unlike the other children, whose faces were filled with wonder and excitement, Aletha's brown eyes grew large with fear.

"It's paradise!" J. threw his arms wide. "It's the promised land. It's where we belong!"

"B-but where are Conrad and Piper?" Jasper was scanning the valley and the surrounding mountains.

Smitty was also searching, but the area was vast and

teeming with life, most of which was unidentifiable to him. "I can't see them."

J. looked toward the distant mountains, squinting at them as though that might make him remember something. It didn't. "We'll just have to start searching. We'll find them sooner or later."

And that was the precise moment when everything went wrong.

On their first foray into the valley they had traveled no more than forty feet down the mountain when Kimber was sucked into voracious flesh-eating quicksand. It took all of Daisy's strength and J.'s strategy to extract her. A full six hours later, Kimber lay panting on the ground and Smitty was pointing out where quicksand holes were dotted throughout the terrain like land mines.

Retreating back to the safety of the cliff for the night, they rested, recovered, and plotted a new course through the valley. The next day they had reached only ten feet down when they were set upon by amorous lilac bushes. Violet had made the mistake of smelling the fragrant flowers and praising them, when the bush sprang to life, wrapped its branches and leaves around the kids, and refused to release them. Happy to have such lovely "babies," the bush rocked them and bloomed over them contently. Another day was taken up figuring out that the only way to escape the flowers' embrace was by sing-ing to them (upbeat Broadway-type melodies were the most effective).

The day after that they were almost scorched to death by volcanic sunflowers. Then there was a rogue river that swept them up and took them on a wild water ride before depositing them back on the cliff. After that, siren fireflies mesmerized them with their lights and enticed them to dance until they reached the point of exhaustion.

No one talked about quitting, but days were starting to stack up with no progress to show for them. The day they were attacked by a freak band of flying monkeys was definitely the low point.

"You've got to be kidding me!" Violet squeaked. "Flying monkeys? I thought they were only in movies."

The monkeys were mischievous blighters and pelted the team with little nuts that turned out to have minds of their own too—when given the opportunity they bit the kids viciously. If the kids managed to catch the nuts and squish them, the nuts screamed like babies and piti-fully begged for mercy, and, if granted, the nasty nuts immediately turned around and set about biting again. The kids took shelter behind rocks and did their best to fend off the monkeys and their dreadful nut-bombs.

"Apparently flying monkeys are not just in movies," J.

said, picking up a wiggling nut and lobbing it back at a passing monkey.

Hours later the monkeys grew bored and went looking for new entertainment. They departed as quickly as they arrived and left the kids, who did not share the monkeys' sense of humor, disheartened, tired, and riddled with bite marks.

"Forget about getting to those mountains; we can't even get into the stupid valley," Lily moaned. "It's impossible."

"Yeah," agreed Kimber. "The wildlife here has issues."

"Yesterday I saw a herd of leaping lizards down there." Smitty shook his head. "How are we gonna deal with that?"

Myrtle sighed. "It's impassable."

"Maybe that's the point," J. considered. "It's a natural barrier to keep people out."

"T-too bad Piper's n-n-not here," Jasper mused. "She'd fly over it in a second."

"You can say that again," Violet said.

"Yes, yes, she would, wouldn't she?" J. sat up straight. "This is never going to work unless we have a flyer."

"Well, Piper's out there somewhere and we're here, so it's not really an option," Lily sighed.

"But"—J. turned to the bedraggled group, his face animated and hopeful—"if we could find a flyer, wouldn't that be the answer to our problems?"

"S-sure." Jasper shrugged. "But where are we going to find a flyer?"

J. paused. All the kids' attention was trained on him, their faces trusting and open, waiting for what he'd say next. He was aware that what he was about to suggest would change their mood drastically.

"I happen to know where there is another flyer."

"A-a-another flyer?" J. had Jasper's full attention. "Who?"

"She's different than when you knew her," J. said quickly. "Her name is Letitia Hellion and she's my sister. But she'll help us."

A ripple of undisguised horror passed across the kids' faces.

"No!" Kimber said emphatically.

"Double no." Lily crossed her arms over her chest.

"You've got to be crazy."

"Dr. Hellion is evil."

"I disagree," J. stated calmly. "And I would say that at this moment she is our only hope. And the decision isn't up to you anyway. Jasper is the leader, so he must decide."

Everyone turned to Jasper, who felt himself shrink.

"Well?" J. was not a patient man. "Jasper?"

Dr. Hellion had so terrified Jasper that she had literally made him forget what his ability was. To seek her out was nothing short of sheer madness. Even to this day he would wake up in the middle of the night, his heart beating wildly, his forehead feverish, afraid that she was coming for him.

But one simple question made Jasper pause as he considered the matter: *What would Conrad do?*

CHAPTER

30

*F*OR THREE DAYS CONRAD AND PIPER relentlessly searched every square inch of Xanthia. Poor AnnA was peppered with questions and forced to explain anything and everything from the reason why Xanthian families shared a sleeping space ("Why would anyone wish to sleep alone through the darkness?") to why the mountain rumbled and shook from time to time ("Mother Mountain is happy and her spirit is jumping.").

Each day followed the same gentle rhythm, and it washed over Piper and Conrad and lulled them into a calm that felt foreign and strange. After Aldo sang in the morning, crystal bells chimed, calling everyone to the breakfast offering. "Offerings," or meals, were shared in a large chamber on the main plateau next to the waterfall's pool. Long tables were heaped with food that had been lovingly grown on the garden ledges. Piper and Conrad experienced a culinary awakening with the foreign flavors, which were sometimes sharp, often sweet, and always unexpected.

After the morning offering the children sang their way to the Celebration Center, where Sergei, their learning facilitator, was waiting for them. Meanwhile the adult Xanthians devoted their mornings to heart tasks. A heart task, as Piper and Conrad discovered, was anything that was accomplished with the use of the unique talent of a Chosen One.

After the noon offering many Xanthians gathered in the southern gardens, where they whiled away their afternoons listening to the storyteller. As the sun set, the crystals on the mountain ignited in an orange glow and a chorus of singers gave thanks to the day. In the center of the plateau in the evenings musicians played as the children were lulled to sleep.

The more Piper saw of Xanthia the more enchanted she became. While Conrad could not deny its appeal, he found Xanthia inscrutable and maddeningly calm. The more he looked for answers the fewer he found, and as the days ticked by his frustration grew.

On their fifth night in Xanthia the entire mountain was buzzing with excitement. After great preparation there was to be a Celebration. Torches had been lit leading a path to the Celebration Center, which was blooming with woven flower garlands. When Piper and Conrad arrived all the young ones had begun dancing and playing bells. Crystal bells of every color hung from the trees, and when the bells were hit with a rock the crystals lit up and sounded like laughing—a high-pitched, tinkling trill.

AnnA met them, flushed with excitement, and escorted them to where everyone else gathered in front of the steps to the Celebration Center. Conrad noticed that wherever he went with Piper the Xanthian people would discreetly melt away, leaving a berth of space around them.

"Equilla will lead Priscilla out," AnnA told them excitedly, forgetting her shyness for the moment. "Priscilla is the Chosen One to be celebrated tonight and will show her talent for the first time. Look, those are Priscilla's parents over there."

Piper saw a man and a woman laughing and talking proudly with others.

"Does everyone have a Celebration?" Conrad asked.

"Yes. On your twelfth birthday the Celebration is a way for all of Xanthia to recognize your achievement and welcome you."

Music swelled and the crowd quieted as Equilla led a beaming Priscilla out of the Celebration Center. Priscilla wore a golden robe with bees embroidered so artfully throughout it that it appeared that they were actually alive. When they reached the center of the steps Equilla held up her arms and those gathered found silence.

"I present to you Priscilla!" Equilla's rich voice carried across the plateau and a cheer rose from all gathered. "Priscilla now stands before you as an adult and shall be recognized for her ability to make friends with the bees. From this day forward Priscilla will be awarded the role of Beekeeper of Xanthia."

It was an emotional moment for Priscilla's parents and for many other Xanthians who had watched her grow. They reached out for one another's hands and held them tight, remembering the day that Priscilla was born, or perhaps the day she took her first step, or learned her first word. They took pride in her and every child, and the ceremony not only celebrated what Priscilla had become but the work of the entire community in creating her.

Equilla held Priscilla's hand up high over her head in a position of triumph, and the gathered crowd burst into a loud cheer. Mother Mountain rumbled, echoing the fever of the Chosen Ones.

Piper was hit by an unexpected wave of emotion as she watched Priscilla's face flush with happiness and pride. *Imagine*, Piper thought, *what it must be like to be celebrated for your ability and your contribution*. It was a powerful passage for a young person and a strong affirmation of the path that she was on—an affirmation that Piper had only ever dreamed of. Her heart ached. Would they allow a former Outsider to have their own Celebration ceremony? Would Betty and Joe be able to attend when she was celebrated? Piper resolved to speak to the matter at once with AnnA. Surely, she would know the way of things on this.

When at last the cheer died away, Equilla lowered Priscilla's hands and took a step back so that the girl was front and center.

"Welcome, Priscilla, Keeper of the Bees. All of Xanthia honors and celebrates you." As Equilla's last syllable was uttered the bells on the trees began to ring and Priscilla summoned the bees. Up and down the mountain and throughout the valley the sound of buzzing began to fill the air. Soon a large swarm was gathering and growing. Priscilla waved her hand and the bees proceeded to circle over her head like a massive buzzing halo.

All eyes were fixed on the bees as Priscilla sent them hurtling up into the sky until no one could see them again, and then just as suddenly they fell out of the sky like rain. They were mere inches from the ground when they recovered.

Finally Priscilla called the bees to her and they landed

on her legs, arms, back, and head until she was completely covered and it was impossible to see any part of her. Slowly she began to turn around and around, and as she did the bees fell from her. She spun faster and faster and the bees swarmed around her, and finally her arms bolted up and the bees shot away like lightning.

By this point tears were streaming down Piper's face and her body was vibrating with some urgent need. Would she be twisting in the air and would they all clap for her? And what then? How would her life be when she was celebrated and seen for her true self by everyone around her? The tingling grew.

Conrad was surprised to see the tears on Piper's face.

"It's real nice here, Conrad," Piper said. "Maybe we should stay. After we find your father we could bring the others back here too."

"Maybe," Conrad said, unconvinced.

Soon there was dancing and Conrad and Piper and everyone else circled around Priscilla, clapping their hands and stomping their feet and cheering. When it was time for the feast Conrad found himself drifting away to a remote corner of the plateau where he could be alone with his thoughts.

The stars were shining over the valley and Conrad could see that there was so much to appreciate about

Xanthia, and yet the inner turmoil that bubbled inside him was at odds with his surroundings. What was his father doing at that moment? And how was he going to find him? He wondered about Smitty and Jasper and all the other kids and told himself that they were safe.

As his thoughts continued to spiral in different directions, a metal anchor suddenly flew through the air and lodged in the stone rail inches away from where Conrad was leaning. Conrad started, looking around but seeing no other movement.

"Look out!" yelled a voice.

Following the sound, Conrad looked down and discovered a boy dangling from a rope that was attached to the anchor lodged not more than a foot from his arm. The boy climbed quickly and expertly.

"Dude, get outta the way!" the boy yelled with great urgency.

Conrad did nothing of the sort but continued to stare and wonder why the boy wanted him out of the way. All at once the answer was painfully clear: climbing up the mountain not twenty feet behind the boy were two giant spiders. The spiders had bodies the size of large boulders attached to legs as long as the wings of an airplane. They were black and hairy with hungry mouths jammed full of pointy teeth. They leaped at the boy, who only just evaded their grasp. The boy was climbing hand over fist, pulling himself up while rappelling against the mountain.

Conrad's mind snapped to with crystalline clarity—there were large rocks by the water and he grabbed two of them.

The lead spider lunged for the boy and Conrad lobbed one of the rocks, hitting the spider squarely between its fifty eyes. The startled arachnid fell back before regaining its footing. The boy was five feet from the railing and Conrad let his second rock fly at the next spider—but the crafty beast dodged the missile completely.

"Grab my hand," Conrad yelled.

The boy swung and grasped Conrad's hand. Just as the spider leaped for him, Conrad pulled with all his might and propelled the boy over the railing. The two of them fell in a painful pile on the rock.

Neither had the time to enjoy a single inhalation before the spider climbed over the side and pounced on top of them.

Conrad was wrenched upward at the end of the spider's right front leg. The boy was treated similarly by the spider's left front leg. Crouching triumphantly, the hairy beast opened its wretched mouth and dangled its tasty prey above the filth of it.

"Looks like it's a good day to die." The boy shrugged good-naturedly as the spider lowered them to its mouth.

The comment infuriated Conrad. "I'm not dying here!"

Twisting his body around, Conrad kicked the spider's leg with all his might.

*T*HE FORCE OF CONRAD'S BLOW ACCOM-
plished exactly nothing. Or at least nothing good.

Infuriated by the feeble attack, the spider tossed the
other boy away like trash so that he ricocheted off the side
of the mountain and fell to the ground. It then focused
all its attention on Conrad, opening its mouth wide and
baring its fangs.

"Dude, if it bites you're a goner," shouted the boy.
"Its venom can stop an elephant's heart cold."

Conrad's feet dangled by the spider's teeth and he drew
them away to no use—the nasty creature was stuffing
him into its mouth. With death imminent and options
limited, Conrad made five quick decisions based on
his knowledge of basic spider anatomy. First, he spring-
boarded off the front fang with enough force to pull
himself free. Next he used his forward motion to jump
on top of its eyes. He then stamped on the many eyes

mercilessly, blinding and confusing the beast. The spider began throwing itself against the mountain in an attempt to dislodge Conrad, but he held on to the bucking arachnid, grabbing hold of a sharp branch, which he then stabbed into the back of the spider.

"ARH!" An unholy howl came out of the spider's mouth.

Jumping off the spider's back, Conrad rolled to the ground and the boy pulled him out of the way of being trampled. Together they dodged as the spider spun around and finally fell off the side of the mountain altogether.

"Whoa, like that was pretty awesome!" The boy was excited. "You've got some moves on you, dude."

"Not really. When competing against a foe of superior strength and size you must use the element of surprise and attack with stealth and precision."

"Righteous!" The boy's smile broke wide open and he took Conrad's hand and began to shake it vigorously like an overexcited puppy. "I'm Maximillian, but no one calls me that. Just Max, that's what you can call me. Max."

"Okay, Max." With difficulty Conrad extracted his hand out of Max's grip. His shoulder had completely healed but after all the roughness with the spider he was feeling prickles of pain. "I'm Conrad."

Even in the darkness, Conrad could see that Max looked much like himself; blond hair, pale skin that set off blue eyes, and the same jaw. But that was where the similarity ended and striking differences emerged—the boy's face was open and his smile was easy and wide. Unlike Conrad, Max wasn't glaring at him with open distrust and angry eyes, but instead had a sparkle in his eye and an excited inquisitiveness in the curves of his mouth, as though some great discovery was soon to be made that was sure to delight him. Conrad guessed his age to be about sixteen.

"Where did those spiders come from?"

Max reached into the bag strapped around his shoulders. "I just snatched one of their eggs." Max pulled out a pale yellow egg about the size of a football. "I thought it'd be like way fun but the spiders went freaky deaky and I was like 'whoa' and hotfooted it outta there."

The egg glowed and made strange sounds as though there was a demon wriggling inside, seeking to escape.

"There's a legend that says if you eat the yolk you'll be able to see the future," Max said, mesmerized by the orb.

"It's spectacular," Conrad agreed. "But not exactly worth the risk."

"Relax." Max smiled devilishly. "You've gotta have fun."

Before Conrad could respond he caught a fast-moving black blur out of the corner of his eye. In a flash the lead spider, which he'd conked on the head with the rock, was back and gunning for the egg.

Max swiveled to get out of the way, but not fast enough, and the spider knocked the egg out of his hand. In the same movement, it pushed Conrad to the ground while leaping on top of Max.

Max didn't have time to respond before the angry spider bit him with all that it had.

"Agggggggg," Max moaned.

Its task complete, the spider scooped up the egg, leaped back over the side, and was gone.

"Max?" Conrad was half crawling and half running in his effort to get to where the spider had left Max in a heap. *"Max?"*

"Uhhhh."

Max looked up toward the stars with glassy eyes. Conrad quickly laid him out flat and felt for the wound. He probed gently but couldn't find anything.

"Max, where did it bite you?"

Max gurgled, sucking in a long, thin breath. With what seemed like a great effort he turned his head so that he could look at Conrad.

"The egg?" he croaked.

"Forget the egg." Conrad waved his hand dismissively. "You were bitten."

"I—" Max began.

"What?"

Max seemed to fade away and then blinked a few times. Conrad grabbed him and shook him.

"Tell me where you were bitten?"

"I—"

Conrad waited but Max's body went limp and his eyes closed. Laying him on the ground, Conrad got up and looked around to see what might be on hand. Besides the water and some flower bushes there was nothing of use.

He clenched his fists in frustration. "Darn it all!"

Silence settled and Conrad stamped his foot, kicking at the dirt. First his father had been shot and snatched away from right in front of him, and now this! It was too much.

"*Stop!*" Conrad yelled at the mountain. His echo taunted him.

"I don't know what your problem is," said Max calmly.

Conrad spun around. Max's eyes were open and he suddenly looked as fresh as a daisy.

"Seriously, I'm the one who's out an egg. I'm the one who should be screaming like an idiot." Max sat up. "Like, dude, you should'a grabbed it. I'll never get another one now."

Conrad stared at Max in disbelief.

"I'm not saying I'm mad, but they only lay eggs once every hundred years, and it's a total buzzkill trying to find 'em. So it's not your fault but . . ." Max dusted himself off and hopped up on his feet. "It's kinda your fault. Next time you could maybe like help out a little bit more."

Conrad eyed Max closely. "I just saw that spider bite you."

"Chill. I'm fine."

"I see that you're fine. But how?"

"It's no big deal."

Conrad wasn't buying it. "Do you have an immunity?"

"Oh yeah, you're the new kid. Genius, right?" Max smirked. "Alright, genius, figure it out. I'll give you three guesses."

"Is everything a game to you?"

"Do you always ask this many questions?"

"No. I'm rarely around someone who knows more than I do." Conrad wasn't bragging, simply stating a fact.

Max rubbed his hands together. "Let's see what you got."

Conrad eyed him and decided to go with it. "If you had an immunity to spider bites, you would have told me when I asked. If you'd had antivenom, I would have seen you administer it, so I'll rule that out. You've made this into a game because you think that I won't guess.

So it's something unexpected, something most people wouldn't think of."

"Very good. And your questions are?"

"I don't need three questions, I only need one. Do you have a self-healing ability?"

Max shook his head, his eyes feverishly bright with anticipation.

"Then," concluded Conrad, "you must be immortal."

Max clapped appreciatively like he was watching a magic show. "Dude, you rock!"

"So, it's true? You're immortal?"

"Let's just say I haven't bit the dust yet."

"Wow!" Conrad's eyes lost focus as he considered Max. He swayed ever so slightly, and stepping back, he stumbled on a rock that sent him tumbling to the ground.

CHAPTER

32

*T*HE ROUND GRAY ROCK THAT CONRAD SAT
on was no rock at all but a miniature elephant that
had achieved a very deep, very happy sleep when Conrad unceremoniously thudded on his back.

"Errrrr—" the elephant trumped angrily, jumping
to his feet and tossing Conrad to the ground.

Several other rock elephants awoke and sounded in
sympathy. Then the group of them huffily charged off
into the night, leaving Conrad with a sore behind in the
dirt. He regarded Max speculatively. "And how long have
you been around?"

"I'm not a real big numbers guy." Max would have
happily left it at that, but it was clear that Conrad was
going to keep at him until he came up with something
more substantial. "You know, it was like way, way back
when—well, before the Romans and Greeks and there
weren't any cities and things were really simple."

"Before the Mayan calendar?"

"Sure. I'd been kicking around for a while before that."

"So, you're talking about four thousand B.C.?"

"Sounds about right. Give or take a hundred here or there."

"You've lived all these years and . . ." Conrad mused aloud, as though the elephant-rock incident hadn't happened. He struggled to come to terms with the nature of Max's life and existence. "Well . . . what exactly have you been doing with your time?"

"Having fun."

"Fun?"

"Yeah, it's great." Max affably settled himself in the dirt next to Conrad. "I've got stories that'd make your toes curl. Like the time I swam with fifty-foot blue whales. And there was this other time I had a chariot race with Nero. He's a sore loser, lemme tell you. Anyway, that's all there is to life—fun. It's the only thing worth doing. I figured that out pretty quick. You see, most people think life is serious. W-R-O-N-G. That's why I made up the golden rules of fun."

"The golden rules of fun?"

"Sure, they're key. Rule one, always have your next fun thing planned. That's huge; you gotta keep your momentum going. Rule two, never repeat yourself.

Boredom is a big buzzkill. And three, kick out all the unfun. Like all the Outsiders are pretty unfun 'cause they die so easily. It sucks."

"I believe they think that sucks too."

"Oh." Max shrugged as though he'd never thought of it that way. Dawn was already breaking and the sky in the east held the glow of the coming sun. Max impatiently got to his feet. "Good talking to you, but I've gotta check out this tsunami that's going to hit South America. It'll be awesome."

Max threw his bag over his shoulder and began to walk. Conrad immediately followed behind him.

"How do you know that's going to happen?"

" 'Cause of the energy globe."

"What's the energy globe?"

"In the Knowledge Center, dude." Max snorted in surprise. "Haven't you seen the Knowledge Center yet?"

"No; AnnA hasn't taken us there." Conrad fumbled in his pocket, pulling out the bloodstone. "Max, have you ever seen one of these in your travels?"

Max looked quickly and shrugged. "Sure, I've seen lots of rocks."

"No, but this one is different. Look!" Conrad shoved the rock in Max's hand and dodged in front of him to block his path. "See. It's not a naturally forming rock.

It's something that had to be engineered. I'm trying to find out about it. It's important."

"Huh." Distracted, Max batted away some bright red butterflies that were humming a lively tune and handed the rock back to Conrad. "Sorry, dude, but you're asking the wrong guy. I'm not into rocks and I've got somewhere to be."

"Do you know where my father is?" Conrad tried not to sound desperate, but failed miserably.

"Just 'cause I've lived a long time doesn't mean I'm like omniscient or something. Who's your father? Is he an Outsider? I don't really pay attention to Outsider stuff."

"His name is Harrington. President Conrad Harrington."

Max let out a low whistle. "Your father's the president? What's that like?"

"Not so good. But that's not the point. I'm looking for him."

"It takes talent to lose the President of the United States. Sorry, dude, can't help you with that one."

"But he's not the only one. My friends were taken too and it has something to do with this rock. I need a way to find more information. I need . . . help."

Max kept on walking. Conrad floundered for a way to grab Max's attention, because his current strategy wasn't working. Obviously, he was going to have to start talking a language that Max would understand.

"Hey, no problem, dude." Conrad shrugged. "If you have somewhere to be, then I'll catch you later. Just didn't want you to miss out on the *fun*."

This time Conrad turned away and Max was the one to stop.

"What kind of fun?" Max was intrigued.

"Well, it's a mystery, isn't it? A mystery that needs to be solved. Who knows what answers I might find. It could be exciting and dangerous and . . . fun." Conrad walked away. "But you have to go. I don't want to keep you."

Conrad held his breath and silently counted backward from ten. When he reached seven Max was by his side.

"I've never solved a mystery before. Lemme see that rock again?"

Conrad casually handed it to him.

"See the way the light travels through it and how dense it is? Whoever engineered this had a plan for it."

"It just looks like a rock to me." Max tried to see the fun in it and was sorely disappointed.

"It's a clue," Conrad corrected him. "They've been left in key places on the Outside, and finding the connection is when things will get fun."

"Hmm." Max looked at the sky and back at the rock.

"Hold it. I just had an idea. Like I know exactly where you can figure all this out, dude. It just came to me like *bam*."

"Really?" Conrad waited hopefully.

"Sure. Like I already said, the Knowledge Center." Max pointed to the corner of the top tier. "You can find anything in that place: books, artifacts, anything really. If you're into that sort of stuff I guess it's okay."

Conrad was intrigued.

"It's all about the Outsiders, but most Chosen Ones aren't really interested so no one goes in there much. A kid like you would totally dig it, and I bet we can find out about this rock if it was on the Outside."

Conrad's heart began to race as he considered the possibilities. "Sounds like fun. Let's go!"

CHAPTER

33

$\mathcal{T}$HE KNOWLEDGE CENTER WAS TUCKED away at the top of the plateau. It was a massive cavernous chamber lined with shelves, in the center of which stood long tables holding strange and amazing contraptions.

"Just like I said." Max waved his arm. "You can find anything in here."

Conrad's eyes went wide; all around the walls were ancient books thickly stacked against one another, and parchment and papyrus scrolls were tightly rolled up in bins. There were artifacts of every kind from every era; a bow and arrow was perched next to the first Apple computer beside which was a dinosaur bone. There was a gramophone, an axe from the Paleolithic Period, a hammer used by a blacksmith in the 1700s, and a pair of Cleopatra's goblets. The unmistakable work of Pablo Picasso and Marc Chagall hung next to unknown artists with superior skill. Statues of Caesars sat next to a golden Buddha underneath a glowing Virgin Mary. Fragments of rocks with ancient cave paintings were stacked five deep.

The place was part museum, part library, and part treasure trove. It was like nothing Conrad had ever seen, and indeed, if there was any place that could have captured and excited his hungry brain, this was it.

In the center of the chamber, rows of tables held the strangest artifacts. The first thing that caught Conrad's eye was a large spinning globe of the earth. It was composed of particles of light and certain areas glowed. Conrad stepped closer to study it.

"That gizmo tracks the energy patterns around the earth," Max explained. "Any major stuff goes down like an earthquake or a volcano and it'll light up like Vegas, baby."

"Unbelievable."

"But wait, you gotta see this, too. This is a complete record of history." In a rather grand fashion, Max pointed to a tree stump about the size of a stool. "Of course, you've got everything that you'd expect to find on the internet, but I haveta say, the internet is way lame. Don't get me wrong, I like stupid cat videos as much as the next guy, but if you're looking for the hardcore stuff you might as well just shoot yourself in the head 'cause you're gonna find zilch. I'm not even exaggerating. There's at least a hundred times as much info that's been tossed or burned or whatever and no one even knows about it. Taa-daaa. We've got it all here for you. So let your fingers do the walking."

After such a grandiose introduction the stump seemed less than impressive. It was withered but the roots delved into the mountain. Conrad approached it cautiously, delicately touching the rings. He turned suddenly to Max with a shocked look on his face.

"Is this the tree of knowledge? You cut down the tree of knowledge?"

"As if. Naw, the Outsiders chopped this baby down. I saved what was left and brought it here." Max's jaw took on a hard line. "You know, the Outsiders'll never understand. That's why we had to take off and not be around them anymore." Shaking away his dark mood, Max waved Conrad to the stump. "Sit, sit."

As soon as Conrad's flesh connected with the tree he suddenly saw a huge green leafy canopy above him as though the tree was intact once again.

"Give this baby a spin. You've got every word ever written down under this hood ready to go. C'mon, say a name and watch what happens."

"Aristotle Stagiritis, son of Nicomachus."

At once large volumes of books appeared, hanging

from the branches of the tree and all within arm's reach. Conrad plucked a thick volume entitled *Nicomachean Ethics* from out of the air and began to thumb through it. "Is this Aristotle's handwriting?"

"You bet."

"Incredible," Conrad breathed.

"It rocks your world, right?" Max waited for Conrad to look up from the book, but Conrad was enthralled. "I got other cool tricks, but those babies are your best bets for tracking this red rock."

"Mmmmm." Conrad turned the page of the book, delving deeper, when suddenly a flash of light caught his eye. At the far end of the room a beam of sunlight was reflecting off the surface of a rather strange device. Intrigued, Conrad stepped away from the tree of knowledge to investigate.

"What's this?" Conrad touched the top of a wooden wand mounted on the wall.

"Uh, I dunno. Lemme think." Max picked it up and turned it over and then started carelessly throwing it in the air. "Oh yeah, I remember. It's a water-thingy. It purifies water or something, but I can't get it to work anymore. Once I was talking to this guy and he told me that all the water is going to like dry up. Wait, what was that dude's name again? Nost-something."

"Nostradamus?"

"Whoa, how'd you know that? You've got like a gift. Anyway, he said the world was gonna go thirsty and it was gonna happen real sudden. And it'd be bad, too, and throw the whole planet into a dark age, cause without clean water everyone would lose their minds and fight and stuff. So one of the folks up here cooked up this water purifier. It'll turn sand into clean drinking water. Amazing, right? Except they died and I can't make heads or tails of it. Too bad 'cause it'd have saved millions of lives. Or maybe billions."

Suddenly bored, Max tossed the water purifier aside and forgot about it. "Anyway, it's a cool, fun, party-time up here, right?" Max flung his arms open wide. "Betcha never seen stuff like this."

Conrad nodded. "It's impressive." Turning around and surveying the new domain, he took a deep breath of satisfaction. "Let's get to work."

BY THE TIME THEY ARRIVED AT AREA 63 Jasper was so nervous he could hardly put two words together.

"H-H-Hellion," he struggled, unable to say more.

"Yes, yes, they're keeping Letitia in there. We'll break in and get her out." J. spoke in his usual no-nonsense manner. He'd led the kids to a thicket of trees under the cover of darkness where they could gather themselves before breaking into the facility.

"And why is this a good idea, again?" Kimber eyed the guard towers and armed security forces lurking within.

"Without my sister there's no way to fly across that valley. Letitia's probably the only person alive who can help us figure out how to get to Conrad and Piper." J. tied a rope around his waist and attached night-vision goggles around his head. "There are seven separate checkpoints, sensors on all walls, some of which are activated by body heat. Violet and Lily will go in first and—"

"We don't need you to tell us what to do," Nalen said stiffly.

"We can figure it out ourselves," Ahmed agreed.

J. noticed how the kids all stood close together, glaring at him. He threw up his hands. "Fine," he surrendered. "Lead the way."

If J. was impressed by what he saw over the next ten hair-raising minutes, he managed not to show it. Ahmed and Nalen created lightning, which they directed to hit the main power grid, blowing it out and allowing them a sliver of opportunity to enter the facility before the power transferred over to generators; Smitty located every sensor, and Kimber disabled them with electrical bursts; Lily moved a shrunk-down Violet up to the cameras, and Violet directed them away.

J. took them to Letitia's room and Daisy broke the door open so that they could silently creep inside.

Letitia Hellion had her back to the door and sat on the side of her bed, looking at the wall in front of her. She'd been fitted into a straitjacket and her arms were tied securely at the back of it. There was a ghostly silence in the room so that their footfalls sounded ominous and clumsy.

When Letitia didn't move or respond to their arrival the tension mounted.

"Are you sure that's her?" Violet whispered to J. The mat of black hair looked familiar but nothing about the woman before them was as they remembered her.

"Of course," J. returned. He cleared his throat and spoke gently. "Letitia, it's me, Jeston. I've come to get you out."

Letitia did not respond.

"Letitia?"

"I thought you said she was okay," Smitty hissed.

J. raised his hand to silence Smitty, his brow furrowed with concern. "I found it, Letitia. It was just like you said, and I can take you there now. I've come to get you out."

Letitia remained like a statue.

The small hairs on the back of J.'s neck stood at attention. "Stay here," he commanded the kids, and cautiously approached Letitia.

J. was conscious of the way he placed his feet, wanting to ease toward his sister without startling or upsetting her. He had expected her to be excited to see him. What could have happened since he'd been gone?

Coming around the side of her bed, J. kept his eyes fixed on her and what he saw sent shivers down his spine, stopping him in his tracks.

Letitia Hellion's face was frozen in a position of abject terror; her eyes open and large, her pupils fixed on something only she could see. Her mouth quivered open but made no sound. It looked like she was screaming: a scream only she could hear.

"Letitia!" J. rushed to her, placing his hands on her shoulders. "Letitia, what is it?"

Letitia Hellion seemed unaware of J. Whatever she was seeing was so terrible she couldn't move.

J. grabbed for the straitjacket and roughly pulled at it. Now that they could see that Letitia was not a threat, the kids rushed forward to help, and Daisy promptly shredded the jacket off of her.

With her arms free Letitia threw them forward as though reaching for someone. J. tried to take her hands but she reached past him.

"Look!" Smitty pointed at Letitia's throat.

All eyes focused on a necklace made of twisted gold with a flashing red stone mounted in the center that made the children recoil.

"How did Dr. Hellion get a bloodstone?" Violet breathed in a hushed voice.

J. quickly yanked it from her neck, threw it to the

ground, and crushed it beneath his heel. A bright red light exploded from underneath his foot.

Letitia sank into herself like a deflated balloon. Her arms fell and her face slackened but still she did not acknowledge the presence of J. and the kids.

"She's falling and I can't reach her," she babbled in a whisper. "Must save her. Can't let her fall."

"Letitia?" J. touched her shoulder. "Letitia, it's all right."

"She's falling. She's falling!" Letitia continued to whisper in frantic tones. "No! No!"

J. let his hand drop and rubbed his fingers against his jaw.

"What's she saying?" Kimber leaned closer to Letitia. "What's the matter?"

"She thinks she's back with Sarah. Sarah was our younger sister and Letitia accidentally dropped her while she was flying in a rainstorm." J. sighed deeply. "It's her worst nightmare."

"Dr. H-H-Hellion?" Jasper was by far the most frightened of Letitia, but he also happened to be the most kindhearted of the group, and it pained him to see anyone in such a state. "Dr. Hellion, it's o-okay."

Letitia was out of reach of Jasper's words and so he rubbed his hands together until they glowed and lay them on her. But his healing light seemed to have no effect on her, for better or worse, and she continued her muttering.

"Grab my hand. Hold on," Letitia panted. "Don't let go."

Jasper looked to J. for direction.

"He got to her before we could," J. growled, "and trapped her inside her worst fears. Probably so she couldn't help us."

Smitty looked over his shoulder, scanning the hallway for movement. "He who?"

"Exactly," J. agreed. "Who? The same *who* that left these bloodstones at the accident sites and shot Conrad. That *who*."

"But what do we do now?" Violet worried. "How will we get across the valley?"

As a beeping siren sounded in the depths of Area 63 the gathered group stood watching a madwoman, lost and muttering.

For once J. had no plan. He sat down next to his sister, defeated.

"It's n-n-no good staying here." Jasper's thin voice quavered. "L-let's go."

"What about her?" Lily nodded at Dr. Hellion.

J. looked to Jasper with haunted eyes and for once Jasper made a decision without first thinking what Conrad would do.

"We'll take her with us," Jasper said, tossing J. his backpack.

Moments later when the guards stormed the room they found it empty, making Letitia Hellion the first and only prisoner ever to escape Area 63.

CHAPTER

AT LAST CONRAD GOT A PROPER
glimpse at the inner workings of the bloodstone, thanks to Max. Max rummaged through the deepest reaches of the Knowledge Center and pulled an eyeball
the size of a loaf of bread from a back shelf and dusted it
off. Max explained to Conrad how he'd salvaged the eye
from the carcass of a giant a few thousand years ago, and
showed him how to strap it over his own eye and peek
through it. When Conrad did so the eye granted un-
earthly vision and the secrets of the bloodstone appeared
before him.

Conrad wasn't surprised to confirm that the bloodstone was mainly comprised of beryllium and lanthanum.
But an unidentifiable mystery component mixed in held
the stone together and gave it the deep red color. For lack
of a better word Conrad described the component as
"intelligent."

"It's reactive!" Conrad explained to Max.

"I don't get it." Max lounged on a Ming dynasty chair and was amusing himself by throwing nasty-nuts into an old vase he'd placed on a table several feet away.

"Whatever is in the bloodstone, it's adapting, changing right before my eyes." Conrad quickly pulled together a few nearby materials and created a small explosion on the table.

This caught Max's attention. "Whoa."

"Watch!" Conrad pointed at the rock as it began to glow and suck the explosion toward it. "It's absorbing the energy. It's acting like a giant magnet, pulling the energy into its core and then holding it there like a battery."

Max repeated Conrad's experiment and created a similar result. "Awesome. Now what?"

Conrad bent over the rock, studying it further. "It's adapting. Which means it's trainable and . . . it's learning." Conrad remembered the rock around his father's neck. "I'm willing to bet that you can program these to live off someone's life force like a parasite."

"How'd you do that?" Max was poking at the rock now with one of the instruments.

"I don't know the *how* yet." Conrad stood up and began to pace.

Max got up and paced too, like he was trying on a role for size. "I dunno what's happening, but something is happening and it's totally wild. So what are you going to do now?"

"I need to create a model that will allow me to extrapolate and predict future events."

"Huh?"

"I don't have a statistically relevant pool of data." Conrad was talking more to himself than to Max. "I need to create search criteria that will isolate similar global events that match the pattern I have already identified. I'll have to work my way through history—not all of history, just the last thousand years. . . ."

With great fervor Conrad began moving through the room, collecting information and bits of equipment. Obviously, his Direct Brain Interface was in perfect working order, but without access to the internet in Xanthia he was bereft of large online data pools. This was no longer a problem with the resources of the Knowledge Center at his fingertips.

The thoughtful and stationary aspect of this work suddenly discouraged Max. "Oookay." He sat back down. "That sounds time-consuming." His foot tapped back and forth impatiently. "Dude, I'm hungry. You hungry?"

"Mmm." Conrad was giving Max only a small portion of his available attention.

"Well, I'm gonna get some grub. You want some too?"

"Mmmm."

Max headed for the door.

"Oh, Max?" Conrad had suddenly snapped back to the moment at hand. "Can you find Piper? She'll want to be part of this and she doesn't know where I am."

"Piper?" Max looked confused. "You mean the flyer?"

"That's the one."

Max pointed at Conrad and made a clicking noise. "You got it, big guy. Back in a flash."

Conrad hardly noticed when Max returned.

"Piper wants to hang with AnnA. Apparently AnnA's going to show her the singing caves," Max reported. "She says she'll catch you later."

Conrad nodded and continued with his work.

After Max had eaten his food and then eaten Conrad's food he began to rappel from the ceiling of the Knowledge Center. When that got boring he jumped from bookshelf to bookshelf without touching the floor. That got old too so he dressed up in a suit of armor from a fifteenth-century English castle and began attacking imaginary foes.

———•———

A DAY LATER MAX HAD EXHAUSTED ALL POSsible variations of jumping, climbing, fighting, and juggling the many artifacts in the room. He lounged on a guillotine and made popping sounds with his mouth.

"Clu, clu, clu." Max varied the volume, playing with the echo in the room.

Conrad was no longer aware of the passage of time. His days and nights were marked by only one thing: quantifying damage and assigning a numeric amount to each encounter. Every war, every disaster created surges in energy and those surges created patterns that were not accidental. There was a purpose to it all. There was a plan. . . .

He was learning that whoever was behind these events would be striking again soon—and in a big way. The pattern suggested that every few years there was one disaster or another. According to Conrad's estimation the next one was due to be a big one, and it was imminent. He was getting closer to it—so close, until . . .

"Done!" Conrad completed what he was writing with a flourish and held up a piece of paper with six numbers on it.

Max jerked himself upright. Conrad hadn't spoken in so long that he hung on his every word. "What's that?"

"Those are the coordinates of the next disaster site," Conrad said with certainty.

Once again Max was disappointed: Where and when exactly was the promised fun going to materialize? "I don't get it."

"Okay, listen—it's simple. To predict the future you must understand the past and break down the pattern. Once you know the pattern you can predict the future. Get it? So I used the disaster sites I personally visited and found bloodstones at as markers to identify other similar events throughout history. From these I was able to create an algorithm based on location, frequency, and level of destruction. These numbers"—Conrad handed the piece of paper to Max—"are ninety-nine percent accurate."

Max looked at the numbers on the page like they were dirty. "I can't read this crap. And ninety-nine percent accurate of what?"

"These numbers are the coordinates of the location where the next major disaster will occur. And according to my calculations it's going to happen in approximately twenty-four hours, give or take thirty minutes." Conrad's energy was electric. "They call them accidents but they're not. Someone is making them happen and that someone is the same person who created the bloodstones and kidnapped my father. And this time I'll be there and I'll stop them once for all. And if I find whoever is behind it, I will find my father."

Finally some action and excitement: Max was all in. "And I'll come too, right? 'Cause we're partners?"

"Where's Piper?" Conrad suddenly remembered that he hadn't seen her since the Celebration.

"I just talked to her again, like you told me." Max shrugged. "She said she wants to go to the Celebration Center with AnnA and show the little ones how she can fly. She's been flying around a lot."

Conrad sighed. "I guess Piper deserves to finally stop hiding and fit in."

"Whatever you need, I'm your guy," Max offered. "And I know how to get in and out of Xanthia like no one's business, and lemme tell you, that ain't no small thing. So where are we going?"

"Here, give it to me." Conrad took the paper back from Max and marched over to the globe. "They're latitude and longitude." He spun the globe, getting quickly to the point.

"Is it Mongolia? It's so festive this time of year!" Max watched hopefully, as if he were waiting for a game show prize.

"No, it's right . . . here." Conrad's finger came down in the middle of North America. Max crowded in close to catch a glimpse.

"Oh, dude, that's like—what is that? A river?"

"Yes, it is." Conrad picked up on the disappointment in Max's voice. "It's the Colorado River, to be exact."

Max slouched away. "I've seen that a million times. Yawn."

"Well, the Colorado River is . . . it's largely unpopulated. There's a lot of wildlife." Conrad was thinking out loud. "It's also the largest source of drinking water in the region." As soon as the words came out of his mouth everything clicked into place. "That's it!"

Max looked up with the clear expectation that something exciting was about to happen. But all Conrad did was pick up the water purifier.

"Don't you see?! They are going to attack the water source." Galvanized into action, Conrad was quickly grasping the mechanics of the instrument. "And here's the thing—we can stop it!"

For someone who hadn't aged for the last several thousand years, Max looked tired. "Dude, this is taking way too long and *nothing* is happening." Max flung himself on the floor of the Knowledge Center in a bored-attack pose that was accompanied by a pout. "Dude, I'm BORED. Like losing my mind, going crazy, ready to jump off a cliff for the heck of it, B-O-R-E-D. Listen, I'm gonna catch the next wave outta here."

"No, you can't." Conrad turned quickly, holding parts of the water purifier in his hand. "Let me get this working and then we'll go down to the Colorado River together.

I can have it going by the morning, and think—if we get there and catch whoever it is that is doing this, we'll solve the mystery! It'll be *fun!*"

Max was swayed but was definitely at the end of his tether. He shrugged in a noncommittal way. "For sure?"

"Promise."

———— ❖ ————

TRUE TO HIS WORD, CONRAD PLACED A WORKing water purifer in Max's hands at first light.

Max swished the wand about excitedly. It was a rather ordinary stick that forked at the end. The extraordinary thing about it was that it glowed bright blue from within, humming with incredible power.

"Dude, you rock! I never thought you'd fix it. How'd you do it?"

"It wasn't actually broken." Conrad had dark smudges of tiredness beneath his eyes. "It just needed a power source, and it would only accept a connection with a biological agent. After that it was simply a matter of targeting an organic source to provide power."

"I totally didn't understand a word you just said. Were you even speaking human?"

"Look." Conrad turned his head to the side and pushed his hair out of the way, displaying the pronged metal device the size of a quarter that was stamped into his flesh behind his ear. Small lights on it flickered and jumped about.

"What the heck!" Max was enthralled.

"It's my Direct Brain Interface. I connected the water purifer to my DBI and created a subprogram that captured my brain energy and routed it to the water purifier. Basically, as long as I am thinking, the purifier will have power."

"Gnarly." Max fingered the device, pulling on it.

"Hey, watch it!" Conrad stepped away. "It's hardwired in."

"You mean you can't take it off? Not ever?"

"Not unless I want to blow my brain apart."

"Whoa!" Max headed for the door. "Alright, let's scram!"

Conrad collected his notes. "I'll meet you down there."

"I'm leaving in five."

"I'll be down in two."

$\mathcal{P}$IPER WAS TOO ANGRY TO FLY STRAIGHT. She bobbed up and down, suddenly slowing and then zipping ahead hotly. She was breathing in outraged gasps and her fingers twitched with angry flicks. Up ahead she spotted Conrad and her anger detonated at the sight of him.

"Conrad!" Piper called out loudly so anyone on the mountain could easily have heard her. Still Conrad didn't turn around. "CONRAD!"

The fact that Conrad was obviously ignoring her only increased Piper's fury. He'd been hiding from her for over a week now. This time she would not be denied. This time she would have his full attention.

Flying up behind him, Piper landed with a thud and grabbed his shoulder, swinging him around.

"Conrad, I was calling you!"

Piper gasped and stepped back—standing before her

was not Conrad but someone entirely different, someone she had never met before. From behind she could
have sworn he was Conrad's exact twin, but now that
she was looking at him face-to-face the differences were
obvious.

"Oh! Sorry—"

"Good thing I don't bruise—you've got a grip on you."
Max twitched any discomfort out of his shoulder and
then put his hand out in greeting. "I'm Max."

"Max? Oh. I'm Piper."

"Oh yeah. You're the flyer, right?"

Piper took a step away, suddenly unsure.

"Can you take me for a spin? You know, like in the
air."

Max's exuberance and overly friendly manner took
Piper off guard. "I have to go," she said, hovering upward.
"I need to find Conrad."

"He's where he always is."

Piper was affronted. "And where exactly is that?" How
did this Max know where Conrad had been all this
time when she didn't?

"The Knowledge Center. It's down there." Max
pointed to the last chamber at the far end of the balcony.

"Uh, okay. Thanks." Piper headed for the place he
pointed out.

"Catch you later, fly girl," Max called out after her.

Piper flew into the Knowledge Center, ignoring all the wonders inside and focusing her attention on Conrad, who was bending over a table. She barreled up behind him and slammed her hand on the table, causing him to jerk upright.

"What the—"

"You need to listen to me, Conrad." Piper pointed her finger at him to further emphasize her point. "Do you have any idea what is going on here?"

"What are you talking about?"

"I was just with AnnA, and do you know what she's doing?"

Conrad had no idea. How could he? He shook his head.

"She's giving away all of her stuff. Do you know why?" This time Piper didn't wait for the answer. "Because it's her twelfth birthday next week and she should be having her Celebration ceremony but she's not. She's not having it because she doesn't have a gift. And if you don't have a gift and you live in Xanthia, do you know what that means?" Bits of spittle escaped Piper's mouth as she spoke. "It means that they kick you out. The elders, everyone, is going to force AnnA to leave. And not only that, but they'll erase her memory and dump her in the outside world like a piece of trash."

This was news to Conrad, and he let out a long breath in response. "Who told you this?"

"AnnA did. I forced her. She was so embarrassed she didn't even want us to know. She was afraid we wouldn't want to be her friend if we found out." Piper waved her arms about passionately as she spoke. "No one wants to be her friend here, either. She told me that she is the only kid on the mountain who doesn't have a father, and she's too afraid to ask her mother about it. They treat her like an outcast. Which, of course, you wouldn't know because all you do is run off and hide with that Max guy. Whoever he is."

"What are you talking about? I haven't been hiding. You're the one who's been too busy to see me!" Conrad placed a bag over his shoulders.

"Did you even hear what I said?"

"Yes, of course. But I have something really important to do. Can we talk about it later?"

"Later is too late!" Piper planted her feet. "They are going to erase her memory this afternoon."

Conrad continued with his task.

"What is going on with you? This should be a no-brainer. AnnA is our friend and she needs our help— end of story."

"Piper, what I'm working on could change everything. It could change the world."

This startled Piper. "How come I don't know about this? What is it?"

Conrad pushed past her. "Maybe you'd know if you weren't with AnnA all the time and too busy to see me."

"What do you mean too busy? Says who?"

Conrad bristled, painfully aware that time was ticking away. "We're going to have to talk about this later. I have to go now."

Piper's eyes drifted to the wall that Conrad had covered in notes and diagrams and charts. It towered over her, reaching to the ceiling—a massive array of mad scribbles next to pictures and dates and charts all arranged in some order that was impossible for Piper to decipher. The sheer monstrous mass of it took her breath away. "Conrad, what have you done?"

"Hey, dude!" Max suddenly appeared, slamming into the wall by the door. "You said two minutes. It's been like four." He looked at his watch. "Now four and a half. You comin' or what?"

Conrad stood in the center of the chamber with Max behind him and Piper in front of him.

"Conrad," Piper said quietly. "We've always done everything as a team—together. And I need your help. Right now."

"What's the holdup?" Max called, swinging himself from a hook like a monkey. "Stay or go, go or stay! Make the call, smart guy."

"It's likely that I won't be able to do anything to help AnnA," Conrad reasoned.

"You can try." Piper's voice fell to a searing whisper. "I don't know what is happening here, Conrad, but something weird is going on. You have to stay with me!"

Piper's words and the intensity of her voice stunned Conrad, shaking him from the adrenaline of the chase.

"DUDE!"

"Don't make me choose!" Conrad begged Piper.

"I will. I am." As Conrad hesitated Piper's eyes burned into him. "Who is this Max? What is going on? How come he looks so much like you?"

"He looks like me?" Piper's words stopped Conrad dead. His skin puckered into prickles like it had been blasted with a cold wind. "We look alike?"

"I was just outside and I actually thought Max was you."

"You did?" Conrad took his bag off his shoulder and let it thud to the ground. "I see."

Piper watched the color drain from Conrad's face until he became as white as a sheet. "What?"

"Max, you go on ahead. I'll catch up with you," Conrad said, not taking his eyes from Piper.

Max jumped off the hook. "Naw way! What if you miss it?" He looked from Conrad to Piper. "'Cause of her? Pffff. Fine. Your loss. But I'm not missing it. I'm gonna go."

With a wave of the water purifier, Max turned to leave. "And dude, this is choice! You did good. It's something you'll be remembered for."

"Thanks."

"Here." Max pulled from around his neck a chain, on the end of which was an old key. He tossed it to Conrad, who caught it.

"What's this?" Conrad looked at the key in his hand. It was made of ancient iron with deep grooves circling in the handle.

Max was already out of sight. "A gift. You deserve it. Later," he called over his shoulder.

"Good riddance." Piper snorted. "Now *what* is going on, Conrad?"

"That is what we're going to find out."

37

*E*QUILLA SEEMED NEITHER SURPRISED nor upset when Conrad and Piper abruptly burst in and proceeded to detail AnnA's plight.

"This is a very complicated matter," she said, calmly pruning her dragon plant. The plant was the size of a Labrador retriever and each stem contained a snapping dragonhead of a different color. As with all things, she handled the vicious plant with equanimity and brushed aside the snapping jaws before her finger was dislodged. Several times a flame burst came her way, and this too she neutralized with a small breath.

"There's nothing complicated about it. It's just plain wrong!" Piper was still fighting mad.

Equilla placed the pruning shears down and took off her gloves, one finger at a time. "There are things you need to know about us and our past. Our history here is a long one."

She led Piper and Conrad out to the balcony and motioned to comfortable chairs. After pouring them a special blend of juices and herbs, which they drank and which made them feel strangely calm, she sat down in front of them.

"In the very beginning," she began, "we all lived in a great city by the sea. Everyone was exceptional and there was a lasting peace among all the people. One day a boy was born named Primus, and it was discovered that he had no ability. No one had ever seen anything like it; every child was born with some ability, and to not have one was unthinkable. People shunned Primus and his parents feared that he had some sort of sickness and would die. Fortunately he began to grow and was healthy.

"Over the years Primus watched as all his friends grew into their abilities, and the day came when this made him angry. His anger grew into jealousy, particularly toward his closest friend, Agios, who had a very special ability that was widely celebrated. Agios could part the waters of the sea and walk from the shore to an island without one drop of water falling on him.

"Next to Agios, Primus felt insignificant. So one day he played a trick on him. Primus took Agios's puppy and secretly chained it next to the water. Then he challenged

Agios to part the waters, which caused the puppy to drown. When Agios discovered what had happened to his dog he was overwhelmed by grief and remorse. Primus told Agios that it was his ability that was to blame. He explained to Agios that his gift was dangerous and he warned him that if he continued to use it there would be more deaths. At first Agios did not believe him but Primus argued his point so passionately that finally Agios did believe.

"With one follower under his belt Primus moved on to others and soon they, too, turned their backs on their unique abilities for what they believed to be the safety and well-being of all concerned."

"They believed it even though it wasn't true?" Piper interjected.

"Yes, Primus lied and hid the truth. His deception transformed peaceful people into a fearful, argumentative, and conflicted mob. Concerned parents refused to use their abilities and forced their children to do the same. Others refused to let their talents go. Those who wanted to be normal did not wish to live next to neighbors who chose to keep their gifts. Children with special abilities were taught not to play with children without them. Generations went by and the tension and anger built and people forgot the name Primus but remembered in gory detail the stories their parents told them of danger and fear. Anything that went wrong—a bad crop, an unexpected accident—was blamed on those with what were now 'special' abilities. Finally the day came when there were so few of us left that we were led by the Guardian to Mother Mountain for our own safety."

Equilla looked back and forth between the two of them and sighed.

"You are not safe down there, in the outside world. You are hunted and tortured and they will never accept you. It is not safe for us to have AnnA here when she is not like us. It will create problems and unrest even if that is not her intent. The two worlds have separated and never shall they meet. It is for good reason and it has been so now for thousands of years."

"But AnnA . . ." Piper began.

"AnnA will be treated kindly and with great care. All her memories of this place will be erased and she will know nothing about it. She will be taken below, where the Outsiders will care for her."

"In an orphanage or a foster home or—"

"In a place where she will be with people like herself, where she will fit in and be accepted." Equilla's voice was even and rational. "It would be unkind for her to remember Xanthia when she can never return. We take her memories away for her happiness as well as our own safety."

"But—" Piper began.

"No one person can be allowed to threaten the safety of this place." Equilla was quiet but definite. "There have been very few children born this way, but on the rare occasion it does happen, our rule on this is firm: AnnA must go."

"Then the rules need to be changed!"

"My child, it is not for me to make these rules. I simply uphold them by the will of the people."

Conrad got to his feet, putting a hand on Piper's shoulder to calm her. "I can understand your rules. As much as we may not like them, they certainly make sense."

Equilla nodded, pleased at his clear thinking.

"Let me ask you," Conrad continued in even tones. "In the beginning, who was it that created the rules?"

"When we first came here our Guardian set down the rules for our happiness, safety, and protection."

"And who is the Guardian now?"

Equilla shook her head calmly at Conrad's naive mistake. "There has only ever been one Guardian."

The color drained from Conrad's face and he unwittingly took a step backward. Piper was perplexed both by what Equilla said and by Conrad's reaction to it.

"But you said Xanthia has been around for thousands of years. It's not possible to have the same Guardian for that long."

"Actually, Piper, it is," Conrad said, "if the Guardian happened to be immortal."

"But . . ." Confusion knit Piper's brows.

Conrad put the pieces together for her. "The Guardian is Max."

"That . . . guy? Max?"

"Oh, you've met the Guardian?" Equilla was impressed. "He rarely visits. He is so busy with other matters. I myself have only seen him once."

"But Conrad's been with him this whole time in the Knowledge Center."

"The Knowledge Center?" Equilla was momentarily perplexed. "Oh, you mean the Guardian's chambers. He does not like his things disturbed, and so out of respect we do not enter."

Abruptly, as though he were on fire, Conrad turned to go and then stopped mid-stride. "And the decision to bring us here?"

"The Guardian insisted. I myself felt it would be too difficult for Outsiders, even ones as exceptional as you, to settle into Xanthia, but the Guardian was adamant."

Conrad inhaled this information deeply into his lungs and held it there while his skin puckered into goose bumps. "I see," he said, grabbing hold of Piper's arm and pulling her away with him. Piper flinched at the contact; all warmth had drained from Conrad's hand and his fingers were icy—as if someone had just walked over his grave.

CONRAD LEFT EQUILLA IN A CONTROLLED frenzy; his face was flushed, his hands brushed his hair back absently while he mumbled disjointed words beneath his breath. Piper could only catch a few snippets as she trotted next to him.

"Conrad, what's going on?"

"Not now, Piper."

Piper bolted into the air and zipped in front of Conrad, landing in his path. "Yes, now." She crossed her arms over her chest. "What does all of this mean?"

"Max is not who he seems."

"So what?"

"If he is the Guardian then it was his decision to bring us here, right?"

Piper followed this. "Right."

"Why? If no Outsider has ever set foot in Xanthia, then why did he choose us and why now?"

"Maybe he wanted to help us out."

"Max doesn't care about anyone. Against all odds and all reason he brought us here for a very important, very specific reason. He wanted something."

Piper thought about what Conrad said and it made sense to her. "We were perfectly well and good on the farm until everything blew up at the Fall Festival." Suddenly Piper stopped short with her mouth open. "It was Max!"

"What was Max?"

"At the festival. It was him!" Piper's hands came to her head in alarm. "I was walking on the balcony and I saw you walking ahead of me, but it wasn't you—it was Max. From behind you guys look like you're twins."

"Yes, I know. As soon as you pointed that out to me earlier I knew that Max had been at the festival. That's why I didn't go with him."

"But why would he do that?" Piper looked to Conrad to help her understand and make sense of this too. "Why would he deliberately put us in danger and expose us?"

"So that we would have no choice but to come here."

Conrad pushed past Piper and ran to what he had always thought of as the Knowledge Center, but now knew were Max's chambers. Even though he'd left only an hour earlier and nothing had changed, the place looked entirely new in his eyes. The eyes in a painting of Cleopatra suddenly bored into him. The manacles from a slave ship tossed carelessly on a shelf loomed ominously, and a row of longbows pointed in his direction with menace.

Conrad feverishly rummaged through the room, pushing aside priceless vases, not caring if they remained whole or not. Piper, who appreciated their antiquity, followed behind Conrad and attempted to stop what destruction she could.

"Careful with that painting. No, you'll make those parchments tear. Conrad, what are you *doing*?"

"Max is hiding something and I'm going to find it. He's been one step ahead of me all this time. It was his decision to force AnnA to leave, and he knew she would tell you. He was also the one who selected her to be our guide. And he knows me well enough to know that I'd go to Equilla to try and change her mind. He knew that we would learn he is the Guardian."

"You think he figured *all of that* out?"

"He wasn't exactly born yesterday, and this last week he's developed a pretty good understanding of how my mind works. So, yes, he would have known all of that." Conrad tossed aside some armor only to find a few books and a Civil War cavalry sword behind it. Useless.

"What exactly are we looking for?" Piper wondered.

"Something out of place. Something that doesn't belong." Conrad barreled through parchment rolls, searching, searching. "Max has a secret, and if I know him he wants us to find it. It's like a big game for him."

"This is crazy, Conrad. It would take us months to go through this mausoleum."

"Mausoleum?" In a very quiet, slow way Conrad looked at the chamber and nodded. "Yes, it is. That's exactly what it is: a place of dead things."

As the dank, low smell of rotting and death hit the back of his nostrils, Conrad's eyes settled upon a painting of a young woman. Unlike everything else, she appeared to be a beacon of life, entirely different from everything around her. Around her neck was a necklace with a red stone in the middle—a bloodstone. Her image was so striking it surprised Conrad that he hadn't taken notice of it before. There was a hopeful expression on her face, the kind of hope born from naïveté and unfettered innocence.

That very innocence, Conrad knew, could only be found in one place—Xanthia.

Piper was awed by the lifelike depiction too. "Jeez, she's beautiful. You think she lived in ancient Greece?"

"No, I think she's probably still alive."

Piper reacted in surprise.

"The paint hasn't cracked or faded. It's no more than fifty years old. Look at the robes she's wearing," Conrad pointed out. "They're Xanthian. Whoever she is, she's a Chosen One and she's got a bloodstone around her neck."

He approached the painting and studied every inch, looking for clues. Finally when none could be found he gently placed his hands around the frame and felt for anything that might be unusual. Even though Conrad was not applying pressure the painting suddenly snapped off the wall and crashed to the ground.

Conrad had to leap out of the way or else get clobbered by the heavy frame. When it came to rest on the floor it kicked up a cloud of dust, and Piper and Conrad instinctively started to wave it from their eyes and cover their mouths.

At last the dust settled, revealing a small stone door on the wall where the painting had been. Carved into the center of the door was an intricately designed sun. With delicate and elegant lines the artist had somehow captured the feeling of heat rising off of the sun.

"Is that a snake?" Piper pointed to a strange shape that curved off the top of the sun.

"No, it's not a snake," Conrad said with certainty. Using the cloth on his tunic he began to brush the thick dust away and blow on the carving until it was clearly revealed.

"Oh, it's a sword." Piper could see it plainly now. "A sword in a sun."

The sword was piercing the middle of the sun and droplets of blood dripped from the wound.

Conrad stepped back and allowed himself a full vantage of the entire carving. *There is a sword in the sun. My mother is trapped in the sword in the sun.* That is what his father had said to him on the roof of the White House. How had his father known of this carving? And what did it mean?

Even as possibilities were whizzing from one side of Conrad's brain to the other he was pulling the key Max had given him from around his neck. He slid it into the small keyhole and it fit perfectly.

CLICK! The stone responded by vibrating. A low rumble emanated from the sun and it pushed its way into the rock, crumbling away in big angry chunks.

"What did you do?" Piper came to Conrad's side.

Conrad watched as the sun fell to the floor, creating a hole in the wall. Through that hole was a passage.

Piper sucked a long breath in and held it.

When Conrad started to walk forward she clutched his arm and held him back. "Don't go near that."

"Piper, I have to see what's in there." Shaking his

arm free, Conrad walked to the dark hole and peered inside.

At first all he could see was darkness. As his eyes adjusted he saw the outline of stone steps leading downward.

"I'm going in," Conrad said.

CHAPTER

39

*T*HE STAIRS WERE NARROW AND SLANTED down at a steep incline. The ceiling was rounded and low, the air thick and close. Conrad had created a small torch to illuminate their journey down, down and into the belly of Mother Mountain. The descent seemed endless so that when Conrad's foot finally hit the bottom it felt awkward as his body readjusted to level ground. Even with the light from the torch the darkness was bottomless.

The hallway that they found themselves in was wide and the ceiling was high, making them feel small and helpless. Thirty feet later the hallway ended and they stopped at the threshold to something much bigger. Foreboding kept Piper rooted to the spot. She grabbed Conrad's arm and her fingers dug into him. "Let's go back now. No farther."

"You go back. I have to keep going. My father might be down here."

Piper sighed deeply. As he watched Piper's chest heave with a terrible fear, it seemed to Conrad that she might collapse on the spot. He remained still and in a few seconds she settled and started to float next to him. Getting her feet off the ground was having a calming effect that allowed her to continue on.

Now the darkness around them had no borders or end; no walls or ceiling could be seen and their footsteps echoed loudly. Because there was nothing to look at Conrad's attention was drawn to the sound of their feet falling on the stone. The more intently he listened the stranger their steps became, as though Piper was limping. Stopping suddenly, Conrad looked back—Piper was still hovering behind him! He hadn't been listening to her footsteps at all.

In complete stillness Piper and Conrad listened to the sound of two feet walking. They sounded something like this:

Thump. *Drag.* Thump. *Drag.*

"What is that?" Piper breathed in Conrad's ear.

Conrad's breath caught in his throat; his skin tingled with fear and dread.

Piper's hand shot out in front of her at the same time she grabbed Conrad's arm. She was pointing straight ahead at a creature that was walking in a hobbled manner, dragging one leg behind it.

Neither of them moved. The creature didn't see them, which was impossible since they were holding torches that burned brightly in this place of darkness.

Tufts of gray hair were dangling from the creature's head and in patches there was no hair at all, but a sort of grayish dirty skin. Its body had rags drawn about it and it moved slowly. Piper's and Conrad's eyes were fully adjusted to the darkness now, allowing them to discern a massive pile of stones on either side of what seemed to be a football-field-size cavern. The stones were piled to the ceiling and about as large as a breadbox each.

At length the creature reached one of the stone piles and with great effort tossed the stone in its arms onto the pile. Next it climbed up, choosing a specific stone, and with the same great effort, took the stone into its arms, curling around it and then limping to the pile of rocks on the opposite side.

Now that the creature was walking straight for Conrad and Piper they could see that she was not a creature at all but a very, very old woman. All but two of her teeth had rotted away, and those last two miserable specimens were sticking out at odd angles from her mouth and praying for release. She was so bent and twisted that her back had formed itself into a hunch almost the size of the rock she carried. She had no shoes on her feet and there were open sores covering every part of them such that each step was its own specific agony. The dirty dagger-like fingernails on her hands made them look more like claws than anything human. As she moved, the muscles in her face tightened and shook from the effort of it all, and perhaps without even knowing that she was doing it, she moaned.

The fear coursing through Piper's body began to give way to another feeling entirely: pity. She found herself rooting for the woman; there was such determination on her face and her body was so feeble, surely too weak to make it to the massive pile of rocks against the far wall. At any moment Piper worried that the weight of the rock would pull the old woman to the ground and pin her there and possibly even kill her.

Piper held her breath with each step she took, waiting until her foot was safely returned before relaxing again.

"Do you think she knows we're here?" Piper whispered.

Conrad shook his head.

"Hello," he called out.

The old woman continued without interruption on her piteous journey.

With quick steps Conrad positioned himself by the rock pile and waited for the old woman to reach him. As she approached she did not acknowledge the light, nor did she see that Conrad was now standing by the rock pile waiting for her to arrive. Piper flew down next to him, propping the torch on the stone pile.

"Hello," Piper said this time.

The old woman hobbled onward.

"She may have lost her vision and her hearing," Conrad pointed out. He was waiting for her to stop at the base of the pile. Sure enough she did, just as she had done before, and it was then that Conrad reached out and took the rock out of her arms. He was so surprised by its weight he almost fell over.

When the old woman found herself without a rock and no explanation for its absence she stopped suddenly and with great effort opened her eyes. The moment the light hit her corneas she threw the filthy sticks that were her arms over her unsuspecting eyes as a shield.

"Owwwww," she moaned. "Owwww."

Piper reached out to her but Conrad stopped her. "Let her eyes adjust. Who knows how long it's been since she last saw light."

Curling into herself, the old woman moaned, rocking back and forth. Taking the torches, Piper flew with them to the hallway and left them out of sight, reducing the amount of light by half.

Blinking furiously and holding her hand above her head to keep the glare away, the old woman began to blink and squint and coax her tired old eyes back into seeing. As she was always in the darkness, she went days, or was it weeks or even months, without bothering to open them: when there was nothing to see you stopped looking.

She opened her mouth to speak, but began to cough violently. She motioned to her mouth. Conrad looked about and spotted a wooden bucket with a metal cup on a stick hitched against its side.

Piper saw it too and flew to it, dipped the cup in, and filled it with water. She was back at the woman's side moments later and helped her place it to her lips.

The woman slurped it greedily, letting it slop down her face and drench the rags against her chest. When she had sucked the contents of two full cups she waved it away and opened her mouth.

"Danger." Her mouth trembled and worked hard to form the words that seemed foreign to her. "Get out!" She pointed a sinewy arm back the way they had come.

"Can we help you?" Piper offered.

She looked back and forth between the two of them,

then got up and, as they watched with amazement, she picked up another rock and started walking back to the other rock pile. They found themselves following behind her.

"We can show you the way out," Piper offered.

"I cannot talk . . . to you. No one is allowed down here." She looked over her shoulder suddenly. "No one has ever come. He might hear."

Conrad stepped forward quickly. "Who is he?"

She hobbled faster, trying to escape them. "Danger."

"What kind of danger?"

"Stupid boy," she spat. "You know nothing."

"Then educate me!" Conrad's demand was met with silence. "How long have you been down here?"

She snorted. "I have no need of time. I was a young woman when last I saw daylight."

A look passed between Piper and Conrad. "You've been down here all this time moving these rocks back and forth?" Piper was aghast.

"Stupid child. These are not rocks: they are memories."

"You mean your memories were turned into rocks?"

"Some."

Conrad was getting tired of this game. If she was determined to be stubborn it could take considerable time to pry anything out of her, and Max could return at any moment. Conrad decided he was going to have to bluff the old woman to get her talking. It was a gamble but one he calculated would pay off.

"Max sent us down here. Do you know Max?"

She said nothing.

"I'm going back to meet him now." Conrad started to walk away. "I'll tell him that I met you and I'll tell him that you told me a lot of interesting things."

She stopped walking toward the rock pile. "I told you *nothing*."

"You told us *everything*." Conrad continued to walk and the woman started to hobble after him desperately.

"Noooo," she wailed. "Noooo."

Piper was distressed to see her so upset. "Conrad!"

Conrad spun around and charged up to the old hag's face, pointing his finger at her threateningly. "If you tell us nothing, I will go to Max and say that you have told us everything. If, though—" He paused a beat to make sure he had her attention. "If you tell us everything then we will say nothing and you will be safe. You choose."

She dropped the rock. "No one is safe around Max. You are a fool."

"We know that Max is the Guardian. We know that he is immortal," Conrad said quickly. "Piper and I are Outsiders and we know about the rest of the world too."

She rested her weary bones upon the rock. "Max is

not immortal," she moaned. "He lets people believe that, but . . . it is not truth."

"If he's not immortal how has he lived so long?"

"He—" She searched for the word and at the same time put her hand to her mouth as though she were putting imaginary food in it. "He's a—a Gobbler."

Piper repeated the word like she could taste it. "A Gobbler?"

"That is so, yes. He eats energy. But not all energy is equal. Grief, suffering, creates a lot of energy and it keeps him young. The more he eats the longer he remains young."

"My god," Conrad breathed. "He's like a vampire."

"That is his gift." She nodded. "Without that energy he would wither and die."

"And you're the only one who knows this and so he keeps you down here," Conrad considered.

"He feeds on my suffering too, but it is not why I am down here. He keeps me here because I would destroy him if I could." She said this calmly and without malice, and it made her declaration all the more chilling.

Piper wondered what possible series of events could have led up to such a terrible end. "What happened to you?"

The sincerity of Piper's question melted the old

woman's hardness and she sighed deeply. "So long ago. I think of it little." Her attention turned inward and she got lost in her thoughts.

Conrad could see that she was ready to talk and so he approached her gently. "How was it that you learned Max is a Gobbler?"

"Because I broke the law. And because I am his wife."

"*I* WAS EIGHTEEN THE FIRST TIME I MET Max. I was shy and excited. He seemed to know all about me, but then he knew all about everything. He told me that he'd been to the moon. Imagine, going to the moon!"

"Nothing much to look at up there, but way fun bouncing up and down and the earth looks a sight," is what he said.

Now that the old woman had started talking she became oblivious to Piper and Conrad and went into a world all her own.

"My mother always said that I was very beautiful. She said I shone like the stars and that is why she named me Starr. When I was still very young it was discovered that I had the ability to read other people's memories. My mother told me that memory keepers are rare. She said it was my job to take the memories that people offered me and to hold them safe. I did as I was told. I ate the memories of the elders. I swallowed the memories of the storyteller. Any memory I was offered I held on to. I was filled with memories.

"Max started to visit me but I didn't notice for some time that he only came when no one else was around. He said he was busy but the truth is that he likes to stay out of sight and in the shadows. The truth is that he— well, the truth is complicated."

The old woman grew silent, and Conrad and Piper waited patiently for her to continue.

"He was so mysterious, so thrilling, so full of things that I fell deeply in love with him. He never loved me. I know that now, but I believed that he did at the time. Just like I believed that he was immortal. He never really told me that he loved me and he never told me that he was immortal, in so many words. The thing about Max is that he directs your attention and then allows you to believe what you want to believe."

"At dawn one day we married ourselves. No one else was there. I was thrilled by the secrecy. There are no secrets in Xanthia and to have one was exciting. When I became pregnant Max told me to go to the elders and explain to them that my child was a special child. I did as he told me.

"The elders were not surprised. It was then that I

learned this wasn't the first time this had happened. Over the history of Xanthia there had been other children born in this way. It didn't happen very often and when it did no one talked about it. After that Max went away and didn't come back, not even when our child was born. I had a little boy and I named him Peter. He was . . . extraordinary, with a heart so pure and good. He was always happy, always looking for ways to help people and bring them joy. He filled me with a deep contentment and I no longer cared or thought about Max.

"As Peter grew he became worried about his gift. It seemed to me that he had a strong gift; the way he made people happy, the way he would calm them if they were upset. Almost like he could place thoughts into their heads. I saw the gift growing, but one day it went away, and after that he was often confused and sometimes angry.

"He was eleven and his celebration was a week away when I was told that he was going to have to leave— that they were going to take him to the outside world. I swore I would never let him go. I kicked up such a fuss Max himself returned. He was angry with me and told me that I was ungrateful, that Peter was his child too and he could do with him what he wanted.

"He would listen to nothing I said. I was so angry I did to him the very worst thing I could think of—the thing that no Xanthian has ever done before: I used my ability with ill intent. It wasn't an offered memory—I took it. Without his permission, I saw everything."

The old woman who had once been a beautiful young woman named Starr shuddered. Her thin lips curled back from her two pointy teeth and her tongue darted out and licked them. Her eyes shifted back and forth as she remembered.

"In his mind I saw how he fed upon the pain and misery of others. And oh, how much pain he had caused. How relentless he had been. The Outsiders were powerless against him. He was so clever, so devious, and they were so unaware. I saw how he had taken his children before from Xanthia, and how those children had great gifts that he would manipulate: how he used those children as instruments of his terrible will. That is the very thing that he had planned for my Peter.

"He knew that I had seen what he was. 'I will tell everyone,' I said. 'It is time you stopped this and our peoples were together again.'

"Max went wild and said the Outsiders and the Chosen Ones would never be together—he would make sure of that. I ran from him and hid with Peter. Sure enough he found us in a cave and he gave me a choice: either Peter would spend the rest of his life suffering, or I would. Of course, I chose myself. Then he had Joseff the stone maker turn the memories that I had stolen into these rocks. He locked me down here with them and you are the first I have seen since that time. When the day comes that I stop moving the stones Peter will be put to death. He is a good boy, my Peter."

"But—" Conrad hated to interrupt the story but he was on the edge of his seat and couldn't wait a moment longer. "What about Peter? What happened to him?"

"Max would have erased his memory and left him to fend for himself among the Outsiders."

"Are you sure?"

"He did that with all his other children. It is certain Peter would have been the same. When he grew older Max would have used him to do his work."

Conrad stood up and walked away. On the White House rooftop his father had said his name was Peter. *My mother was so beautiful and she sacrificed everything for me,* his father had said. The truth was snapping into place in quick motions inside his head.

"Conrad?" Piper whispered, interrupting his thoughts.

Conrad looked up to see that Piper was right in front of him, her face full of concern. He filled his lungs with the damp black air and shook his head. "Peter is my father."

Piper didn't understand him. "What?"

"My father told me his name was Peter. Remember J. was investigating my father and said that he was abandoned in the desert? Her Peter and my father are the same person."

"But . . . that means she's your grandmother!"

Conrad nodded, looking at Starr, who was slumped over and shaking. Suddenly he put his head in his hands.

"Are you okay?" Piper waited for him to recover.

"If she's my grandmother, then Max is my grandfather, and . . . he knows that. Max knows who I am."

"Wow," was all Piper could say, and the moment lingered while Conrad processed this.

"I'm gonna have to say it," Piper sighed finally. "Your family has some serious issues. I think you're going to need therapy or something."

"I think you're right," Conrad agreed.

"What are you going to do now?"

Conrad was watching Starr, who had grumbled herself to her feet and was hobbling back toward the rocks. "We have to help her."

As she was struggling to pick up a memory rock, Conrad approached her and tried to take the weight of the rock away.

"Leave me be," she snapped. "I have told you everything and now you must go."

She snatched the memory rock and Piper could see that it was a very heavy memory indeed.

"Please"—Conrad attempted to help her—"you don't need to do that anymore."

"*No!*" She hobbled away. "Let me be."

"We can help you," Piper called after her.

"Help yourselves. I have made my choice. Now you must make yours."

"Maybe," Conrad began with the utmost care, following next to her, "something happened. Peter was hurt and it's possible that he's no longer alive."

"No," she said, shaking her head harshly. "Peter is alive. I know this."

"But how can you know?" Piper asked with equal sensitivity.

The old woman dumped the rock and took a moment to gather her strength again before rummaging in her rags to pull out a necklace that had been hanging from her scrawny neck. Conrad instantly recognized it from the painting. Just like his father's bloodstone, there was a heartbeat in the center of it, opening and contracting to a steady beat.

The old woman looked at the light and reassured herself. "This sits against my own heart so that I know. See? He is alive. If he were dead it would not beat."

"But . . ." Conrad reached out to touch the pulsing red stone. "Where is he?"

"Fool. Max has him. He's hiding him from me in the cave at the top of the mountain. The same cave where I tried to hide him."

Conrad's eyes went wide. "How do you know?"

She snorted. "Because Max likes to gloat. He likes the fact that I tried to hide him there and now he's hiding him there from me. Irony is what he calls it." She reached for another rock and turned her back on them. "He wants you to find him but he will not let you take him, foolish boy. Don't even try."

Conrad heard the old woman's words but disregarded their meaning because he was already running to find the cave, and Piper was flying behind him.

CHAPTER

41

B Y THE TIME HE STOOD OVERLOOKING the Colorado River, Max's blood was jumping with anticipation.

There was a silence around the river. The usual chatter of birds and frogs brought Max back to quieter times that he had known and remembered with nostalgia.

The world, Max had come to realize, was no longer as fun as it used to be. There was too much organization, too much peace, education, justice, and far too many medical advances. People no longer dwelled in superstition and ignorance, but relied on rational thinking, research, and science. Everything was examined and connected; kids tweeted and Twittered and took pictures that they posted on a Facebook. Everyone was looking at everyone else and nothing was hidden. And it was just the beginning, of that Max was certain. There were advances just around the corner that would eradicate war, and not long after that there would be a true global village based on peace and equality.

The very thought of it made Max shiver—there was no fun in peace.

Now, the Dark Ages had been a party. In the Dark Ages man was scattered and ignorant—helpless against the elements and one another. No one communicated, no one knew what was going on from one village to the next, empowering Max to roam freely and find, or create when necessary, adventure as he saw fit. If only those sweet Dark Ages could return again. . . .

The water purifier crackled, bursts of electrical sparks popping out and pulling Max's thoughts back to the task at hand. He wielded the purifier like a magic wand, feeling its motion through the air. Slipping his free hand into his pocket, Max removed a small orange worm that he thumbed onto the wood of the purifier. Upon contact, the worm dug into the grain of the wood, burrowing inside like the hungry parasite it was. When it had disappeared from sight the purifier shivered and shook and the blue light grew dim, flickering out. A moment later an orange glow erupted inside the wand and it emitted a high whistle, like that of a siren.

Wouldn't Conrad be surprised when Max showed

him this! Of course, Conrad had no experience with the Antipode worm. Time was when the worm could be found on every continent on the globe causing havoc of every delicious nature. But as always happened, the Outsiders got wigged out and hunted down the Antipodes until they had eradicated every single last one of them. The fact that the worm was the cause of death and destruction anywhere and everywhere that it was found probably had something to do with the Outsiders' violent feelings toward it and its eventual extinction. Outsiders hated death and destruction and thus hated the worm.

Fortunately Max had the foresight to save a few of them for his own personal use. What the Outsiders didn't understand was that the worm wasn't destructive, but brilliant, not to mention the fact that the little wriggler had a great sense of humor. The creature naturally and organically played the "opposite" game, and what could be more fun than that? Children liked the opposite game—the opposite of "up" is "down"; "in" for "out"; "hard" for "soft." The worm played the same game on a grand scale and in the most creative ways. If you were a kind, helpful person and the worm got into you it would turn you into a killer. The worm would turn a hot fire into ice, a fish into a bird, and now, thanks to Max's foresight, the worm had turned the purifier from something that could transform sand into clean drinking water into a machine that changed cleaning drinking water into sand. Ha!

It was all so fabulous and amazing that the only thing that saddened Max was that no one else was around to witness his genius. He wanted credit where credit was due; he wanted to be appreciated and admired, and more than anything he wanted a round of applause.

At the edge of the river Max hesitated only a moment before wading in up to his waist. The water was cold and ran around him quickly. Fish darted away from his feet and a water snake retreated to the reeds.

He didn't want to rush things: he wanted the moment to linger. Max held the wand up in his arms and turned around slowly, taking in the delicate balance of nature.

The water was pure and sparkling: basic but essential. It was easy to take water for granted until you didn't have it anymore. Max remembered the time he was stuck in a settlers' outpost surrounded on all sides by bloodthirsty natives—he couldn't really remember which natives; frankly, after a while they all sort of blended. Anyway, it was okay fun: unexpected things were popping up, skirmishes and attacks followed by counterattacks and the usual man-trying-to-survive-against-a-ruthless-environment sort of scenario. It was on the point of becoming ho-hum when the clean water ran out and suddenly things amped up to a whole new fun-level. The settlers started fighting among themselves over what was left of the water. Desperation was so deliciously dramatic—Max had never felt so young or so vibrant.

Then there was that time on the Viking ship when Sventlek the Red had poisoned the water and the crew went blinking mad and burned the ship from underneath themselves and drowned like rats. What a riot!

It had only occurred to Max recently that since the world was so globalized, the only way to really achieve the fun-charge he was looking for was to "encourage" global problems. And nothing said global catastrophe like a good old-school water shortage. The Colorado River would be first but others would follow: the Yangtze, the Nile, the Danube. Then Max would sit back and just watch the fun, soaking in all that delicious hysteria.

With Conrad's intelligence at his disposal Max was back in business again; water shortages would be only the beginning. Maybe it could be a one-two punch: first the water, and then he'd get Conrad to engineer a really bad virus. The Black Plague was a great thing when it happened; Max remembered those days well and fondly.

Yes sir, with genius on your side the possibilities are endless.

Max turned around and around in the water and

when the anticipation overtook him he tapped the top of the water with the wand like an orchestra conductor. Upon contact the cold water instantly turned to sand. The effect rippled outward as more water came into contact with the wand and a wave of sand began to travel up and down the river.

Max was now buried up to his waist in golden granules. A two-foot-long trout came thrusting upward out of the sand in confusion, gasping and flailing. Max watched it wiggling in panic and then placed his hand lovingly on top of its head as it flipped and flopped, its gills opening and shutting more and more slowly.

Max listened to the frogs chirping at a hysterical pitch and the birds going frenzied. In the distance a black bear began howling. He could feel his energy rising and his body growing younger by the second.

And then Max gave himself, because no one else would, a long, loud round of applause.

"Hooray for Max," he cheered like he was a fan in the stands. "Max is amazing! What an achievement!"

He continued to clap for quite a while because, frankly, this was the sort of thing that deserved a long round of applause. Finally he stopped and bowed. It felt good. Not as good as if someone else had been there, but still it was better than nothing.

Max would have lingered longer but he'd given

Conrad ample time to figure things out in Xanthia and it was time for him to get back. He didn't want to miss out on a drop of that drama.

Yes. Max sighed happily. *The world is my oyster and life is good!*

CHAPTER

42

CONRAD TOOK THE STEPS TWO AT A TIME. He was panting from the effort and sweat beaded his face and chest. Piper had to fly to keep up with him. Neither of them bothered with the torches as the thing they most feared was no longer below them but above them.

"Wait up!"

"There's no time." Conrad was panting. "We have to get to my father before Max gets back!"

They didn't stop until they had gone all the way up the stairs and into the Knowledge Center, where they found the energy globe flashing like a red-hot siren.

"What the heck?" Piper reached out to touch it.

Conrad immediately identified the Colorado River as the focal point of a major shift in the planet's energy. No doubt Max had done damage of some sort, and Conrad felt a sick foreboding in the pit of his stomach.

Conrad pulled Piper out of the Knowledge Center

and into the sunlight, where the events of a normal afternoon were unfolding in Xanthia exactly as they always did. He had no time to consider this but craned his neck to look up to the top of the mountain. "I can't see a cave."

Piper rose into the air, cupped her hands over her eyes to block out the rays of the setting sun. "I see something near the top. Maybe that's it."

"You'll have to fly me up there." Conrad lifted his arms away from his sides so that Piper could grip him.

Piper swooped behind Conrad and grunted from the effort of picking him up. "Watch my shoulder," Conrad warned. "It still hurts sometimes."

Slowly they ascended, when AnnA spotted them and came racing their way, climbing up onto a balcony railing as though to catch them.

"Piper!" AnnA reached up to Piper, out of breath, relieved to see her friend. "I've been looking for you everywhere."

"AnnA!" Suddenly Piper remembered AnnA's plight. Over the last week she and AnnA had spent every waking moment together and had become good friends. She had promised AnnA that she would help her, but the revelations of the last few hours had completely distracted her from that purpose.

"Piper, what do I do?" AnnA's face was red and anxious. "Equilla has sent for me."

"Come with us," Piper said impulsively.

"Piper, no!" Conrad warned. "It's too dangerous."

"Not as dangerous as going to Equilla. C'mon, AnnA."

AnnA hesitated, wrapping her fingers around the stone railing and looking up in confusion. "Where are you going?"

"We have to get to a cave at the top of the mountain. Do you know where it is?"

"Over there." AnnA pointed in the opposite direction from where they had intended to go. "It's behind the floating rocks."

"I see it." Conrad pointed to the rocks. "Go. Go."

"But . . ." AnnA's face furrowed with confusion and fear. "How do I get up there?" It was clear that Piper was only just able to manage Conrad's weight and couldn't handle AnnA, too. "And we are not allowed in the caves. The Guardian says that they're not safe and we are not to go there."

Conrad snorted. "I bet he does."

Tears welled in AnnA's eyes. "I . . . I cannot break the rules." Her face was flushing a deep red. "I am . . . frightened. And I am not like you—you are Outsiders."

Despite Conrad's urgency, Piper slowed down and lowered herself until she was eye level with AnnA.

"We are frightened too, AnnA. You have to do it in spite of your fear." Piper gazed with compassion into

AnnA's pale face. "And you are like us, AnnA. We are all the same, the Outsiders and the Chosen Ones; we all came from the same place but we were tricked into forgetting."

"Piper," Conrad urged, wary of the time.

Piper sighed, wishing she could do more for her friend. "AnnA, I can't take you, you've gotta do it yourself—but you can. I know you can." Piper tipped her head in salute and swooshed up.

AnnA watched Piper ascend. It caused a fluttering inside her chest that was entirely foreign to her, and she was only just able to place a name to the feeling: yearning. As she considered what she was to do with her yearning heart, Nuttle the squirrel leaped up on the railing next to her.

"AnnA, I am waiting for you," Nuttle said in the voice of Equilla. "Please come to me at once."

AnnA's breath caught in her throat. She handed the squirrel a nut and then carefully climbed down from the railing. When her feet were back on Mother Mountain she looked from Nuttle to where Piper and Conrad had flown away, painfully aware that nothing she had ever learned in the Celebration Center or for that matter in all her years in Xanthia had adequately prepared her for a moment like this. Yet in the last seven short days with Piper McCloud, AnnA's world had been turned upside down—Piper was a revelation on every level, opening

AnnA to ideas she had never thought possible. AnnA considered, for the first time in her life, that somewhere, deep inside her, resided the same courage and spirit of Piper McCloud. And that maybe, just maybe, that was a good thing.

———◆———

THE FLOATING ROCKS BOBBED BACK AND forth, bumping into one another with loud thuds, making it necessary for Piper to dodge through them like an obstacle course. At the mouth of the cave, Piper set Conrad on the ground and paused to take in the fact that the cave was not dark but had a blue glow emerging from deep inside it.

Like AnnA, Conrad was afraid: afraid his father was dead, afraid of finding his father, and afraid of not finding him. He was strangely aware of his breathing all of a sudden, as though the cave had absorbed all sound and only the noise within could remain; the thud of his heart beating, the wheeze of his lungs pulling air in and pushing it out.

"Look! There's snow," said Piper, but she sounded impossibly far away, like she was in a distant land and calling out to him.

Conrad saw that his feet were in white powder. Along the walls of the cave ice was forming, and around the bend it was possible to see that the snow got deeper. The cold air now stung his lungs and his breath formed little clouds as it came out of his mouth.

His father's hands had often felt cold; Conrad remembered how on his second birthday his father had carried him around his party and his hands had felt icy against his arms. There had been a lot of people at the party and they had all wanted to touch Conrad and talk to him and hold him and he didn't like it. He was glad when his father had taken him back to his nursery and sat with him. They were dressed in the same outfit, a costume of some sort. As he thought on it Conrad's memory sharpened and he remembered that the costume had been a Superman outfit: his mother's idea, no doubt.

His father had looked like he truly was Superman to Conrad, though: strong, wise, powerful. He was his hero, and just being near him made Conrad glow inside and filled him with the urgent need to please him—and be like him.

For several months Conrad had been disassembling his electronic toys and reforming them in better ways. This was something his mother had reprimanded him for, thinking that he was ruining the toys, not making them smarter. Conrad hoped his father would celebrate and maybe even participate in this thing he felt compelled to do.

While his father watched, Conrad pulled apart his toy, reprogrammed it, and set it out for him to see.

"Call South America," Conrad told the toy.

"Hola," a voice in South America said soon after.

Conrad was delighted with the result and looked to his father with hope and anticipation. But the reaction he saw on his father's face terrified him. His father's eyes became small, his pupils dilated and strange. His hands shook and he spoke in a voice that was not his own before savaging the toy, hitting it until there was nothing but small parts scattered across the floor.

Even as Conrad thought about it now he felt the same sharp pain in the spot between his ribs. For years afterward in one form or another Conrad had attempted to please his father over and over again, hoping that at last his father would understand. Without fail his father treated his endeavors with revulsion and horror. It was more than confusing and disheartening to Conrad—it was dangerous. The satellite incident had been the final straw, pushing his father to throw Conrad at the mercy of Dr. Hellion and abandon him completely.

What would Conrad give to know then what he knew now? How much easier would it have been for his two-year-old self if he had understood that his father was under a powerful spell and suffering under his own wounds? In the file that J. had given to Conrad there were police reports on his father, and Conrad read about the day he had been discovered on the side of the road. An Officer Gonzalez had picked him up while wandering on a deserted Nevada highway, a scrawny eleven-year-old alone for an indeterminate amount of time without food or water and suffering severe burns from the punishingly hot sun. Child Services had questioned his father at length but he'd been robbed of all memory and knew nothing of his home or family. They held him, and the boy waited patiently for a loving family to claim him.

It was a futile and painful hope because, of course, no one ever came for him and he never had a home again. In foster care he was beaten and bullied by the other boys, enduring years of loneliness and mistreatment. When he was sixteen years old, the abuse had become too much and he'd run away to make it on his own in a cold and lonely world. For several years, he lived on the streets begging for change, when out of the blue one day, a mysterious benefactor took an interest in him. Suddenly unheard of opportunities were handed to him, and all the benefactor asked in exchange was a simple pledge of loyalty, which Harrington was all too happy to give. Years later, when that benefactor revealed himself as Max and his diabolical plans were laid bare, Harrington found himself caught in a web so deep and tangled, he was unable to free himself. And in this web he had remained, trapped and desperate.

What was it like, Conrad wondered, to have a feeling deep inside that could not be remembered or reasoned with, a longing for the peace of his home and justice for his mother? How had his father endured it?

Now that there were no longer secrets between them, would he be able to save his father from his past? No question; Conrad's fears mounted.

The cave walls were coated in thick ice now; the snow was several inches deep and the blue light was growing brighter. As they rounded the bend the light was so blinding that Conrad was forced to raise his arm to shield his eyes.

As his vision refocused from a bright blur, Conrad's heart skipped a beat.

In the middle of a cavern layered with ice was a frozen upright slab, and in the center of that slab was his father. Peter Harrington's face was contorted with pain and his hand reached to the wound in his chest. He was frozen in place with the thick coldness, his skin tinted blue.

"Oh no!" Piper breathed, floating up and down behind Conrad's shoulder.

Conrad took the last few steps and finally reached his father. He placed his hands on the ice above where his father's hands were and willed with a raging ferocity to melt the cold and free him. The ice cared nothing for Conrad's feelings and remained, burning his skin and firmly holding Harrington in frozen isolation.

Was it irony, Conrad wondered, or just some sort of nasty piece of destiny that was seeing to it that even though at long last he was physically with his father, he was still unable to reach him? The unfairness of it all erupted out of him and, using both fists, Conrad began pounding against the ice block.

"Ahhhhhh!" There was a raging scream and Conrad was surprised to hear that it sounded like his voice.

"No, Conrad. Stop!" Piper pulled at Conrad's arms, holding them back. "The ice is too thick. You'll only hurt yourself doing that."

Conrad jerked himself away, pacing around the ice block with no purpose.

Piper hated to see Conrad in such a state and raised her hands up as though directing fidgety traffic. "We'll just thaw him out. Look," she said, pointing to the ceiling where blue crystals emitted a sharp coldness. "I'll knock those crystals out and it'll warm up lickety-split." She impulsively flew to them. "As soon as your father thaws we'll get going home."

"Don't touch them!" Conrad shouted with alarm. "Piper, don't!"

Piper stopped in mid-swing, her hand about to make contact with the largest crystal.

"If you thaw the ice my father will die. He had a bullet pass through his heart, and Max couldn't fix it . . . so he froze him."

"So . . ." Piper waited for Conrad to give her a plan. "Then what do we do?"

Conrad looked into his father's face. "Max didn't want him dead because he needed him as a bargaining chip; he's using him now just like he's used him his whole life. It was Max who saw to it that my father was given power, and as the President of the United States he could make him cover for all the mischief and destruction he caused. Then we came along and started to cause problems and Max didn't like it. But Max being Max, he didn't want to miss out on an opportunity, either, so he chose us to serve him."

"Serve him? How?"

"Good question. Why don't you ask him yourself?" Conrad said. "I'm sure he's more than happy to explain it."

Turning around, Conrad faced Max, who was now standing at the threshold of the cavern. Max was breathing hard as though he had been running a great distance but had a delighted expression on his face like he was expecting to open a fabulous present.

"Did I miss anything?" Max panted. "I got here as soon as I could."

"Your timing is impeccable," Conrad commented wryly, "as always."

"Buddy." Max threw his arms wide and rushed at Conrad, capturing him in a bear hug and shaking him with vigor. "WE ARE GONNA HAVE FUN!"

43

*J*ERKING HIS BODY AROUND, CONRAD whacked his elbow into Max's spleen. Max crumpled at the same time Conrad pulled his knee up to smash him in the face.

"Uhhh." Blood spurted out of Max's nose, but it only lasted a few short seconds before it healed and the flow stopped. Moments after that Max shook it off completely. "Dude, what was that?"

"Cut the crap, Max." Conrad crossed his arms furiously over his chest. "So what is it you want me to do? What's your grand plan?"

"I just need a plague." Max shrugged. "And I thought up some other gadgets, weapons of mass destruction mostly, that'd come in handy. You could whip them up in no time."

"No."

"But I got you the T-shirt and everything." Max

unfurled a bright yellow T-shirt that read THE ULTIMATE WEAPON. He tossed it at Conrad.

Conrad dropped the T-shirt in the snow. "Yellow isn't my color."

"You're not funny, Max," said Piper, disgusted. "You've hurt a lot of people."

"True. But your dad is depending upon your cooperation." Max nodded to Harrington's frozen form. "It's not going to be pretty if he thaws."

"Yes, if he thaws he'll die," Conrad agreed. "So now you'll hold my father's life over my head just like you did to Starr. But I still won't help you. My father wouldn't want me to."

Despite the danger, Piper felt her whole body swell with pride.

Max exhaled dramatically. "What? You mean you won't do as I say?"

Conrad stood, immovable.

"Rats! And I thought I had everything all figured out. What am I going to do now?" Max sagged, sighing for a second time as though to drive home the point that his extreme disappointment could not be contended with. "All this planning for nothing."

"You can't outsmart Conrad," Piper gloated.

Max threw up his hands, defeated. "You win. I lose. You're smart. I'm not." Thrusting his hand into his pocket,

Max pulled out a bunch of bloodstones and popped one into his mouth like it was a piece of candy. He sucked on it and then spat it onto the floor and quickly put a fresh stone into his mouth. Conrad immediately noticed that the discarded stone was black, as though Max had sucked the red out of it, and not only that, but as Max sucked on the stone he looked younger, reenergized.

"What—" Conrad leaned down and picked up the discarded black stone.

"Don't interrupt!" Max waved his hand at Conrad impatiently. "You're like a little obsessed with these things. FYI—the ingredient you couldn't figure out—it's my blood. My blood sucks up energy, so I created the rocks as an easy way to get a snack. Anyway, that wasn't what I was about to say. You made me lose my train of thought!"

He tossed a couple more bloodstones into his mouth and they seemed to jog his memory. "That's it . . . Hold your knickers, I almost forgot."

With a flourish Max pulled the purifier out of his pocket. It glowed bright orange in the blue ice light. "Ta-da. Problem solved!"

Conrad didn't understand. "What do you think you're going to do with that?"

"I fixed it," Max explained gleefully. "Made it better. You know all about that, Conrad. You fix things all the time. Just not like this. Let me demonstrate." He waved it about like a magician on a stage and then leveled it at Conrad. "Lick my boot."

Suddenly Conrad felt an explosion ignite in the back of his head at the site of his Direct Brain Interface. It seared a pain into the core of him so deep that he fell to his knees clutching his skull.

Piper bent over, reaching to him. "Conrad? What's wrong?"

"It's his head," Max explained. While Conrad writhed on the ground Max took his own sweet time walking up to him, the purifier leveled and pointing.

"You see, Piper, Conrad powered this by connecting it to the device on the side of his head. His brain sends it signals and those signals power it and allow it to function. But here's the amazing thing, Conrad, and I know you in particular will appreciate this part—I've got this special thingamajig and it reversed the direction of the current. Meaning that instead of your brain sending signals to it, I can send signals back to your brain."

"Stop it!" Piper begged.

"It'll stop whenever Conrad wants it to. Con, if you want the pain to go away all you gotta do is obey what I say. You're fighting against me and that's why it hurts. Now lick my boot."

"No!" Conrad's entire body was shaking from the effort of disobeying. Max waved the purifier over him.

"What this is designed to do is to relieve you of executive function. Do you know what that means?"

Conrad's face was white. He felt his hands shaking as he pushed himself to sit up. "It means that it can take away my free will."

"Exactly." Max smiled. "Your brain will do as I say and follow my instructions. I will then have the benefit of your genius for my own uses." He looked at Piper, who was filled with horror. "In case you're not following all of this, tootsie, this means that I win and you lose."

"Stop hurting him."

Conrad's face curled with outrage as he felt his body standing up and walking toward Max. As he did so the pain went away. With all his might he tried to stop himself from walking, then from kneeling in front of Max, and finally from licking his boot. It was disgusting, it was exhausting, and ultimately it was futile. His body did just as Max told him to.

"Now sit down."

Conrad's body immediately sat on the floor as though he were a puppet.

Max clapped his hands, thrilled with the results. "This baby works like a charm. And the more we do it, the better it'll work too."

Conrad's face was red and flushed. The internal war going on inside his brain was fierce. "You're sick."

"That's funny, 'cause I feel fine. Well, this was fun, but it's time to get to work. Conrad, go to the Knowledge Center right now."

Conrad got up. Piper grabbed his arm, pulling him back. "Conrad, don't do it. Stop!"

"Hit her!" Max told Conrad.

Conrad immediately slapped Piper across the face. The force of his blow left a red welt across her cheek and she reached for the pain in shock and horror.

Conrad's jaw dropped, his hand tingling. "I—I . . ." There was no excuse.

"Congratulations—this is your purpose now, Piper." Max smirked. "Whenever Conrad doesn't work fast enough I will tell him to hurt you. It's a wonderful incentive for him to do as he's told." Max threw his head back and laughed maniacally like a stock villain in a penny dreadful. He stopped as quickly as he started. "Seriously though, Connie—can I call you Connie? I'll make you do real damage to her, and it's not gonna be fun to watch, so let's just not go there. Okay?"

"Let Piper go," Conrad begged. "I won't fight you if you let her go."

"You're hardly in a position to negotiate," Max pointed out. "Now, no more dilly to this dally, let's get down to some good old mass destruction. Go team!"

*T*HE BELL FOR THE EVENING OFFERING had rung, calling Xanthia to the large chamber on the plateau. Laughter and music from the gathering wafted along the mountain as Max escorted Conrad and Piper through the shadows to the Knowledge Center. Max was several paces behind them, the purifier pointed at Conrad lest there be any funny business. Piper was walking next to Conrad and they had their hands held up in the air because Max had demanded it (*Reach for the stars, partner. Keep your hands where I can see 'em.*) and Conrad had immediately obeyed.

"Conrad," Piper whispered. "What are we gonna do?"

Conrad didn't answer.

"Conrad?" Piper could see that Conrad's hands were trembling.

Conrad's eyes flicked to the side, checking on Max. Max was highly distractible, and after looking at the back of Conrad's head for fifteen whole seconds he'd reached a sufficient level of boredom so that he allowed his attention to get caught up in a group of skunk birds. He giggled to himself when a blue skunk bird sprayed a yellow one in the face with his stink.

"Whoooa, face-stink," he snickered.

"There's only one way out," Conrad whispered to Piper.

Piper immediately felt a bubble of relief forming in her chest. "Anything. Just tell me what to do."

"You have to fly home and tell the others."

"No problem."

"Max will try to stop you." Conrad spoke quickly. "We are the only people who know what is going on, and he can't let that get out. He'll do whatever it takes to make sure you don't go anywhere."

"I can handle it. Just say when."

They walked in silence for several yards, listening as Max chuckled over the birds. "Bam! Stink 'em up, yellow."

"See that arch ahead?" Conrad flicked his eyes at a graceful archway twenty feet in front of them.

"Uh-huh."

"Take off when we get to it. Just go and don't look back. And Piper?"

"Yeah?"

"When you have the others and it's safe, come back for my father and set him free."

"Just tell me what to do and I'll do it."

"But there's one last thing." He was careful to whisper and keep himself from looking at Piper. "I won't be going with you."

Piper inhaled sharply, angrily. "Then I'm not going. I won't leave you behind."

"It's not your choice; it's mine. Don't fight me on this: there isn't time. As long as my brain is functioning Max has power. It's as simple as that. The only way to stop him is for me to stop thinking." Conrad was strangely calm and assured. "I'd rather not be able to think at all than have my thinking used for Max's ends."

"You can't stop thinking. That's not possible."

"Actually it is."

Piper looked at Conrad out of the corner of her eye and he tilted his head, showing her the blinking lights on his Direct Brain Interface. She instantly understood. "You're going to pull it out?" Piper gasped. "But it'll kill you."

"Yes. No. Maybe. It'll fry my brain for sure. Whether it will cause my death is pure guesswork on my part."

Horrified tears sprung to Piper's eyes, which added to her stress of having to keep everything perfectly quiet. "But . . . you can't."

"I will. In another ten yards it will be over." Conrad took a measured breath. "You are the only friend I ever had, Piper. And you are the best friend anyone could have ever hoped for. My life has been blessed by you."

"Please—please—"

"Max will turn me into a monster. One day he will order me to kill you, and I can't watch you die. If you are my friend you will do as I say and get out of here. Don't look back."

Time was not slowing but speeding up for Piper. If this truly was their only option (and when had Conrad ever been wrong?) it was far worse than she could ever have imagined. She wanted to argue but knew it would do no good. She wanted to plead and beg and rage and hurt Max and save Conrad, but the archway was before them.

"It's alright, Piper." Conrad could see his friend's misery and pain. "I'm not afraid and I'm not sad. I swore that I would unravel this secret and I did: I now know the truth. It was a terrible secret and it is a terrible truth but it no longer has any power over me, and that is freedom." Even now Conrad was impeccably rational. "There are things worse than not being able to think. It's nice being smart, but it's nicer to have a friend like you. Choosing you is the smartest thing I could ever do."

Piper placed one shaking hand over her lips to stop her sobs.

"I don't think I told you what my father said to me before Max shot him." Conrad wanted to give Piper something to make her strong so that she could get through what was to happen next: his father's words seemed fitting. "He told me about a prophecy. The prophecy says that there is a girl who can fly and a boy who knows everything and that they can change this world. It says that they alone will have the power to stop Max. And do you know what?"

Piper shook her head. "No," she whispered.

"I believe that's true. That boy and girl are you and me." Conrad smiled thinking about this. "I'm sorry I can't go the rest of the way with you but I know you are strong enough to do it alone. Okay?"

Piper was far from okay.

"I need you to tell me that you'll be okay. Please do that for me."

Piper heard her friend's voice crack and it made her aware that Conrad needed her to be strong. He was being strong for her, but it was a burden he could no longer lift alone. If she truly was his friend and this was the last thing she could do for him, she would do it with all she had. Piper swallowed her sobs and inhaled fire.

"Me? Okay? I'm gonna kick his butt!"

Conrad grinned. "That's my girl!"

At the archway Conrad stopped walking and turned to Piper. "Tell my father it was worth it and I wouldn't change anything. Now go."

Piper didn't hesitate but flew like the wind.

"Hey, dude!" Max shook the wand at Conrad furiously. "Stop the chitter chatter and get clippety-clopping to the Knowledge Center. And tell Piper to fly back here. I order you."

Waves of pain erupted in Conrad's brain. With all the strength he possessed he reached his hand up to his head, wrapped his fingers around the metal DBI, and ripped it from his skull.

"DUDE!"

Piper did not look back. She did not see Conrad crumple to the ground, tremors pulsing through his body as though an internal earthquake was silently erupting in places unseen.

Max grabbed Conrad's shoulders, shaking him, but Conrad was past the place of responsiveness. Max was no longer playful or telling jokes or having a good time. His face was no longer cleverly hidden behind a mask of youth and beauty, but laid bare by the hard lines of the oldest man in the world.

"*Nooo*," he screamed.

Reaching for the purifier, he pointed it at Conrad,

but the orange light was flickering. Max hit the side of the wand like it was a broken toaster, knocking it against the railing.

The orange light dimmed and then died out completely.

"Ahhhh!" Furious, Max threw the wand aside and rushed to the railing, looking for Piper in the sky. He spotted her at once flying fast over the plateau toward the valley.

Max bent down and placed his hands on the mountain. "Mother Mountain, I have given you my people." He spoke quickly and quietly like he was praying. "I command you now to give me a thunderstorm."

Beneath Max's hand Mother Mountain rumbled in response, the distant sound of lightning making the air shake.

"Strike her," Max growled. "Strike her down for me!"

Clouds pushed together closely and like a switch had been pulled, the rain fell in thick angry pellets. Piper was instantly soaked.

BOOM! The thunder was so loud it made the air around her reverberate with electricity and danger.

"Fly home," Piper coached herself. Repeating Conrad's words gave her comfort.

Gaining altitude, Piper began her journey across the valley. The cloud cover blocked the moon and visibility was a struggle with the rain hitting at her face. The force of the wind pushed her off course, but she corrected by dipping her left arm down.

Suddenly Piper felt the air around her change; her hair rose up and her skin tingled, and a moment later a brilliant blinding flash of lightning sliced, striking her arm.

"Owww," Piper yelped. Losing her balance, she spun out of control.

"Strike one," Max shouted from his vantage at the edge of the plateau. He was gripping the railing, watching Piper's progress. She had just started across the valley on what Max predicted would be her last flight.

Throwing her weight up, Piper managed to stop the spin and regain control. Back on course, she started across the valley. Her arm was black at the impact site and throbbing wildly. The cool balm of the rain was welcome relief. "It's okay," she told herself. "I'm fine. I can make it."

Once again Piper felt her hair rise and skin tingle but this time she rolled in the air and changed direction wildly, just avoiding another direct hit by a thick bolt of lightning.

"Ugh." Max grimaced, pounding his fist against Mother Mountain. "Strike again. Strike again."

In the valley below Piper, a surge of hot lava from a volcanic minefield burst upward, striking her full force.

"Ahhh!" she screamed.

The boom of thunder rocked her next and she prepared for the telltale signs of lightning. Below her volcanic lava bursts erupted and she had to make split-second dodges to avoid them.

Max leaned forward in anticipation, rubbing his hands. "Come on, come on," he cheered. "Gimme a direct hit."

CRACK!

Piper rolled to her left and a moment later a dagger of lightning was behind her, hitting her left foot.

CRACK!

No time to react this time. Piper was momentarily jolted but was able to shake it off.

BOOM! went the thunder.

Piper was tired. She rolled away from a bolt of lightning sluggishly.

BOOM!

Even after her skin started to prickle, Piper didn't swerve. The rain was punishing her and the darkness suffocated her. Piper was now halfway across the valley, but the entrance to the tunnel might as well have been solar systems away.

Lightning sliced through her thigh.

"A direct hit." Max jumped to his feet, his two hands rising into the air in triumph.

"Give her another whack," Max shouted to the sky. "One more'll do it."

Piper started counting numbers in her head. *Ten times two is twenty. Twenty divided by two . . .*

BOOM!

Lightning sliced to her right, and then right in front of her. Her shoulder was hit and the now familiar jolt of electricity bounced through her fragile system.

Twenty divided by two . . . I don't know that one, Conrad. How do I do that?

CRACK!

The sound was so loud and so close that Piper lost her hearing altogether.

A lightning strike directly in her path made Piper pull up and stop. Suddenly she was disoriented. Looking this way and that, she completely forgot what she was doing. She shook her head several times.

It's raining, Conrad. I want to go home.

Piper waited for Conrad to answer her but he didn't.

Conrad, I don't know what to do. Where do I go . . .

Piper didn't hear the boom, didn't see the light. She was hit directly through her back.

Max yelped with joy and watched as Piper remained still in the air for a moment and then fell down toward a pool of lava below.

"*Adios*, Piper McCloud." Max toasted her with an invisible glass. "You flew well but not well enough. You tried hard but not hard enough. I win. Again. 'Cause I'm a winner. And all that you and Conrad learned will die with you." He bowed to her as the adrenaline that had been pounding through his body began to fizzle and die. Without him realizing it his foot began tapping of its own accord, restless for new adventure. Max found himself considering how the waves off the coast of Morocco would be something to see at this time of year. . . .

Piper felt nothing as she fell. Her body was in so much pain, a switch was flicked inside her brain that allowed her to feel peaceful nothingness. The rolling clouds, the lightning and thunder were all around her and a part of her now. The heat rising up to meet her as she fell was comforting and she wasn't aware that it was burning her skin. It was a quiet and painless drifting away.

CHAPTER

"*P*IPER IS FALLING!" KIMBER SCREAMED frantically.

They could all see quite plainly that Piper was falling from where they stood on the cliff, but still Kimber yelled it, such was the state of her panic.

The whole group of them had returned to their perch overlooking the valley the day before and had sat listlessly, gazing toward the mountain. All hope that Letitia Hellion would fly them across the valley was entirely abandoned; indeed the only thing Letitia had done since leaving Area 63 was rock back and forth and mutter nonsense to herself.

"I'm coming, Sarah. Hold out your hand," she'd gibber feverishly as though seeing her little sister in front of her. "I won't let you fall."

Sitting on the hard rocks of the cliff hour after long hour with nothing to do and no hope of reaching Piper and Conrad, the kids were driven to distraction listening to Letitia moan and beg. As another day came mercifully to an end Smitty unexpectedly jumped to his feet and rushed forward, pointing to the mountain with great excitement. "Piper! I see Piper."

Immediately they all snapped upward, rushed to Smitty's side, and squinted to see where he pointed. It didn't take long before they were able to see Piper too.

"I see her now. Look, she's over there!"

"Can Piper see us? Does she know we're here?"

"Is Conrad with her?"

And their first glimpse of Piper had caused such an eruption of gladness that a cheer spontaneously burst from their throats. But no sooner had they started to celebrate than there was rain and thunder and their excitement turned to concern.

"Why is Piper flying in this storm?"

"Did you hear that thunder? She needs to get out of the sky."

And then when the lightning struck Piper again and again all became horror. Althea covered her eyes with shaking hands, and Nalen and Ahmed tried to draw the storm away, only to find that its power was beyond their reach, while Smitty, who could see in agonizing detail what the others could not, wept bitter tears.

"STOP!" Kimber yelled at the storm.

Myrtle grasped Jasper's arm, crying, "We have to save her!" Which, of course, Jasper agreed with but had no immediate solution to achieve.

Wet, helpless, and defeated, the entire group watched as Piper McCloud was struck by one last bolt of lightning and hung in the air without moving. For a heartbeat some of them felt hope, but that hope was fleeting—Piper fell from the sky.

46

*L*ETITIA KEPT HER HAND OUTSTRETCHED and ready, waiting in a state of hyperalertness for Sarah to take it. Sarah was falling and she knew that if she closed the gap and found her, grasped hold of her tiny fingers and held them tight, she would finally stop her from hitting the ground. . . .

Sometimes when she was looking for Sarah a strange face would suddenly flash before her eyes, a child or someone who looked like her brother Jeston. It was fleeting and confusing but thankfully passed quickly. Once she imagined that she was sitting with a group of children on a cliff overlooking a valley, but the dream evaporated as fast as it came.

But then there was lightning and thunder and it was terribly, terribly loud: louder even than Sarah's screams for help. The noise caused the dream of the cliff to grow more sharply in focus and it was then that she realized a whole group of children were right there with her. They were begging her and pointing to the sky. It was very confusing.

"Save her," one of the children screamed.

She reached out her hand farther. *Can they see Sarah? Can they help her?*

"She's struck by lightning!" one of the children yelled, and her voice had agony in it. It was the agony that made her listen because it was a feeling she knew well and made sense to her; made her want to hear more.

"We have to do something!" shouted another.

"Look! Piper's falling!"

She looked and saw what the boy saw—a girl was falling . . . and it was Sarah! *My Sarah.*

At last she had found her and could save her.

Without hesitation she leaped off the cliff and flew like an arrow. Her body was stiff and sore, her muscles weak and unprepared, but her spirit full to bursting.

The storm was raging around her, thunder and lightning to her left and right and in front of her.

The girl was falling fast, tumbling through the air. Letitia reached out her tired arms and they tingled with hopeful longing to hold her.

"Sarah!" she called. "I'm coming."

Fiery liquid shot up from below, splattering her limbs and burning her flesh. To avoid further injury she would have to pull up and carefully navigate her way through it, but there was no time for such maneuvers.

With a last burst of energy she plunged through a lava spray, came out the other side, and at long last grabbed the girl, plucking her from the air and encircling her with her arms.

"Sarah, my Sarah."

Tears clouded her vision and a burst of wind carried them upward to safety.

"You're safe. I've got you." She breathed in the girl's scent, touched her hair, feeling her sweetness and reveling in her wholeness. At long last, she had saved her and they were released from the endless cycle of reaching and falling.

For the first time in her life she felt forgiven and free. Letitia Hellion had found peace.

CHAPTER

47

JASPER BLEW INTO HIS HANDS AND THEY shone white-hot, brighter than the moon. He was ready when Letitia Hellion placed Piper in front of him, pale and burned. He positioned his hands on either side of Piper's chest, and the light jumped into her, and for a terrible moment she remained motionless until at last she sucked a shallow, painful breath into her lungs.

Relief rippled through the kids, who were gathered thickly around Piper, closely monitoring the way Jasper healed her battered body again and again until she opened her eyes, looking up at them in confusion.

Violet threw herself on Piper, hugging her tight. "Oh, Piper, we thought you were dead."

J., who hung in the shadows next to his sister, squeezed her hand. "You did it, sis. You saved her!"

Piper was startled to find herself among her friends and it took long moments to orient herself. She opened her mouth to speak but her throat was hoarse, causing her to heave and cough.

"Give her room," Violet ordered, propping Piper up. Myrtle handed Piper a water canteen and after she pulled a long drag she found that she could talk again.

"How did you get here?" Piper croaked.

"Long story," Smitty said, and smiled.

"We've been trying to get across the valley but it's impossible," Lily explained. "So we've been waiting and waiting."

"Oh." Piper was glad to see them, but her thoughts remained on Conrad and she dreaded sharing that news, particularly with little Aletha, who was curled next to her, staring up at her with large brown eyes. Piper would not allow herself to think of Conrad as being dead—no, that thought was too terrible. Instead, she only considered the possibility that he was gone and gone in such a way that there was a chance that he would come back. It was for this reason she was able to collect herself and think what she must do next, and it was then that Piper suddenly caught sight of Letitia Hellion.

"What's Dr. Hellion doing here?" she croaked. The sight of Letitia sent shivers down Piper's spine and her first instinct was to fly as far away from her as possible.

"Piper," Jasper said quietly, "if it wasn't for Dr. Hellion

you would have died. We couldn't get to you, and she flew out to save you when you were struck by lightning."

"Really?" Piper looked from Jasper to Dr. Hellion.

"Really. You were unconscious, so you don't remember." Jasper nodded slowly and seriously. "She saved your life."

As this news settled into Piper she felt a tingling in her stomach. "Dr. Hellion saved my life? And she was flying?" Of all the people she had ever met none had held such deep-seated hatred for exceptional abilities as Letitia Hellion.

Breaking away from the others, Piper walked on unsteady legs to her old foe. Two paces in front of her, Piper inhaled sharply at the sight of the nasty burns that covered much of Letitia's body. With effort she refocused her eyes and met Letitia's gaze.

"Tell me, why . . . why did you fly, Dr. Hellion?"

Letitia Hellion searched within herself. "I flew because . . ." All her delusions had fallen away and reality was laid before her in stark, beautiful lines. She could clearly see that Piper was not Sarah, and yet her happiness was not diminished by that knowledge. "I flew because I can."

Piper considered this answer. "If you hadn't flown I would've died."

"Yes," said Letitia with a shaking voice. "It was good—my flying helped."

Piper offered Letitia her hand and Letitia placed her trembling fingers on Piper's small ones.

"There is a boy named Max, and he has tricked us all into being afraid of our abilities and made other people afraid of them too."

"Max?" Letitia let the name settle into her and it opened her mind like a key. "Yes, I remember now. Max. Yes, his name is Max. He was the one who took my memory away."

Piper nodded. "He did the same thing to Conrad's father, and everyone else for that matter." Piper turned to the others. "Conrad figured out the truth and Max is behind everything. It's up to us to stop him." Piper knew, without having to ask, that her friends would stay at her side and fight, no matter where that fight might take them. But they weren't enough—they would need everyone.

Piper turned to Letitia. "Will you join us, Dr. Hellion?"

"Me?" Letitia Hellion drew her hand away in surprise. After everything she had done to hurt these kids, how could they possibly want anything to do with her? "You want me?"

"We want everyone, but especially you." Piper

shrugged. "If you're able to change your mind then there's hope for everyone else, too."

Letitia Hellion inhaled Piper's sentiment so that it would reach every place in her body. When she was able she nodded her wholehearted agreement. Not long after that Piper related in detail the happenings of the time in Xanthia, and the kids were shocked to learn the truth, overcome with emotion, passionate about the cause, and ready to do as Conrad had asked of them.

"We should move out." J., in particular, was ready to get going and had already gathered his backpack and prepared to leave. "Max already has a head start and we don't want to lose him."

"No," Piper disagreed. "Conrad wants us to take care of something else first."

Piper then flew them to Xanthia with Letitia's help. Once there, Piper did not look at that beautiful place the same way; the truth had changed everything.

"My son? Where is my son?" were the first words out of Harrington's blue lips once he had been released from his icy prison and healed by Jasper.

It nearly broke Piper's heart to look at Harrington, so striking was the similarity between father and son.

"I am here for Conrad," Piper explained to him, valiantly keeping the quaver out of her voice. "Because he can't be."

And then Piper took Harrington deep into Mother Mountain and Starr stopped what she was doing and put down her rock for the last time. She held out her arms to her son and they held each other for so long and with such joy that Mother Mountain herself trembled with their salvation.

It was with great satisfaction that Harrington broke the bloodstone from around his mother's neck, and no sooner had the evil thing been crushed than Starr's gruesome lumps and humps dispersed. As if by magic, Starr returned to her graceful and lithe form, albeit with a few gray hairs and wrinkles.

Piper was careful to bear witness to every word and feeling because it was such a grand victory: Conrad's victory—a testament to his smarts and his sacrifice—and no one understood that better than she. The next time she saw him, she promised herself, she would tell him everything.

———◆———

WHEN THE KIDS RETURNED TO LOWLAND County, much to the delight of Betty and Joe McCloud, not to mention Fido, they had precious little time to rest with Max on the loose and up to no good. After everything that had happened in Xanthia, Max was more desperate than ever to feed off the energy of havoc and mayhem, and the kids had to react quickly to the various emergencies at hand. First Max staged an international incident designed to ignite a world war and the kids had to rescue hostages and expose key evidence to foil his plans. Next Max showed up in the Middle East with a rare strain of a deadly flu virus and the kids worked as a team to keep it contained. Seemingly there was no end to Max's devious plans, but no matter how tired or disheartened, the kids battled on and on, yearning daily for the genius of their fallen friend.

But even in their darkest hours Piper refused to give up and would say confidently, "We've been through worse. When Conrad gets back he'll want to know that we gave nothing less than our best." To which no one had the heart to suggest to Piper that Conrad would most likely not be coming back—which was what they feared. Not Piper, though.

"Conrad is our friend," Piper would remind them. "He wouldn't leave us. He'll be back as soon as he can and when he gets here he'll know exactly what to do— just like old times." And despite everything the kids would put aside their fears and believe Piper McCloud and rise to the fight with everything they had, exactly as Conrad had trained them to do, and would have wanted.

*B*ELLA LOVELY WAS WEEDING IN HER mother's vegetable garden, preparing it for the winter months ahead. It had been a decent harvest that year but there was nothing but dry stalks and wilting plants now. It was Bella's job to trim away the old to make way for the new growth of the coming spring. She had been working for hours when the sound of birds filled the air, and not just one bird, but hundreds of them. Getting to her feet, Bella scanned the sky, catching sight of an approaching mass of fluttering wings. The flock was flying straight for her and she watched them with curiosity and wonder.

Cupping her hands over her eyes to cut the glare of the sun, Bella suddenly noticed that the lead bird was no bird at all . . . it was a girl.

It was the girl who could fly.

Bella trembled at the sight of the girl, overjoyed and self-righteous all at the same time; she knew it, she'd known it all along. Finally she had proof.

Like a gunslinger in a Western she whipped her iPhone from her back pocket and clicked pictures and took video. There was a growing movement of Seekers just like her, and these pictures would feed them like manna from heaven.

Even after the girl who could fly and all the birds were long gone Bella kept her eyes on the sky. She wished she could go with them, that she could be part of whatever was happening.

Sighing, Bella holstered her iPhone and reluctantly drew her gaze down. No sooner had her eyes lowered than she gasped and started, unable to believe what she saw. Bella was suddenly standing in a garden that was in full bloom! While Bella had been distracted her dead plants had come back to life; the flowers had bloomed and the vines were bursting with ripe fruit and vegetables.

Bella's skin tingled. *How could this have happened? What made my garden transform?*

Bella had no answers, only questions bubbling inside her, and throughout the rest of her day everything she came into contact with began to blossom. That night she uploaded her pictures and videos onto the web. All across the nation Seekers feverishly drank in every pixel and watched the footage over and over. They wrote about it too.

The time has come. The future is here. Rise up. Rise up.

CHAPTER

49

H E HAD NO SHOES, NO WATER, NO IDEN-
tification, and no memory. On a day when the
temperatures hovered above 130° he had been discarded
like a dirty candy wrapper on a lonely stretch of Nevada's
Highway 93. By the time Officer Felt picked him up his
skin was flaming a deep angry red and flowering with
blisters.

"What's your name?" Officer Felt badgered, like he
was accusing him of stealing.

The boy looked at Felt with endless confusion. Everything startled him—the car, the doors, even the way
Officer Felt spoke.

"Where ya from? Vegas?" Felt waited for the boy to
answer. "You get lost or something?"

The boy had no answer.

The precinct in Wells, Nevada, was so small it consisted of nothing more than a small office and a holding

cell. They placed him in the cell with an old man who was sprawled haphazardly on the floor, snoring loudly. He had to gingerly step over him and huddle in the corner.

The woman who came for him introduced herself as a social worker from Child Protective Services. She asked a lot of questions he couldn't answer.

"What's your name?"

He shrugged.

"Where are you from?"

He looked away.

"Who are your parents?"

He had no answer.

He was shivering from dehydration so she gave him some water. He said no more.

No sooner had the social worker completed her assessment than Peter Harrington walked into the small Wells police station and approached the front desk.

Ever since he'd been woken by the kids in Xanthia and learned that Conrad's body had not been recovered, Harrington had been filled with hope. It wasn't a hope he wanted to share with the kids because he didn't want to create false expectations that might or might not come true, and frankly, when you are dealing with someone like Max there's no certainty whatsoever. All the same Harrington knew that Max was a creature of habit and had a thirst for symmetry, as well as a twisted delight in having fun. Nothing would tickle Max quite so much as having history repeat itself again, thanks to him.

It made Harrington feel queasy to see that the precinct hadn't changed in the forty years since the day they had brought him in off the side of the road. The police officer by the front desk lumbered to his feet when he approached.

"Afternoon," said Officer Felt. "Can I help you?"

"Yes," Harrington said, smiling. "I am—"

Before he could continue Officer Felt put his hand up in surprise. "Hey, anyone ever tell you how much you look like President Harrington? God rest his soul."

Harrington nodded and shrugged it off good-naturedly. "Yes, I've heard that before, but my name is Peter."

"It's like you're twins. Got the same eyes, same hair."

"As I said," said Peter, "it's a coincidence."

Officer Felt instantly accepted the explanation and felt no need to think on it further: like a thought had been placed inside his head that wasn't his own.

"I understand that you picked up a boy today," Peter said, and smiled. He'd been monitoring the police frequencies for weeks waiting to hear the call.

"Yeah," said Officer Felt, wiping the sweat from his brow and leaning against the desk. He knew better than to give out information, but there was just something about this Peter guy that was so friendly he couldn't help himself. "I gotta tell you it was the darnedest thing. I was driving down ninety-three and I sees him wandering around like a stray dog. It was hotter than Hades out there and this kid is burnt to a crisp. Heck if I know how long he's been out there. So I pulls over and talks to him and he can't put two words together. Doesn't even know his name. A mess, I tell ya. I got Child Services on the line pronto."

Peter nodded and smiled. "I'll take a look at him."

The idea wormed itself into Officer Felt's brain, but he resisted. "Well, now, that ain't protocol. . . ."

"Of course," Peter said understandingly. "It would be a big help, though."

Officer Felt's face was suspicious, but Peter's words washed the lines off his forehead. He smiled affably and shrugged.

"Guess it couldn't hurt. Right?"

"No, it wouldn't hurt at all," Peter agreed.

"Right this way."

Officer Felt led Peter through the office and into the holding area.

The memory of the place almost knocked Peter off his feet. The boy huddled in the corner of the room, burned and shaking, looking but not seeing with vacant blue eyes.

"I guess you have work to do," Peter said to Officer Felt.

"You bet I do," Officer Felt agreed, even though there was exactly nothing that he needed to do. Still, he turned and left the room.

Peter looked at the sad offering of a boy before him and shook his head in disbelief. The boy's blond hair was full of sand and dust and his clothes were nothing more than shredded rags.

Peter walked slowly to the middle of the room and sat down opposite the boy, crossing his legs. The boy watched him with curiosity.

"My name is Peter, and I have been waiting for you," he told him.

"For me?" The boy's lips were cracked and bleeding and his voice was hoarse.

"Yes. For you."

"D-d-do you know me?" The boy's face created a painful picture of hope.

"I know everything about you. I know where you come from and where you are going. More than that, I know what is in you."

The boy let out a long shaky breath of relief. "Really?"

"Your name is Conrad and today is your birthday."

"My birthday?"

"Yes, you are thirteen years old today. And you are very, very smart."

"But . . . I don't know anything."

"Then I will help you remember again."

Conrad nodded, satisfied and relieved by Peter's calm assurance.

"Peter?"

"Yes."

Conrad struggled to arrange his thoughts. "Who are you?"

"I am your father. I am here to claim you and take you home. Okay?"

"Okay."

For some reason that he would never be able to explain to Child Protective Services, Officer Felt let Peter take the boy away without so much as showing a single piece of identification.

All Peter said was, "It's probably best that the boy comes with me."

The minute Peter said it, it seemed like the most natural and most reasonable course of action in the world to Officer Felt. "Sure thing," he said, and waved them out of the station.

Conrad's body was stiff and sore and he had a hard time walking to where his father had parked the car. Peter slowed his pace and patiently walked next to him. Suddenly they both stopped, arrested by the sound of a thousand birds passing overhead. As they looked up at the sky it began to fill with birds, and leading the birds was a girl.

Conrad's burned and tired face tried to understand this flying girl but couldn't. "Who's that, Dad?"

"That, my son, is the start of a revolution. And you and that flying girl started it just like the prophecy said you would."

This didn't make any sense to Conrad so he just watched the flying girl and the birds and then let his father take him to the car. When they reached the car, Peter opened the back door and Conrad was surprised to see a boy already sitting in the backseat. Next to the boy was the strangest and probably ugliest creature Conrad had ever seen. At the sight of Conrad the creature started to bob up and down with excitement and jostle excitedly to get at him.

"This is Jasper," Peter explained to Conrad. "And Fido." Peter scooped Fido up to stop him from jumping all over Conrad.

"Oh," said Conrad blankly.

Conrad got into the car and sat down. He watched with quiet wonder as Jasper began to rub his hands together and blow into them.

Before Jasper put his hands on Conrad he said, "This w-w-won't hurt."

Conrad didn't flinch when the healing light traveled up and down his body. He only gasped when the synapses in his brain caught fire and his memories slammed into place like a tractor trailer hitting a concrete wall. When it was over Conrad knew he was Conrad and saw his father—saw him completely for who he was.

"Thanks for coming to get me, Dad."

Peter released Fido and he threw himself at Conrad and licked his face with passionate slurps. Conrad hugged and petted him.

Peter started the engine. "It's time to go home, son."

ACKNOWLEDGMENTS

I AM BRIMMING WITH GRATITUDE FOR THOSE who helped me through the long, long journey of this book. At the very beginning, Jean Feiwel wouldn't let me turn her offer down and had faith in me regardless of the fact that I didn't have faith in myself. Jodi Reamer stayed in my corner through the thick and thin of it all (she is an agent-extraordinaire with strange and marvelous powers). At the very end, Liz Szabla was the bright star that guided the book home. Never have I met a more talented and generous soul; no doubt about it, this book was lost without her. In addition to these, I received daily bolstering from an assorted cast of friends and family who believed and believed—but none so much as my sister, Kim; Frances Doel; and my best friend, Marta Anderson, who always cheers the loudest and the longest.

While I was writing *The Boy Who Knew Everything*, I learned that there are real boys (and girls) who do know everything. I can tell you this truly because I have met them. They work silently and often without recognition, but because of them, this world is changed utterly. Here is a short and incomplete list of their names:

Dr. Jean-Nicolas Vauthey, Surgical Oncology, MD
   Anderson Cancer Center
Dr. Scott Kopetz, Oncology, MD Anderson Cancer Center
Dr. Steven Applebaum, Oncologist, UCLA
Dr. James Yoo, Surgeon, UCLA
Saskia de Koomen, RN, UCLA
Ryanne Coulson, PA, MD Anderson Cancer Center

If you start looking for these boys and girls, then you will find them too, or maybe, just maybe, you can become one yourself. . . .

12/15